Hills of Han
A Romantic Incident

by

Samuel Merwin

Double 9
BOOKS

Hills of Han
A Romantic Incident
by Samuel Merwin

ISBN: 978-93-62203-92-2

Published by

DOUBLE 9 BOOKS

2/13-B, Ansari Road
Daryaganj, New Delhi – 110002
info@double9books.com
www.double9books.com
Tel. 011-40042856

ABOUT THE AUTHOR

Samuel Merwin was an American dramatist and author. Merwin was born on October 6, 1874, in Evanston, Illinois, to Ella B. and Orlando H. Merwin. His father was the postmaster in Evanston. Merwin and Edna Earl Fleshiem got married in 1901. The marriage had two sons, Samuel Kimball Merwin, Jr. and Banister Merwin, as well as an adoptive son named John Merwin. After graduating from Northwestern University, he served as Success magazine's associate editor and later editor from 1905 to 1911. In 1907, the magazine sent him to China to examine the opium trade. He died of a stroke while dining at The Player's Club in Manhattan on October 17, 1936.

CONTENTS

Hills of Han

Slumber on! The sunlight, dying,
Lingers on your terraced tops;
Yellow stream and willow sighing,
Field of twice ten thousand crops
Breathe their misty lullabying,
Breathe a life that nei'er stops.

Spin your chart of ancient wonder,
Fold your hands within your sleeve,
Live and let live, work and ponder,
Be tradition, dream, believe...
So abides your ancient plan,
Hills of Han!

What's this filament goes leaping
Pole to pole and hill to hill?
What these strips of metal creeping
Where the dead have lain so still.
What this wilder thought that's seeping
Where was peace and gentle will?

Smoke of mill on road and river,
Roar of steam by temple wall...
Drop the arrow in the quiver...
Bow to Buddha.... All is all!
Slumber they who slumber can,
Hills of Han!

NOTE

The slight geographical confusion which will be found by the observant reader in *Hills of Han* is employed as a reminder that the story, despite considerable elements of fact in the background, is a work of the imagination, and deals with no actual individuals of the time and place. S. M.

CHAPTER I
THE SOLITARY

I

ON a day in late March, 1907, Miss Betty Doane sat in the quaintly airy dining-room of the Hotel Miyaka, at Kioto, demurely sketching a man's profile on the back of a menu card.

The man, her unconscious model, lounged comfortably alone by one of the swinging windows. He had finished his luncheon, pushed away his coffee cup, lighted a cigarette, and settled back to gaze out at the hillside where young green grasses and gay shrubs and diminutive trees bore pleasant evidence that the early Japanese springtime was at hand.

Betty could even see, looking out past the man, a row of cherry trees, all afoam with blossoms. They brought a thrill that was almost poignant. It was curious, at home—or, rather, back in the States—there was no particular thrill in cherry blossoms. They were merely pleasing. But so much more was said about them here in Japan.

The man's head was long and well modeled, with a rugged long face, reflective eyes, somewhat bony nose, and a wide mouth that was, on the whole, attractive. Both upper lip and chin were dean shaven. The eyebrows were rather heavy; the hair was thick and straight, slanting down across a broad forehead. She decided, as she sketched it in with easy sure strokes of a stubby pencil, that he must have quite a time every morning brushing that hair down into place.

He had appeared, a few days back, at the Grand Hotel, Yokohama, coming in from somewhere north of Tokio. At the hotel he had walked and eaten alone, austerely. And, not unnaturally, had been whispered about. He was, Betty knew, a journalist of some reputation. The name was Jonathan Brachey. He wore an outing suit, with knickerbockers; he was, in bearing, as in costume, severely conspicuous. You thought of him as a man of odd attainment. He had been in many interesting corners of the world; had known danger and privation. Two of his books were in the ship's library. One of these she had already taken out and secreted in her cabin. It was called *To-morrow in India*, and proved rather hard to read, with charts, diagrams and pages of figures.

The sketch was about done; all but the nose. When you studied that nose in detail it seemed a little too long and strong, and—well, knobby—to be as attractive as it actually was. There would be a trick in drawing it; a shadow or two, a suggestive touch of the pencil; not so many real knobs. In the ship's diningroom she had his profile across an aisle. There would be chances to study it.

Behind her, in the wide doorway, appeared a stout, short woman of fifty or more, in an ample and wrinkled traveling suit of black and a black straw hat ornamented only with a bow of ribbon. Her face wore an anxious expression that had settled, years back, into permanency. The mouth drooped a little. And the brows were lifted and the forehead grooved with wrinkles suggesting some long habitual straining of the eyes that recent bifocal spectacles were powerless to correct.

"Betty!" called the older woman guardedly. "Would you mind, dear... one moment...?"

Her quick, nervous eyes had caught something of the situation. There was Betty and—within easy earshot—a man. The child was unquestionably sketching him.

Betty's eagerly alert young face fell at the sound. She stopped drawing; for a brief instant chewed the stubby pencil; then, quite meekly, rose and walked toward the door.

"Mr. Hasmer is outside. I thought you were with him. Betty."

"No... I didn't know your plans... I was waiting here."

"Well, my dear... it's all right, of course! But I think we'll go now. Mr. Hasmer thinks you ought to see at least one of the temples. Something typical. And of course you will want to visit the cloisonné and *satsuma* shops, and see the Damascene work. The train leaves for Kobe at four-fifteen. The ships sails at about eight, I believe. We haven't much time, you see."

A chair scraped. Jonathan Brachey had picked up his hat, his pocket camera and his unread copy of the Japan *Times*, and was striding toward her, or toward the door. He would pass directly by, of course, without so much as a mental recognition of her existence. For so he had done at Yokohama; so he had done last evening and again this morning on the ship.

But on this occasion, as he bore down on her, the eyes of the distinguished young man rested for an instant on the table, and for a brief moment he wavered in his stride. He certainly saw the sketch. It lay where she had carelessly tossed it, face up, near the edge of the table. And he certainly recognized it for himself; for his strong facial muscles moved a very little. It couldn't have been called a smile; but those muscles distinctly moved. Then, as coolly as before, he strode on out of the room.

Betty's cheeks turned crimson. A further fact doubtless noted by this irritatingly, even arrogantly composed man.

Betty, with desperate dignity, put the sketch in her wrist bag, followed Mrs. Hasmer out of the building, and stepped into the rickshaw that awaited her.

The brown-legged coolie tucked the robe about her, stepped in between the shafts of the vehicle; a second coolie fell into place behind, and they were off down the hill. Just ahead, Mrs. Hasmer's funny little hat bobbed with the inequalities of the road. Just behind, Doctor Hasmer, a calm, patient man who taught philosophy and history in a Christian college fifteen hundred miles or more up the Yangtse River and who never could remember to have his silvery beard trimmed, smiled kindly at her when she turned.

And behind him, indifferent to all the human world, responsive in his frigid way only to the beauties of the Japanese country-side and of the quaint, gray-brown, truly ancient city extending up and down the valley by its narrow, stone-walled stream, rode Mr. Jonathan Brachey.

The coolies, it would seem, had decided to act in concert. From shop to shop among the crowded little streets went the four rickshaws. Any mere human being (so ran Betty's thoughts) would have accepted good-humoredly the comradeship implied in this arrangement on the part of a playful fate; but Mr. Brachey was no mere human being. Side by side stood the four of them in a toy workshop looking down at toy-like artisans with shaved and tufted heads who wore quaint robes and patiently beat out designs in gold and silver wire on expertly fashioned bronze boxes and bowls. They listened as one to the thickly liquid English of a smiling merchant explaining the processes and expanding on the history of fine handiwork in this esthetic land. Yet by no sign did Mr. Brachey's face indicate that he was aware of their presence; except once—on a crooked stairway in a cloisonné shop he flattened himself against the wall to let them pass, muttering, almost fiercely, "I beg your pardon!"

The moment came, apparently, when he could endure this enforced companionship no longer. He spoke gruffly to his rickshaw coolies, and rolled off alone. When they finally reached the railway station after a half-hour spent in wandering about the spacious enclosure of the Temple of Nishi Otani, with its huge, shadowy gate house, its calm priests, its exquisite rock garden under ancient mystical trees—the tall journalist was pacing the platform, savagely smoking a pipe.

At Kobe they were united again, riding out to the ship's anchorage in the same launch. But Mr. Brachey gave no sign of recognition. He disappeared the moment of arrival at the ship, reappearing only when the bugle announced dinner, dressed, as he had been each evening at the Grand Hotel and the previous evening on the ship, rather stiffly, in dinner costume.

Then the ship moved out from her anchorage into that long, island-studded, green-bordered body of water known as the Inland Sea of Japan. Early on the second morning she would slip in between the closepressing hills that guard Nagasaki harbor. There another day ashore. Then three days more across the Yellow Sea to Shanghai. Thence, for the Hasmers and Betty, a five-day journey by steamer up the muddy but majestic Yangtze Kiang to Hankow; at which important if hardly charming city they would separate, the Hasmers to travel on by other, smaller steamer to Ichang and thence on up through the Gorges to their home among the yellow folk of Szechwan, while Hetty, from Hankow, must set out into an existence that her highly colored young mind found it impossible to face squarely. As yet, despite the long journey across the American continent and the Pacific, she hadn't begun so much as to believe the facts. Though there they stood, squarely enough, before her. It had been easier to surrender her responsive, rather easily gratified emotions to a day-by-day enjoyment of the journey itself. When the constant, worried watchfulness of Mrs. Hasmer reached the point of annoyance—not that Mrs. Hasmer wasn't an old dear; kindness itself, especially if your head ached or you needed a little mothering!—why then, with the easy adaptability and quick enthusiasm of youth, she simply busied herself sketching. The top layer of her steamer trunk was nearly full now—sketches of the American desert, of the mountains and San Francisco, of people on the ship, of the sea and of Honolulu.

But now, with Yokohama back among the yesterdays and Kobe falling rapidly, steadily astern, Betty's heart was as rapidly and as steadily sinking. Only one more stop, and then—China. In China loomed the facts.

That night, lying in her berth, Betty, forgot the cherry blossoms of Kioto and the irritating Mr. Brachey. Her thoughts dwelt among the young friends, the boy-and-girl "crowd," she had left behind, far off, at the other edge of those United States that by a queerly unreal theory were her home-land. And, very softly, she cried herself to sleep.

2

Betty Doane was just nineteen. She was small, quick to feel and think, dark rather than light (though not an out-and-out brunette). She was distinctly pretty. Her small head with its fine and abundant hair, round face with its ever-ready smile, alert brown eyes and curiously strong little chin expressed, as did her slim quick body, a personality of considerable sprightly vigor and of a charm that could act on certain other sorts of personalities, particularly of the opposite sex, with positive, telling effect.

Mrs. Hasmer, who had undertaken, with misgivings, to bring her from suburban New Jersey to Hankow, found her a heavy responsibility. It wasn't that the child was insubordinate, forward, or, in anyway that you could blame her for, difficult. On the contrary, she was a dear little thing, kind, always amusing, eager to please. But none the less there was something, a touch of vital quality, perhaps of the rare gift of expressiveness, that gave her, at times, a rather alarming aspect. Her clothes were simple enough—Griggsby Doane, goodness knew, couldn't afford anything else—but in some way that Mrs. Hasmer would never fully understand, the child always managed to make them look better than they were. She had something of the gift of smartness. She had, Mrs. Hasmer once came out with, "too much imagination." The incessant sketching, for instance. And she did it just a shade too well. Then, too, evening after evening during the three weeks on the Pacific, she had danced. Which was, from the only daughter of Griggsby Doane—well, confusing. And though Mrs. Hasmer, balked by the delicacy of her position, had gone to lengths in concealing her disapproval, she had been unable to feign surprise at the resulting difficulties. Betty had certainly not been deliberate in leading on any of the men on the ship; young men, by the way that you had no means of looking up, even so far as the certainty that they were unmarried. But the young mining engineer on his way to Korea had left quite heart-broken. From all outer indications he had proposed marriage and met with a refusal. But not a word, not a hint, not so much as a telltale look, came from Betty.

Mrs. Hasmer sighed over it. She would have liked to know. She came to the conclusion that Betty had been left just a year or so too long in the States. They weren't serious over there, in the matter of training girls for the sober work of life. Prosperity, luxury, were telling on the younger generations. No longer were they guarded from dangerously free thinking. They read, heard, saw everything; apparently knew everything. They read openly, of a Sunday, books which, a generation earlier, would not have reached their eyes even on a week-day. The church seemed to have lost its hold (though she never spoke aloud of this fact). Respect for tradition and authority had crumbled away. They questioned, weighed everything, these modern children.... Mrs. Hasmer worried a good deal, out in China, about young people in the States.

But under these surface worries, lurked, in the good woman's mind, a deeper, more real worry. Betty was just stepping over the line between girlhood and young womanhood. She was growing more attractive daily. She was anything but fitted to step into the life that lay ahead. Wherever she turned, even now—as witness the Pacific ship—life took on fresh complications. Indeed, Mrs. Hasmer, pondering the problem, came down on the rather strong word, peril. A young girl—positive in attractiveness, gifted, spirited, motherless (as it happened), trained only to be happy in living—was in something near peril.

One fact which Mrs. Hasmer's mind had been forced to accept was that most of the complications came from sources or causes with which the girl herself had little consciously to do. She was flatly the sort of person to whom things happened. Even when her eager interest in life and things and men (young and old) was not busy.

In the matter of the rather rude young man in knickerbockers, at Kioto, Betty was to blame, of course. She had set to work to sketch him. Evidently. The most you could say for her on that point was that she would have set just as intently at sketching an old man, or a woman, or a child—or a corner of the room. Mrs. Hasmer had felt, while on the train to Kobe, that she must speak of the matter. After all, she had that deathly responsibility on her shoulders. Betty's only explanation, rather gravely given, had been that she found his nose interesting.

The disturbing point was that something in the way of a situation was sure to develop from the incident. Something. Six weeks of Betty made that a reasonable assumption. And the first complication would arise in some quite unforeseen way. Betty wouldn't bring it about. Indeed, she had quickly promised not to sketch him any more.

This is the way it did arise. At eleven on the following morning Mr. and Mrs. Hasmer and Betty were stretched out side by side in their steamer chairs, sipping their morning beef tea and looking out at the rugged north shore of the Inland Sea. Beyond Betty were three vacant chairs, then this Mr. Brachey—his long person wrapped in a gay plaid rug. He too was sipping beef tea and enjoying the landscape; if so dry, so solitary a person could be said to enjoy anything. A note-book lay across his knees.

Mrs. Hasmer had thought, with a momentary flutter of concern, of moving Betty to the other side of Doctor Hasmer. But that had seemed foolish. Making too much of it. Betty hadn't placed the chairs; the deck steward had done that. Besides she hadn't once looked at the man; probably hadn't thought of him; had been quite absorbed in her sketching—bits of the hilly shore, an island mirrored in glass, a becalmed junk.

A youngish man, hatless, with blond curls and a slightly professional smile, came up from the after hatch and advanced along the deck, eagerly searching the row of rug-wrapped, recumbent figures in deck chairs. Before the Hasmers he stopped with delighted greetings. It came out that he was a Mr. Harting, a Y. M. C. A. worker in Bttrmah, traveling second-class.

"I hadn't seen the passenger list, Mrs. Hasmer, and didn't know you were aboard. But there's a Chinese boy sitting next to me at table. He has put in a year or so at Tokio University, and speaks a little English. He comes from your city, Miss Doane. Or so he seems to think. T'ainan-fu."

Betty inclined her head.

"It was he who showed me the passenger list. At one time, he says, he lived in your father's household."

"What is his name?" asked Betty politely.

"Li Hsien—something or other." Mr. Harting was searching his pockets for a copy of the list.

"I knew Li Hsien very well," said Betty. "We used to play together."

"So I gathered. May I bring him up here to see you?"

Betty would have replied at once in the affirmative, but six weeks of companionship with Mrs. Hasmer had taught her that such decisions were not expected of her. So now with a vague smile of acquiescence, she directed the inquiry to the older woman.

"Certainly," cried Mrs. Hasmer, "do bring him!"

As he moved away, Betty, before settling back in her chair, glanced, once, very demurely, to her left, where Jonathan Brachey lay in what might have been described, from outer appearances, supercilious comfort.

He hadn't so much as lifted an eyelid. He wasn't listening. He didn't care. It was nothing to him that Betty Doane was no idle, spoiled girl tourist, nothing that she could draw with a gifted pencil, nothing that she knew Chinese students at Tokio University, and herself lived at T'ainan-fu!... It wasn't that Betty consciously formulated any such thoughts. But the man had an effect on her; made her uncomfortable; she wished he'd move his chair around to the other side of the ship.

3

Li Hsien proved to be quite a young man, all of twenty or twenty-one. He had spectacles now, and gold in his teeth. He wore the conventional blue robe, Liack skull-cap with red button, and queue. More than four years were yet to elapse before the great revolution of 1911, with its wholesale queue-cutting and its rather frantic adoption, on the part of the better-to-do, of Western clothing—or, rather, of what they supposed was Western clothing.... He was tall, slim, smiling. He shook hands with Betty, Western fashion; and bowed with courtly dignity to Doctor and Mrs. Hasmer.

His manner had an odd effect on Betty. For six years now she had lived in Orange. She had passed through the seventh and eighth grades of the public school and followed that with a complete course of four years in high school. She had fallen naturally and whole-heartedly into the life of a nice girl in an American suburb. She had gone to parties, joined societies, mildly entangled herself with a series of boy admirers. Despite moderate but frank poverty she had been popular. And in this healthy, active young life she had very nearly forgotten the profoundly different nature of her earlier existence. But now that earlier feeling for life was coming over her like a wave. After all, her first thirteen years had been lived out in a Chinese city. And they were the most impressionable years.

It was by no means a pleasant sensation. She had never loved China; had simply endured it, knowing little else. America she loved. It was of her blood, of her instinct. But now it was abruptly slipping out of her grasp—school, home, the girls, the boys, long evenings of chatter and song on a "front porch," picnics on that ridge known locally as "the mountain," matinées in New York, glorious sunset visions of high buildings from a ferry-boat, a thrilling, ice-caked river in winter-time, the misty beauties of the Newark meadows—all this was curiously losing its vividness in her mind, and drab old China was slipping stealthily but swiftly into its place.

She knit her brows. She was suddenly helpless, in a poignantly disconcerting way. A word came—rootless. That was it; she was rootless. For an instant she had to fight back the tears that seldom came in the daytime.

But then she looked again at Li Hsien.

He was smiling. It came to her, fantastically, that he, too, was rootless. And yet he smiled. She knew, instantly, that his feelings were quite as fine as hers. He was sensitive, strung high. He had been that sort of boy. For that matter the Chinese had been a cultured people when the whites were crude barbarians. She knew that. She couldn't have put it into words, but she knew it. And so she, too, smiled. And when she spoke, asking him to sit in the vacant chair next to her, she spoke without a thought, in Chinese, the middle Hansi dialect.

And then Mr. Jonathan Brachey looked up, turned squarely around and stared at her for one brief instant. After which he recollected himself and turned abruptly back.

Mr. Harting dropped down on the farther side of Doctor Hasmer. Which left his good wife between the two couples, each now deep in talk.

Mrs. Hasmer's Chinese vocabulary was confined to a limited number of personal and household terms; and even these were in the dialect of eastern Szechwan. Just as a matter of taste, of almost elementary taste, it seemed to her that Betty should keep the conversation, or most of it, in English. She went so far as to lean over the arm of her chair and smile in a perturbed manner at the oddly contrasting couple who chatted so easily and pleasantly in the heathen tongue. She almost reached the point of speaking to Betty; gently, of course. But the girl clearly had no thought of possible impropriety. She was laughing now—apparently at some gap in her vocabulary—and the bland young man with the spectacles and the pigtail was humorously supplying the proper word.

Mrs. Hasmer decided not to speak. She lay hack in her chair. The wrinkles in her forehead deepened a little. On the other side Mr. Halting was describing enthusiastically a new and complicated table that was equipped with every imaginable device for the demonstrating of experiments in physics to Burmese youth. It could be packed, he insisted, for transport from village to village, in a crate no larger than the table itself.

And now, again, she caught the musical intonation of the young Chinaman. Betty, surprisingly direct and practical in manner if unintelligible in speech, was asking questions, which Li Hsien answered in turn, easily, almost languidly, but with unfailing good nature. Though there were a few moments during which he spoke rapidly and rather earnestly.

Mrs. Hasmer next became aware of the odd effect the little scene was plainly having on Jonathan Brachey. He fidgeted in his chair; got up and stood at the rail; paced the deck, twice passing close to the comfortably extended feet of the Hasmer party and so ostentatiously *not* looking at them as to distract momentarily the attention even of the deeply engrossed Betty. Mr. Harting, even, looked up. After all of which the man, looking curiously stern, or irritated, or (Betty decided) something unpleasant, sat again in his chair.

Then, a little later, Mr. Harting and Li Hsien took their leave and returned to the second-class quarters, astern.

Mrs. Hasmer thought, for a moment, that perhaps now was the time to suggest that English be made the common tongue in the future. But Betty's eager countenance disarmed her. She sighed. And sighed again; for the girl, stirred by what she was saying, had unconsciously raised her voice. And that tall man was listening.

"It's queer how fast things are changing out here," thus Betty. "Li Hsien is—you'd never guess!—a Socialist! I asked him why he isn't staying out the year at Tokio University, and he said he was called home to help the Province. Think of it—that boy! They've got into some trouble over a foreign mining syndicate—"

"The Ho Shan Company," explained Doctor Hasmer.

Betty nodded.

"They've been operating rather extensively in Plonan and southern Chihli," the educator continued, "and I heard last year that they've made a fresh agreement with the Imperial Government giving them practically a monopoly of the coal and iron mining up there in the Hansi Hills."

"Yes, Doctor Hasmer, and he says that there's a good deal of feeling in the province. They've had one or two mass meetings of the gentry and people. He thinks they'll send a protest to Peking. He believes that the company got the agreement through bribery."

"Not at all unlikely," remarked Doctor Hasmer mildly. "I don't know that any other way has yet been discovered of obtaining commercial privileges from the Imperial Government. The Ho Shan Company is... let me see... as I recall, it was organized by that Italian promoter, Count Logatti. I believe he went to Germany, Belgium and France for the capital."

"Li has become an astonishing young man," said Betty more gravely. "He talks about revolutions and republics. He doesn't think the Manchus can last much longer. The southern provinces are ready for the revolution now, he says—"

"That," remarked Doctor Hasmer, "is a little sweeping."

"Li is very sweeping," replied Betty. "And he's going back now to T'ainan-fu for some definite reason. I couldn't make out what. I asked if he would be coming in to see father, and he said, probably not; that there wouldn't be any use in it. Then I asked him if he was still a Christian, and I think he laughed at me. He wouldn't say."

The conversation was broken by the appearance of a pleasant Englishman, an importer of silks, by the name of Obie. He had been thrown with the Hasmers and Betty in one of their sight-seeing jaunts about Tokio.

Mr. Obie wore spats, and a scarf pin and cuff links of human bone from Borneo set in circlets of beaded gold. His light, usually amusing talk was liberally sprinkled with crisp phrases in pidgin-English.

He spoke now of the beauties of the Inland Sea, and resumed his stroll about the deck. After a few turns, he went into the smoking-room.

Jonathan Brachey, still with that irritably nervous manner, watched him intently; finally got up and followed him, passing the Hasmers and Betty with nose held high.

4

It was early afternoon, when Mrs. Hasmer and Betty were dozing in their chairs, that Mr. Obie, looking slightly puzzled, came again to them. He held a card between thumb and forefinger.

"Miss Doane," he said, "this gentleman asks permission to be presented."

Mrs. Hasmer's hand went out a little way to receive the card; but Betty innocently took it.

"Mr. Jonathan Brachey," she read aloud. Then added, with a pretty touch of color—"But how funny! He was with us yesterday, and *wouldn't* talk. And now...."

"My go catchee?" asked Mr. Obie.

To which little pleasantry Betty responded, looking very bright and pretty, with—"Can do!"

"She gives out too much," thought Mrs. Hasmer; deciding then and there that the meeting should be brief and the conversation triangular.

Mr. Obie brought him, formally, from the smoking-room.

He bowed stiffly. Betty checked her natural impulse toward a hearty hard-grip.

Mrs. Hasmer, feeling hurried, a thought breathless, meant to offer him her husband's chair; but all in the moment Betty had him down beside her.

Then came stark silence. The man stared out at the islands.

Betty, finding her portfolio on her lap, fingered it. Then this:

"I must begin, Miss Doane, with an apology...."

Betty's responsive face blanched. "What a dreadful man!" she thought. His voice was rather strong, dry, hard, with, even, a slight rasp in it.

But he drove heavily on:

"This morning, while not wishing to appear as an eavesdropper... that is to say... the fact is, Miss Doane, I am a journalist, and am at present on my way to China to make an investigation of the political—one might even term it the social—unrest that appears to be cropping out rather extensively in the southern provinces and even, a little here and there, in the North."

He was dreadful! Stilted, clumsy, slow! He hunted painstakingly for words; and at each long pause Betty's quick young nerves tightened and tightened, mentally groping with him until the hunted word was run to earth.

He was pounding on:

"This morning I overheard you talking with that young Chinaman. It is evident that you speak the language."

"Oh. yes," Betty found herself saying, "I do."

Not a word about the drawing.

"This young man, I gather, is in sympathy with the revolutionary spirit."

"He—he seems to be," said Betty.

"Now... Miss Doane... this is of course an imposition..."

"Oh, no," breathed Betty weakly.

"... it is, of course, an imposition... it would be a service I could perhaps never repay..." This pause lasted so long that she heard herself murmuring, "No, really, not at all!"—and then felt the color creeping to her face... but if I might ask you to... but let me put it in this way—the young man is precisely the type I have come out here to study. You speak in the vernacular, and evidently understand him almost as a native might. It is unlikely I shall find in China many such natural interpreters as yourself. And of course... if it is thinkable that you would be so extremely kind as to... why, of course, I..."

"Heavens!" thought Betty, in a panic, "he's going to offer to pay me. I mustn't be rude."

The man plodded on: "... why, of course, it would be a real pleasure to mention your assistance in the preface of my book."

It was partly luck, luck and innate courtesy, that she didn't laugh aloud. She broke, as it was, into words, saving herself and the situation.

"You want me to act as interpreter? Of course Li knows a little English."

"Would he—er—know enough English for serious conversation?"

"No," mused Betty aloud, "I don't think he would."

"Of course, Miss Doane, I quite realize that to take up your time in this way...."

There he stopped. He was frowning now, and apparently studying out the structural details of a huge junk that lay only a few hundred yards away, reflected minutely, exquisitely—curving hull and deck cargo, timbered stern, bat-wing sails—in the glass-like water.

"I'll be glad to do what I can," said Betty, helplessly. Then, for the first time, she became aware that Mrs. Hasmer was stirring uncomfortably on her other hand, and added, quickly, as much out of nervousness as anything else—"We could arrange to have Li come up here in the morning."

"We shall be coaling at Nagasaki in the morning," said he, abruptly, as if that settled *that*.

"Well, of course,... this afternoon....

"My dear," began Mrs. Hasmer.

"This afternoon would be better." Thus Mr. Brachey. "Though I can not tell you what hesitation..."

"I suppose we could find a quiet corner somewhere," said Betty. "In the social hall, perhaps."

It was then, stirred to positive act, that Mrs. Hasmer spoke out.

"I think you'd better stay out here with us, my dear."

To which the hopelessly self-absorbed Mr. Brachey replied:

"I really must have quiet for this work. We will sit inside, if you don't mind."

5

At half past four Mrs. Hasmer sent her husband to look into the situation. He reported that they were hard at it. Betty looked a little tired, but was laboriously repeating Li Hsien's words, in English, in order that Mr. Brachcy might take them down in what appeared to be a sort of shorthand. Doctor Hasmer didn't see how he could say anything. Not very well. They hadn't so much as noticed him, though he stood near by for a few moments.

Which report Mrs. Hasmer found masculine and unsatisfactory. At five she went herself; took her Battenberg hoop and sat near by. Betty saw her, and smiled. She looked distinctly a little wan.

The journalist ignored Mrs. Hasmer. He was a merciless driver. Whenever Betty's attention wandered, as it had begun doing, he put his questions bruskly, even sharply, to call her back to the task.

Four bells sounded, up forward. Mrs. Hasmer started; and, as always when she heard the ship's bell, consulted her watch. Six o'clock!... She put down her hoop; fidgetted; got up; sat down again; told herself she must consider the situation calmly. It must be taken in hand, of course. The man was a mannerless brute. He had distinctly encroached. He would encroach further. He must be met firmly, at once. She tried to think precisely how he could be met.

She got up again; stood over them. She didn't know that her face was a lens through which any and all might read her perturbed spirit.

Betty glanced up; smiled faintly; drew a long breath.

Li Hsien rose and bowed, clasping his hands before his breast.

Mr. Bradley was writing.

Mrs. Hasmer had tried to construct a little speech that, however final, would meet the forms of courtesy. It left her now. She said with blank firmness:

"Come, Betty!"

"One moment!" protested Mr. Brachey. "Will you please ask him, Miss Duane, whether he believes that the general use of opium has appreciably lowered the vitality of the Chinese people? That is, to put it conversely, whether the curtailment of production is going to leave a people too weakened to act strongly in a military or even political way? Surveying the empire as a whole, of course."

Betty's thoughts, which had wandered hopelessly afield, came struggling back.

"I—I'm sorry," she said. "I'm afraid I didn't quite hear."

"I must ask you to come with me, Betty," said Mrs. Hasmer.

At this, looking heavily disappointed, Mr. Brachey rose; ran a long bony hand through his thick hair.

"We could take it up in the morning," he said, turning from the bland young Chinaman to the plainly confused girl. "That is, if Miss Doane wouldn't mind staying on the ship. I presume she has seen Nagasaki."

His perturbed eyes moved at last to the little elderly lady who had seemed so colorless and mild; met hers, which were, of a sudden, snapping coals.

"You will not take it up again, sir!" cried Mrs. Hasmer; and left with the girl.

The Chinaman smiled, clasped his hands, bowed with impenetrable courtesy, and withdrew' to his quarters.

Mr. Brachey, alone, looked over his notes with a frown; shook his head; went down to dress for dinner.

6

Late that night Betty sat in her tiny stateroom, indulging rebellious thoughts. It was time, after an awkwardly silent evening, to go to bed. But instead she now slipped into her heavy traveling coat, pulled on her tam-o'-shanter, tiptoed past the Hasmers' door and went out on deck.

It was dim and peaceful there. The throb of the engines and the wash of water along the hull were the only sounds. They were in the strait now, heading out to sea.

She walked around the deck, and around. It was her first free moment since they left the Pacific ship at Yokohama. After that very quietly— sweetly, even—the chaperonage of Mrs. Hasmer had tightened. For Betty the experience was new and difficult. She felt that she ought to submit. But the rebellion in her breast, if wrong, was real. She would walk it off.

Then she met Mr. Brachey coming out of the smoking-room. Both stopped.

"Oh!" said he.

"I was just getting a breath of air," said she.

Then they moved to the rail and leaned there, gazing off at the faintly moonlit land.

He asked, in his cold way, how she had learned Chinese.

"I was born at T'ainan-fu," she explained. "My father is a missionary."

"Oh," said he. And again, "Oh!"

Then they fell silent. Her impulse at first was to make talk. She did murmur, "I really ought to be going in." But he, apparently, found talk unnecessary. And she stayed on, looking now down at the iridescent foam slipping past the black hull, now up into the luminous night.

Then he remarked, casually, "Shall we walk?" And she found herself falling into step with him.

They stopped, a little later, up forward and stood looking out over the forecastle deck.

"Some day I'm going to ask the chief officer to let me go out there," said she.

"It isn't necessary to ask him," replied Mr. Brachey. "Come along."

"Oh," murmured Betty, half in protest—"really?" But she went, thrilled now, more than a little guilty, down the steps, past hatches and donkey engines, up other steps, under and over a tangle of cables, over an immense anchor, to seats on coils of rope near the very bow.

The situation amounted already to a secret. Mrs. Hasmer couldn't be told, mused Betty. The fact was a little perplexing. But it stood.

Neither had mentioned Mrs. Hasmer. But now he said:

"I was rude to-day, of course."

"No," said she. "No."

"Oh, yes! I'm that way. The less I see of people the better."

This touched the half-fledged woman in her.

"You're interested in your work," said she gently. "That's all. And it's right. You're not a trifler."

"I'm a lone wolf."

She was beginning to find him out-and-out interesting.

"You travel a good deal," she ventured demurely. "All the time. I prefer it."

"Always alone?"

"Always."

"You don't get lonesome?"

"Oh, yes. But what does it matter?"

She considered this. "You go into dangerous places."

"Oh, yes."

"You traveled among the head-hunters of Borneo."

"How did you find that out?"

"There's an advertisment of that book in *To-morrow in India*."

"Oh, have you read that thing?"

"Part of it. I..."

"You found it dull."

"Well... it's a little over my head."

"It's over everybody's. Mine."

She nearly laughed at this. But he seemed not to think of it as humor.

"Aren't you a little afraid, sometimes—going into such dangerous places all alone?"

"Oh, no."

"But you might be hurt—or even—killed."

"What's the difference?"

Startled, she looked straight up at him; then dropped her eyes. She waited for him to explain, but he was gazing moodily out at the water ahead.

The soft night air wrapped them about like dream-velvet. Adventure was astir, and romance. Betty, enchanted, looked lazily back at the white midships decks, bridge and wheelhouse, at the mysterious rigging and raking masts, at the foremost of the huge funnels pouring out great rolling clouds of smoke. The engines throbbed and throbbed. Back there somewhere the ship's bell struck, eight times for midnight.

"I don't care much for missionaries," said Mr. Brachey.

"You'd like father."

"Perhaps."

"He's a wonderful man. He's six feet five. And strong."

"It's a job for little men. Little souls. With little narrow eyes."

"Oh... No!"

"Why try to change the Chinese? Their philosophy is finer than ours. And works better. I like them."

"So do I. But..." She wished her father could be there to meet the man's talk. There must surely be strong arguments on the missionary side, if one only knew them. She finally came out with:

"But they're heathen!"

"Oh, yes!"

"They're—they're polygamous!"

"Why not?"

"But Mr. Brachey..." She couldn't go on with this. The conversation was growing rather alarming.

"So are the Americans polygamous. And the other white peoples. Only they call it by other names. You get tired of it. The Chinese are more honest."

"I wonder," said she, suddenly steady and shrewd, "if you haven't stayed away too long."

His reply was:

"Perhaps."

"If you live—you know, all by yourself, and for nobody in the world except yourself—I mean, if there's nobody you're responsible for, nobody you love and take care of and suffer for..." The sentence was getting something involved. She paused, puckering her brows.

"Well?" said he.

"Why, I only meant, isn't there danger of a person like that becoming—well, just selfish."

"I am selfish."

"But you don't want to be."

"Oh. but I do!"

"I can hardly believe that."

"Dependence on others is as bad as gratitude. It is a demand, a weakness. Strength is better. If each of us stood selfishly alone, it would be a cleaner, better world. There wouldn't be any of this mess of obligation, one to another. No running up of spiritual debt. And that's the worst kind."

"But suppose," she began, a little afraid of getting into depths from which it might be difficult to extreate herself, "suppose—well, you were married, and there were—well, little children. Surely you'd have to feel responsible for them."

"Surely," said he curtly, "it isn't necessary for every man to bring children 'nto the world. Surely that's not the only job."

"But—but take another case. Suppose you had a friend, a younger man, and he was in trouble—drinking, maybe; anything!—wouldn't you feel responsible for him?"

"Not at all. That's the worst kind of dependence. The only battles a man wins are the ones he wins alone. If any friend of mine—man or woman—can't win his own battles—or hers—he or she had better go. Anywhere. To hell, if it comes to that."

He quite took her breath away.

One bell sounded.

"It's perfectly dreadful," said she. "If Mrs. Has-mer knew I was out here at this time of night, she'd..."

This sentence died out. They went back.

"Good night," said she.

She felt that he must think her very young and simple. It seemed odd that he should waste so much time on her. No other man she had ever met was like him. Hesitantly, desiring at least a touch of friendliness, on an impulse, she extended her hand.

He took it; held it a moment firmly; then said:

"Will you give me that drawing?"

"Yes," said she.

"Now?"

"Yes." And she tiptoed twice again past the Hasmers' door.

"Please sign it," said he, and produced a pencil. "But it seems so silly. I mean, it's nothing, this sketch."

"Please!"

She signed it, said good night again, and hurried off, her heart in a curious flutter.

CHAPTER II
ROMANCE

I

UNWILLING either to confess like a naughty child or to go on keeping this rather large and distinctly exciting secret under cover, Betty, at teatime, brought the matter to an issue. The morning ashore had been difficult. Mr. Brachey had severely ignored her, going about Nagasaki alone, lunching in austere solitude at the hotel.

She said, settling herself in the deck chair:

"Mrs. Hasmer, will you ask Mr. Brachey to have tea with us?"

After a long silence the older woman asked, stiffly: "Why, my dear?"

Betty compressed her lips.

Doctor Hasmer saved the situation by saying quietly, "I'll ask him."

It was awkward from the first. The man was angular and unyielding. And Mrs. Hasmer, though she tried, couldn't let him alone. She was determined to learn whether he was married. She led up to the direct question more otariously than she knew. Finally it came. They were speaking of his announced plan to travel extensively in the interior of China.

"It must be quite delightful to wander as you do," she said. "Of course, if one has ties... you, I take it, are an unmarried man, Mr. Brachey ?"

Betty had to lower her face to hide the color that came. If only Mrs. Hasmer had a little humor! She was a dear kind woman; but this!...

The journalist looked, impassively enough, but directly, at his questioner.

She met his gaze. They were flint on steel, these two natures.

"You are obviously not married," she repeated.

He looked down at his teacup; thinking. Then, abruptly, he set it down on the deck, got up, muttered something that sounded like, "If you will excuse me..." and strode away.

Betty went early to her cabin that evening.

She had no more than switched on her light when the Chinese steward came with a letter.

She locked the door then, and looked at the unfamiliar handwriting. It was small, round, clear; the hand of a particular man, a meticulous man. who has written much with a pen.

She turned down the little wicker seat. Her cheeks were suddenly hot, her pulse bounding high.

She skimmed it, at first, clear to the signature, "Jonathan Brachey"; then went back and read it through, slowly.

"I was rude again just now," (it began). "As I told you last night, it is best for me not to see people. I am not a social being. Clearly, from this time on, it will be impossible for me to talk with this Mrs. Hasmer. I shall not try again.

"I could not answer her question. But to you I must speak. It would be difficult even to do this if we were to meet again, and talk. But, as you will readily see, we must not meet again, beyond the merest greeting.

"I was married four years ago. After only a few weeks my wife left me. The reasons she gave were so flippant as to be absurd. She was a beautiful and, it has seemed to me, a vain, spoiled, quite heartless woman. I have not seen her since. Two years ago she became infatuated with another man, and wrote asking me to consent to a divorce. I refused on the ground that I did not care to enter into the legal intrigues preliminary to a divorce in the state of her residence. Since then, I am told, she has changed her residence to a state in which 'desertion' is a legal ground. But I have received no word of any actual move on her part.

"It is strange that I should be writing thus frankly to you. Strange, and perhaps wrong. But you have reached out to me more of a helping hand than you will ever know. Our talk last night meant a great deal to me. To you I doubtless seemed harsh and forbidding. It is true that I am that sort of man, and therefore am best alone. It is seldom that I meet a person with whom my ideas are in agreement.

"I trust that you will find every happiness in life. You deserve to. You have the great gift of feeling. I could almost envy you that. It is a quality I can perceive without possessing. An independent mind, a strong gift of logic, stands between me and all human affection. I must say what I think, not what I feel.

"I make people unhappy. The only corrective to such a nature is work, and, whenever possible, solitude. But I do not solicit your pity. I find myself, my thoughts, excellent company.

"With your permission I will keep the drawing. It will have a peculiar and pleasant meaning to me."

2

Betty lowered the letter, breathing out the single word, "Well!"

What on earth could she have said or done to give him any such footing in her life?

She read it again. And then again.

An amazing man!

She made, ready to go to bed, slowly, dawdling, trying to straighten out the curious emotional pressures on her mind.

She read the letter yet again; considered it.

Finally, after passing through many moods leading up to a tender sympathy for this bleak life, and then passing on into a state of sheer nervous excitement, she deliberately dressed again and went out on deck.

He stood by the rail, smoking.

"You have my letter?" he asked.

"Yes. I've read it." She was oddly, happily relieved at finding him.

"You shouldn't have come."

She had no answer to this. It seemed hardly relevant. She smiled, in the dark.

They fell to walking the deck. After a time, shyly, tacitly, a little embarrassed, they went up forward again.

The ship was well out in the Yellow Sea now. The bow rose and fell slowly, rhythmically, beneath them.

Moved to meet his letter with a response in kind, she talked of herself.

"It seems strange to be coming back to China."

"You've been long away?"

"Six years. My mother died when I was thirteen. Father thought it would be better for me to be in the States. My uncle, father's brother, was in the wholesale hardware business in New York, and lived in Orange, and they took me in. They were always nice to me. But last fall Uncle Frank came down with rheumatic gout. He's an invalid now. It must have been pretty expensive. And there was some trouble in his business. They couldn't very well go on taking care of me, so father decided to have me come back to T'ainan-fu." She folded her hands in her lap.

He lighted his pipe, and smoked reflectively.

"That will be rather hard for you, won't it?" he remarked, after a time. "I mean for a person of your temperament. You are, I should say, almost exactly my opposite in every respect. You like people, friends. You are impulsive, doubtless affectionate. I could be relatively happy, marooned among a few hundred millions of yellow folk—though I could forego the missionaries. But you are likely, I should think, to be starved there. Spiritually—emotionally."

"Do you think so?" said she quietly.

"Yes." He thought it, over "The life of a mission compound isn't exactly gay."

"No, it isn't."

"And you need gaiety."

"I wonder if I do. I haven't really faced it, of course. I'm not facing it now."

"Just think a moment. You've not even landed in China yet. You're under no real restraint—still among white people, on a white man's ship, eating in European hotels at the ports. You aren't teaching endless lessons to yellow children, day in, day out. You aren't shut up in an interior city, where it mightn't even he safe for you to step outside the gate house alone. And yet you're breaking bounds. Right now—out here with me."

Already she was taking his curious bluntness for granted. She said now, simply, gently:

"I know. I'm sitting out here at midnight with a married man. And I don't seem to mind. Of course you're not exactly married. Still... A few days ago I wouldn't have thought it possible."

"Did you tell the Hasmers that you were out here last night?"

"No."

"Shall you tell them about this?"

She thought a moment; then, as simply, repeated: "No."

"Why not?"

"I don't know. It's the way I feel."

He nodded. "You feel it's none of their business."

"Well—yes."

"Of course, I ought to take you back, now."

"I don't feel as if I were doing wrong. Oh, a little, but..."

"I ought to take you back."

She rested a hand on his arm. It was no more than a girlish gesture. She didn't notice that he set his teeth and sat very still.

"I've thought this, though," she said. "If I'm to meet you out here like—like this—"

"But you're not to."

"Well... here we are!"

"Yes... here we are!"

"I was going to say, it's dishonest, I think, for us to avoid each other during the day. If we're friends..."

"If we're friends we'd better admit it."

"Yes. I meant that."

He fell to working at his pipe with a pocket knife She watched him until he was smoking again.

"Mrs. Hasmer won't like it."

"I can't help that."

"No. Of course." He smoked. Suddenly he broke out, with a gesture so vehement that it startled her: "Oh, it's plain enough—we're on a ship, idling, dreaming, floating from a land of color and charm and quaint unreality to another land that has always enchanted me, for all the dirt and disease, and the smells. It's that! Romance! The old web! It's catching us. And we're not even resisting. No one could blame you—you're young, charming, as full of natural life as a young flower in the morning. But I... I'm not romantic. To-night, yes! But next Friday, in Shanghai, no!"

Betty turned away to hide a smile.

"You think I'm brutal? Well—I am."

"No, you're not brutal."

"Yes, I am.... But my God! You in T'ainanfu! Child, it's wrong!"

"It is simply a thing I can't help," said she.

They fell silent. The pulse of the great dim ship was soothing. One bell sounded. Two bells. Three.

3

Aman of Jonathan Brachey's nature couldn't know the power his nervous bold thoughts and words were bound to exert in the mind of a girl like Betty. In her heart already she was mothering him. Every word he spoke now, even the strong words that startled her, she enveloped in warm sentiment.

To Brachey's crabbed, self-centered nature she was like a lush oasis in the arid desert of his heart. He could no more turn his back on it than could any tired, dusty wanderer. He knew this. Or, better, she was like a mirage. And mirages have driven men out of their wits.

So romance seized them. They walked miles the next day, round and round the deck. Mrs. Hasmer was powerless, and perturbed. Her husband counseled watchful patience. Before night all the passengers knew that the two were restless apart. They found corners on the boat deck, far from all eyes.

That night Mrs. Hasmer came to Betty's door; satisfied herself that the girl was actually undressing and going to bed. Not one personal word passed.

And then, half an hour later, Betty, dressed again, tiptoed out. Her heart was high, touched with divine recklessness. This, she supposed, was wrong; but right or wrong, it was carrying her out of her girlish self. She couldn't stop.

Brachey was fighting harder; but to little purpose. They had these two days now. That was all. At Shanghai, and after, it would be, as he had so vigorously said, different. Just these two days! He saw, when she joined him on the deck, that she was riding at the two days as if they were to be her last on earth. Intensely, soberly happy, she was passing through a golden haze of dreams, leaving the future to be what it might.

They sat, hand in hand, in the bow. She sang, in a light pretty voice, songs of youth in a young land—college ditties, popular negro melodies, amusing little street songs.

Very, very late, on the last evening, after a long silence—they had mounted to the boat deck—he caught her roughly in his arms and kissed her.

She lay limply against him. For a moment, a bitter moment—for now, in an instant, he knew that she had never thought as far as this—he feared she had fainted. Then he felt her tears on his cheek.

He lifted her to her feet, as roughly.

She swayed away from him leaning against a boat.

He said, choking:

"Can you get down the steps all right?"

She bowed her head. He made no effort to help her down the steps. They walked along the deck toward the main companionway. Suddenly, with an inarticulate sound, he turned, plunged in at the smoking-room door, and was gone.

Early in the morning the ship dropped anchor in the muddy Woosung. The breakfast hour came around, then quarantine inspection; but the silent pale Betty, her moody eyes searching restlessly, caught no glimpse of him. He must have taken a later launch than the one that carried Betty and the Hasmers up to the Bund at Shanghai. And during their two days in the bizarre, polyglot city, with its European façade behind which swarms all China, it became clear that he wasn't stopping at the Astor House.

The only letter was from her father at T'ainan-fu.

She watched every mail; and inquired secretly at the office of the river steamers an hour before starting on the long voyage up the Yangtse; but there was nothing.

Then she recalled that he had never asked for her address, or for her father's full name. They had spoken of T'ainan-fu. He might or might not remember it.

And that was all.

CHAPTER III
THE SHEPHERD

AT the point where the ancient highway, linking Northern China with Thibet, the Kukunor region and Mongolia, emerges from the treeless, red-brown tumbling hills of Hansi Province there stands across the road—or stood, before the revolution of 1911—a scenic arch of masonry crowned with a curving elaborately ornamented roof of tiles. Some forgotten philanthropist erected it, doubtless for a memorial to forgotten dead. Through this arch the west-bound traveler caught his first view of the wide yellow valley of the Han, with its yellow river, its square-walled, gray-green capital city, and, far beyond, of the sharp purple mountains that might have been cut out of cardboard.

The gray of old T'ainan lay in the massive battle-mented walls and in the more than six square miles of closely packed tile roofs; the green in its thousands of trees. For here, as in Peking and Sian-fu they had preserved the trees; not, of course, in the innumerable tortuous streets, where petty merchants, money-changers, porters, coolies, beggars, soldiers and other riffraff passed freely through mud or dust, but within the thousands of hidden private courtyards, in the yamens of governor, treasurer, and provincial judge, in temple grounds outside the walls, and in the compound of the American Mission. At this latter spot, by the way, could be seen, with the aid of field-glasses, the only two-story residence in T'ainan; quite a European house, built after the French manner of red brick trimmed with white stone, and rising distinctly above the typically gray roofs that clustered about its lower windows.

There were bold gate towers on the city wall; eight of them, great timbered structures with pagoda roofs rising perhaps fifteen yards above the wall and thirty above the lowly roadway. The timber-work under the shadowing eaves had sometime been painted in reds, blues and greens; and the once vivid colors, though dulled now by weather and years, were still richly visible to the near-observer.

Many smaller settlements, little gray clusters of houses, lay about the plain on radiating highways; for T'ainan boasted its suburbs. The hill slopes were dotted with the homes and walled gardens of bankers, merchants and other gentry. On a plateau just north of the Great Highway stood, side by side, two thirteen-roof pagodas, the pride of all central Hansi.

About the city, on any day of the seven, twisting through the hundreds of little streets and in and out at the eight gates, moved tens of thousands of tirelessly busy folk, all clad in the faded blue cotton that spells China to the eye, and among these a slow-moving, never-ceasing tangle of wheeled and fourfooted local traffic.

And along the Great Highway—down the hill slopes, through suburbs and city, over the river and on toward the teeming West; over the river, through city and suburbs and up the hills, toward the teeming East—flowed all day long the larger commerce that linked province with province and, ultimately, yellow man with white, at the treaty ports, hundreds of miles away. There were strings of laden camels with evil-looking Mongol drivers; hundreds and thousands of camels, disdainfully going and coming. There were hundreds and thousands of asses, patient little humorists, bearing panniers of coal lumps and iron ore from the crudely operated mines in the hills. There were hundreds and thousands of mule-drawn carts, springless, many with arched roofs of matting.

Along the roadside, sheltered by little sagging canopies of grimy matting, or squatting in the dirt, were vendors of flat cakes and vinegary *sumshoo* and bits of this and that to wear. Naked children swarmed like flies in the sun.

The day-by-day life of the oldest and least selfconscious civilization in the world was moving quietly, resistlessly along, as it had moved for six thousand years.

2

Reverend Henry B. Withery, on a morning in late March, came, by springless cart, out of Kansu into T'ainan. A drab little man, with patient fervor in his eyes and a limp (this latter the work of Boxers in 1900). He was bound, on leave, for Shanghai, San Francisco and home; but a night at T'ainan with Griggsby Doane meant, even in the light of hourly nearing America, much. For they had shared rooms at the seminary. They had entered the yielding yet resisting East side by side. Meeting but once or twice a year, even less often, they had felt each other deeply across the purple mountains.

They sat through tiffin with the intent preoccupied workers in the dining-room of the brick house; and Mr Withery's gentle eyes took in rather shrewdly the curious household. It interested him. There were elements that puzzled him; a suggestion of staleness in this face, of nervous overstrain in that; a tension.

The several native workers smiled and talked less, he thought, than on his former visits.

Little Mr. Boatwright—slender, dustily blond, always hitherto burning with the tire of consecration—was continually fumbling with a spoon, or slowly twisting his tumbler, the while moodily studying the table-cloth. And his larger wife seemed heavier in mind as in body.

Mr. Withery found the atmosphere even a little oppressive. He looked up about the comfortable, high ceiled room. Mounted and placed on the walls were a number of interesting specimens of wild fowl. Elmer Boatwright, though no devotee of slaughter or even of sport, had shot and mounted these himself.

Withery asked him now if he had found any interesting birds lately. The reply was little more than monosyllabic; it was almost the reply of a middle-aged man who has lost and forgotten the enthusiasm of youth.

There was talk, of course; the casual surface chatter of folk who are deeply united in work. A new schoolroom was under construction. Jen Ling Pu, a native preacher, was doing well at So T'ung. The new tennis court wasn't, after all, long enough.

During all this, Withery pondered. Griggsby was driving too hard, of course. The strongly ascetic nature of the man seemed to be telling on him; or perhaps it was running out, the fire of it, leaving only the force of will. That happened, of course, now and then, in the case of men gifted with great natural vitality.

Then too, come to reflect on it, the fight had been hard, here in Hansi. Since 1900. Harder, perhaps, than anywhere else except Shantung and Chihli. Harder even than in those more easterly provinces, for they were nearer things. There were human contacts, freshening influences... . The Boxers had dealt heavily with the whites in Hansi. More than a hundred had been slain by fire or sword. Young women—girls like these two or three about the dinner table—had been tortured. Griggsby and his wife and the little girl had missed destruction only through the accident of a journey, in the spring, to Shanghai. And he had returned, dangerously early, to a smoldering ruin and plunged with all the vigor in his unusual body and mind at the task of reconstruction. The work in the province was shorthanded, of course, even yet. It would be so. But Griggsby was building it up. He even had the little so-called college, down the river at Hung Chan, going again, after a fashion. Money was needed, of course. And teachers. And equipment. All that had been discussed during tiffin. It was a rather heroic record. And it had not passed unobserved. At the Missionary Conference, at Shanghai, in 1906, Griggsby's report—carefully phrased, understated throughout, almost colorless—had drawn out unusual applause.

Mrs. Doane's death occurred during the first year of that painful reconstruction. Griggsby's course, after that, from the day of the funeral, in fact, as you looked back over it, recalling this and that apparently trivial incident, was characteristic. The daughter was sent back to the States, for schooling. Griggsby furnished for himself, up in what was little more, really, than the attic of the new mission residence, a bare, severe little suite of bedroom and study. The newly married Boatwrights he installed, as something near master and mistress, on the second floor. The other white workers and teachers filled all but the two guest rooms, and, at times, even these. And then, his little institution organized on a wholly new footing, he had loaded himself sternly with work.

Dinner was over. One by one the younger people left the room. And within a few moments the afternoon routine of the mission compound was under way.

Through the open window came a beam of warm spring sunshine. Outside, across the wide courtyard Withery noted the, to him, familiar picture of two or three blue-clad Chinese men lounging on the steps of the gate house; students crossing, books in hand; young girls round and fresh of face, their slanting eyes demurely downcast, assembling before one of the buildings; two carpenters working deliberately on a scaffold. A soft-footed servant cleared the table. Now that the two friends were left free to chat of personal matters, the talk wandered into unexpectedly impersonal regions. Withery found himself baffled, and something puzzled. During each of their recent visits Griggsby's manner had affected him in this same way, but less definitely. The aloofness—he had once or twice ever, thought of it as an evasiveness—had been only a tendency. The old friendship had soon warmed through it and brought ease of spirit and tongue. But the tendency had grown. The present Griggsby was clearly going to prove harder to get at. That remoteness of manner had grown on him as a habit. The real man, whatever he was coming to be, was hidden now; the man whose very soul had once been written clear in the steady blue eyes.

And what a man he was! Mr. Withery indulged in a moment of sentiment as he quietly, shrewdly studied him, across the table.

In physical size, as in mental attainments and emotional force, James Griggsby Duane had been, from the beginning, a marked man. He was forty-five now; or within a year of it. The thick brown hair of their student days was thinner-now at the sides and nearly gone on top. But the big head was set on the solid shoulders with all the old distinction. A notable fact about Griggsby Doane was that after winning intercollegiate standing as a college football player, he had never allowed his body to settle back with the years. He weighed now, surely, within a pound or two or three of his playing weight twenty-four years earlier. He had always been what the British term a clean feeder, eating sparingly of simple food. Hardly a day of his life but had at least its hour or two of violent exercise. He would rise at five in the morning and run a few miles before breakfast. He played tennis and handball. He would gladly have boxed and wrestled, but a giant with nearly six and a half feet of trained, conditioned muscle at his disposal finds few to meet him, toe to toe. His passion for walking had really, during the earlier years, raised minor difficulties about T'ainan. The Chinese were intelligent and, of course, courteous; but it was more than they could be asked to understand at first.

It had worked out, gradually. They knew him now; knew he was fearless, industrious, patient, kind. During the later years, after the Boxer trouble, his immense figure, striding like him of the fabled seven-league-boots, had become a familiar, friendly figure in central Hansi. Not infrequently he would tramp, pack on shoulders, from one to another of the outlying mission stations; and thought nothing of covering a hundred and thirty or forty *li* where your cart or litter mules or your Manchu pony would stop at ninety and call it a day.

Withery was bringing the talk around to the personal when Doane looked at his watch.

"You'll excuse me, Henry," he said. "I've a couple of classes. But I'll knock off about four-thirty. Make yourself comfortable. Prowl about. Use my study, if you like.... Or wait. We were speaking of the Ho Shan Company. They've had two or three mass meetings here during the winter, and got up some statements."

"Do they suggest violence?"

"Oh, yes." Doane waved the thought carelessly aside. "But Pao will keep them in hand, I think. He doesn't want real trouble. But he wouldn't mind scaring the company into selling out. The gossip is that he is rather heavily interested himself in some of the native mines."

"Is Pao your governor?"

"No, the governor died last fall, and no successor has been sent out. Kang, the treasurer, is nearly seventy and smokes sixty to a hundred pipes of opium a day. Pao Ting Chuan is provincial judge, but is ruling the province now. He's an able fellow.".... Doane drew a thick lot of papers from an inner pocket, and selected one. "Read this. It's one of their statements. Pao had the translation made in his yamen. I haven't the original, but the translation is fairly accurate I believe."

Withery took the paper; ignored it, and studied his friend, who had moved to the door. Doane seemed to have lost his old smile—reflective, shrewd, a little quizzical. The furrow between his eyes had deepened into something near a permanent frown. There were fine lires about and under the eyes that might have indicated a deep weariness of the spirit. Yet the skin was clear, the color good.... Griggsby was fighting something out; alone; through the years.

Feeling this, Henry Withery broke out, in something of their old frank way.

"Do knock off, Grigg. Let's have one of the old talks. I think—I think perhaps you need me a little." Doane hesitated. It was not like him to do that. "Yes," he said gravely, but with his guard up, that curious guard, "it would be fine to have one of the old talks if we can get at it."

He turned to go; then paused.

"Oh, by the way, I'm expecting Pourmont. A little later in the day. He's resident engineer for the Ho Shan Company, over at Ping Yang. Pierre François George Marie Pourmont. An amusing person. He feels a good deal of concern over these meetings. For that matter, he was mobbed here in February. He didn't like that."

Withery found himself compressing his lips, and tried to correct that impulse with a rather artificial smile. It wasn't like Griggsby to speak in that light way. Like a society man almost. It suggested a hardening of the spirit; or a crust over deep sensitiveness.

Men, he reflected, who have to fight themselves during long periods of time are often hardened by the experience, even though they eventually win.

He wondered, moving to the window, and thoughtfully watching the huge man striding across the courtyard, if Griggsby Doane would be winning.

3

Up in the little study under the roof Mr. Withery sank into a Morris chair and settled back to read the views of the "Gentry and People of Hansi" on foreign mining syndicates. The documents had been typed on an old machine with an occasional broken letter; and were phrased in the quaint English that had long been familiar to him.

First came a statement of the "five items" of difference between these "Gentry and People" and the Ho Shan Company—all of a technical or business nature. Only in the last "item" did the emotional reasoning common to Chinese public documents make its appearance.... "*Five*. In Honan the company boldly introduced dynamite, which is prohibited. The dynamite exploded and this gave rise to diplomatic trouble, a like thing might happen in Hansi with the same evil consequences." Then followed this inevitable general statement:

"At present in China, from the highest to the lowest, all are in difficulty—the annual for the indemnities amounts to Taels 30,000,000, and in every province the reforms involve great additional expenditure, while the authorities only know how to control the expenditure, but not how to reach fresh sources of income. Those in power can find no fresh funds and the people are extremely poor and all they have to trust to are a few feet of land which have not been excavated by the foreigners. Westerners say that the coal of Hansi is sufficient to supply the needs of the world for two thousand years; in other countries there is coal without iron, or iron without coal, but in Hansi there is abundance of both coal and iron and it forms one of the best manufacturing countries in the world. At present if there is no protection for China then that finishes it, but if China is to be protected how can Hansi be excluded from protection? Therefore all China and all Hansi must withstand the claims of the Ho Shan Company.

"The company's agent general says that the agreement was drawn up with the Chinese Government, but at that time the people were unenlightened and traitors were suffered to effect stolen sales of Government lands, using oppression and disregarding the lives of the people. Now all the Gentry and People know how things are, and of what importance the consequences are for the lives of themselves and their families, and so with one heart they all withstand the company in whatever schemes it may have, for they are not willing to drop their hands and give themselves up to death, and if the officials will not protect the mines of Hansi then we will protect our mines ourselves.

"We suggest a plan for the company, that it should state the sum used to bribe Hu Pin Chili, and to win over Chia Ching Jen and Liu O and Sheng Hsuan Hui and the Tsung Li Yamen, and the Wai Wu Pu and the Yu Chuan Pu, at the present time, and the bribes to other cruel traitors, and a detailed account of their expenditure in opening their mines since their arrival in China, and Hansi will repay the amount. If the company still pushes the claim for damages, in consequence of the delay in issuing the permit then the Hansi people will never submit to it.

"In conclusion the people of Hansi must hold to their mines till death, and if the Government and officials still unrighteously flatter the foreigners in their oppression and flog the people robbing them of their flesh and blood to give those to the foreigners then some one must throw away his life by bomb throwing and so repay the company, but we trust the company will carefully consider and weigh the matter and not push Hansi to this extremity."

Mr. Withery laid the documents on Doane's desk, and gave up an hour to jotting down notes for his own annual report. Then he took a long walk, in through the wall and about the inner city. He was back by four-thirty, but found no sign of his friend.

At five a stout Frenchman arrived, a man of fifty or more, with a long, square-trimmed beard of which he was plainly fond. Doane returned then to the house.

4

The three men had tea in the study. M. Pourmont, with an apology, smoked cigarettes. Withery observed, when the genual Frenchman turned his head, that the lobe of his left ear was missing.

M. Pourmont regarded the local situation seriously.

"Zay spik of you," he explained to Griggsby Doane.

"Zay say zat you have ze petit papier, ze little paper, all yellow, cut like ze little man an' woman. An' it is also zat zay say zat ze little girl, ze student, all ze little jeunes filles, is ze lowair vife of you, Monsieur It is not good, zat. At Paree ve vould say zat it is *se compliment*, but here it is not good. It is zat zay have not bifore spik like zat of Monsieur Doane."

Doane merely considered this without replying.

"That statement of the Gentry and People looks rather serious to me," Mr. Withery remarked.

"It has its serious side," said Doane quietly. "Put you see, of course, from the frankness and publicity of it, that the officials are back of it. These Gentry and People would never go so far unsupported. It wouldn't surprise me to learn that the documents originated within the yamen of his Excellency Pao Ting Chuan."

"Very good," said Withery. "Put if he lets it drift much further the danger will be real. Suppose some young hothead were to take that last threat seriously and give up his life in throwing a bomb—-what then?"

"It would be serious then, of course," said Doane. "But I hardly think any one here would go so far unsupported."

"Yes!" cried M. Pourmont, in some excitement, "an' at who is it zat zay t'row ze bomb? It is at me, *n'est ce pas?* At me! You tlink I forget v'en ze mob it t'rowr ze *bierre* at me? *Mais non!* Zay tear ze cart of me. Zay beat ze head of me. Zay destroy ze ear of me. *Ah, c' était terrible, ça!*"

"They attacked Monsieur Pourmont while he was riding to the yamen for an audience with Pao," Doane explained. "But Pao heard of it and promptly sent soldiers. 1 took it up with him the next day. He acted most correctly. The ringleaders of the mob were whipped and imprisoned."

"But you mus' also say to Monsieur Vitieree zat ze committee of my *compagnie* he come to Peking—*quinze mille kilometres he come!*—an' now *Son Excellence* he say zay mus' not come here, into *ze province.* It is so difficult, ça! An' ze committee he is ver' angry. He swear at Peking. He cool ze—vat you say—-heels. An' ze work he all stop. No good! Noz-zing at all!"

"That is all so, Henry." Thus Doane, turning to his friend. "I don't mean to minimize the actual difficulties. But I do not believe we are in any such danger as in 1900. Even then the officials did it, of course. If they hadn't believed that the incantations of the Boxers made them immune to our bullets, and if they hadn't convinced the Empress Dowager of it, we should never have had the siege of the legations. But I am to have an audience with His Excellency tomorrow, at one, and will go over this ground carefully. I have no wish, myself, to underestimate the trouble. My daughter arrives next week."

"Oh!" said Withery. "Oh... your daughter! From the States, Grigg?"

"Yes, I am to meet her at Hankow. Thc Hasmers brought her across."

"That's too bad, in a way."

"Of course. But there was no choice."

"But zat is not all zat is!" M. Puurmont was pacing the floor now. "A boy of me, of ze *cuisine,* he go home las' week to So T'ung an' he say zat a—vat you call?—a circle.."

"A society?"

"*Mais oui!* A society, she meet in ze night an' *fait l'exercise—*"

"They are drilling?"

"*Oui!* Ze drill. It is ze society of Ze Great Eye."

"I never heard of that," mused Griggsby aloud. "I don't really see what they can do. But I'll take it up to-morrow with, Pao. I would ask you, however, to remember that if the people don't know the cost of indemnities, there can be no doubt about Pao. He knows. And it is hard for me to imagine the province drifting out of his control for a single day. One event I am planning to watch closely is the fair here after the middle of April. Some of these agitators of the Gentry and People are sure to be on hand. We shall learn a great deal then."

"You'll be back then, Grigg?"

"Oh, yes. By the tenth. I shan't delay at all at Hankow."

It seemed to Henry Withery that his friend and host maneuvered to get him to retire first. Then he attributed the suspicion to his own disturbed thoughts.... Still, Griggsby hadn't returned to the house until after M. Pourmont's arrival. It was now nearly midnight, and there had been never a personal word.

But at last, M. Pourmont out of the way for the night, lamp in hand, Griggsby led the way to the remaining guest room.

Withery, following, looked up at the tall grave man, who had to stoop a little at the doors. Would Griggsby put down the lamp, speak a courteous good night, and go off to his own attic quarters; or would he linger? It was to be a test, this coming moment, of their friendship.... Withery's heart filled. In his way, through the years, out there in remote Kansu, he had always looked up to Grigg and had leaned on him, on memories of him as he had been. He had the memories now—curiously poignant memories, tinged with the melancholy of lost youth. But had he still the friend?

Duane set down the lamp, and looked about, all grave courtesy, to see if his friend's bag was at hand, and if the wash-stand and towel-rack had been made ready.

Withery stood on the sill, struggling to control his emotions. Longfellow's lines came to mind:

"A boy's will is the wind's will,

And the thoughts of youth are long, long

thoughts."

They were middle-aged now, they two. It was extraordinarily hard to believe. They had felt so much, and shared so much. They had plunged at missionary work with such ardor. Grigg especially. He had thrown aside more than one early opportunity for a start in business. He had sacrificed useful worldly acquaintances. His heart had burned to save souls, to carry the flame of divine revelation into what had then seemed a benighted, materialistic land.

Grigg would have succeeded in business or in the service of his government. He had a marked administrative gift. And power.... Distinctly power.

Withery stepped within the room, closed the door behind him, and looked straight up into that mask of a face; in his own deep emotion he thought of it as a tragic mask.

"Grigg," he said very simply, "what's the matter?"

There was a silence. Then Doane came toward the door.

"The matter?" he queried, with an effort to smile.

"Can't we talk, Grigg?... I know you are in deep trouble."

"Well" —Doane rested a massive hand on a bedpost—"I won't say that it isn't an anxious time, Henry. I'm pinning my faith to Pau Ting Chuan. But... And, of course, if I could have foreseen all the little developments, I wouldn't have sent for Betty. Though it's not easy to see what else I could have done. Frank and Ethel couldn't keep her longer. And the expense of any other arrangement... She's nineteen, Henry. A young woman. Curious—a young woman whom I've never even seen as such, and my daughter!"

"It isn't that, Grigg."

At the moment Withery could say no more. He sank into a chair by the door, depressed in spirit.

Doane walked to the window; looked out at the stars; drummed a moment on the glass.

"It's been uphill work, Henry... since nineteen hundred."

Withery cleared his throat. "It isn't that," he repeated unsteadily.

Doane stood there a moment longer; then turned and gazed gloomily at his friend.

The silence grew painful.

Finally, Doane sighed, spread his hands in the manner of one who surrenders to fate, and came slowly over to the bed; stretching out his long frame there, against the pillows.

"So it's as plain as that, Henry."

"It is—to me."

"I wonder if I can talk."

"The question is, Grigg—can I help you?"

"I'm afraid not, Henry. I doubt if any one can." The force of this sank slowly into Withery's mind. "No one?" he asked in a hushed voice.

"I'm afraid not.... Do you think the others, my people here, see it?"

"The tone has changed here, Grigg."

"I've tried not to believe it."

"I've felt it increasingly for several years. When I've passed through. Even in your letters. It's been hard to speak before. For that matter, I had formulated no question. It was just an impression. But today... and to-night..."

"It's as bad as that, now."

"Suppose I say that it's as definite as that, Grigg. The impression."

Doane let his head drop back against the pillows; closed his eyes.

"The words don't matter," he remarked.

"No, they don't, of course." Withery's mind, trained through the busy years to the sort of informal confessional familiar to priests of other than the Roman church, was clearing itself of the confusions of friendship and was ready to dismiss, for the time, philosophically; the sense of personal loss.

"Is it something you've done, Grigg?" he asked now, gently. "Have you—"

Doane threw out an interrupting hand.

"No," he said rather shortly, "I've not broken the faith, Henry, not in act."

"In your thoughts only?"

"Yes. There."

"It is doubt?... Strange, Grigg, I never knew a man whose faith had in it such vitality. You've inspired thousands. Tens of thousands. You—I will say this, now—you, nothing more, really, than my thoughts of you carried me through my bad time. Through those doldrums when the ardor of the first few years had burned out and I was spent, emotionally. It was with your help that I found my feet again. You never knew' that."

"No. I didn't know that."

"I worried a good deal, then. I had never before been aware of the church as a worldly organization, as a political mechanism. I hadn't questioned it.

It was Hidderleigh's shrewd campaign for the bishopric that disturbed me. Then the money raised questions, of course."

"There's been a campaign on this winter, over in the States," said Doane, speaking slowly and thoughtfully. "Part of that fund is to be sent here to help extend my work in the province. They're using all the old emotional devices. All the claptrap. Chaplain Cabell is touring the churches with his little cottage organ and his songs."

"But the need is real out here, Grigg. And the people at home must be stirred into recognizing it. They can't he reached except through their emotions. I've been through all that. I see now, clearly enough, that it's an imperfect world. We must do the best we can with it. Because it is imperfect we must keep at our work."

"You know as well as I what they're doing, Henry. Cabell, all that crowd, haven't once mentioned Hansi. They're talking the Congo."

"But you forget, Grigg, that the emotional interest of our home people in China has run out. They thought about us during the Boxer trouble, and later, during the famine in Shensi. Now, because of the talk of slavery and atrocities in Central Africa, public interest has shifted to that part of the world."

"And so they're playing on the public sympathy for Africa to raise money, some of which is later to be diverted to Central China."

"What else can they do?"

"I don't know."

"You find yourself inclined to question the whole process?"

"Yes."

"Aren't you misplacing your emphasis, Grigg? We all do that, of course. Now and then.... Isn't the important thing for you, the emphatic thing, to spread the word of God in Hansi Province?" He leaned forward, speaking simply, with sincerity.

Doane closed his eyes again; and compressed his lips.

Withery, anxiously watching him, saw that the healthy color was leaving his face.

After a silence that grew steadily in intensity, Doane at last opened his eyes, and spoke, huskily, but with grim force.

"Of course, Henry, you're right. Right enough. These things are details. They're on my nerves, that's all. I'm going to tell you..." He sat up, slowly swung his feet to the floor, clasped his hands.... "I'll spare you my personal history of the past few years. And, of course, captious criticism of the church is no proper introduction to what I'm going to say. During these recent years I've been groping through my own Gethsemane. It has been a terrible time. There have been many moments when I've questioned the value of the struggle. If I had been as nearly alone as it has seemed, sometimes... I mean, if there hadn't been little Betty to think of..."

"I understand," Withery murmured.

"In a way I've come through my Valley. My head has cleared a little. And now I know only too clearly; it is very difficult; in a way, the time of doubt and groping was easier to bear... I know that I am in the wrong work."

Withery, with moist eyes, studied the carpet.

"You are sure?" he managed to ask.

He felt rather than saw his friend's slow nod.

"It's a relief, of course, to tell you." Doane was speaking with less effort now; but his color had not returned. "There's no one else. I couldn't say it to Hidderleigh. To me that man is fundamentally dishonest."

Withery found it difficult to face such extreme frankness. His mind slipped around it into another channel. He was beginning to feel that Grigg mustn't be let off so easily. There were arguments....

"One thing that has troubled me, even lately," he said, hunting for some common ground of thought and speech, "is the old denominational differences back home. I can't take all that for granted, as so many of our younger workers do. It has seemed to me that the conference last year should have spoken out more vigorously on that one point. We can never bring missionary work into any sort of unity here while the denominational spirit is kept alive at home."

Doane broke out, with a touch of impatience: "We approach the shrewdest, most keenly analytical people or; earth, the Chinese, with something near a hundred and fifty conflicting varieties of the one true religion. Too often, Henry, we try to pass to them our faith but actually succeed only in exhibiting the curious prejudices of narrow white minds."

This was, clearly, not a happy topic. Withery sighed.

"This—this attitude that you find yourself in—is really a conclusion, Grigg?"

"It is a conclusion."

"What are you going to do?"

"I don't know."

"It would be a calamity if you were to give up your work here, in the midst of reconstruction."

"No man is essential, Henry But of course, just now, it would lie difficult. I have thought, often, if Boatwright had only turned out a stronger man...."

"Grigg, one thing! You must let me speak of it.... Has the possibility occurred to you of marrying again?"

Doane sprang up at this; walked the floor,

"Do you realize what you're saying, Henry!" he cried out.

"I understand, Grigg, but you and I are old enough to know that in the case of a vigorous man like yourself—"

Doane threw out a hand.

"Henry, I've thought of everything!"

A little later he stopped and stood over his friend.

"I have fought battles that may as well be forgotten," he said deliberately. "I have won them, over and over, to no end whatever. I have assumed that these victories would lead in time to a sort of peace, even to resignation. They have not. Each little victory now seems to leave me further back. I'm losing, not gaining, through the years. It was when I finally nerved myself to face that fact that I found myself facing it all—my whole life.... Henry, I'm full of a fire and energy that no longer finds an outlet in my work. I want to turn to new fields. If I don't, before it's too late, I may find myself on the rocks."

Withery thought this over. Doane was still pacing the floor. Withery, pale himself now, looked up.

"Perhaps, then," he said, "you had better break with it."

Doane stopped at the window; stared out. Withery thought his face was working.

"Have you any means at all?" he asked.

Doane moved his head in the negative.... "Oh, my books. A few personal things."

"Of course"—Withery's voice softened—"you've given away a good deal."

"I've given everything."

"Hum!... Have you thought of anything else you might do?"

Doane turned. "Henry, I'm forty-five years old. I have no profession, no business experience beyond the little administrative work here. Yet I must live, not only for myself, but to support my little girl. If I do quit, and try to find a place in the business world, I shall carry to my grave the stigma that clings always to the unfrocked priest." He strode to the door. "I tell you, I've thought of everything!... We're getting nowhere with this. I appreciate your interest. But... I'm sorry, Henry. Sleep if you can. Good night."

They met, with M. Pourmont and the others, at breakfast.

There was a moment, on the steps of the gate house, overlooking the narrow busy street, when they silently clasped hands.

Then Henry Withery crawled in under the blue curtains of his cart and rode away, carrying with him a mental picture of a huge man, stooping a little under the red lintel of the doorway, his strong face sternly set.

CHAPTER IV
THE RIDDLE OF LIFE, AND OF DEATH

1

DOANE stood on the Bund at Hankow, by the railing, his great frame towering above the passers-by. He had lunched with the consul general, an old acquaintance. He had arranged to stop overnight, with Betty, in a missionary compound. In the morning they would take the weekly Peking Express northward.

The wide yellow Yangtse flowed by, between its steep mud cliffs, crowded with sampans—hundreds of them moored, rail to rail, against the opposite bank, a compact floating village that was cluttered and crowded with ragged river-folk and deck-houses of arched matting and that reared skyward a thick tangle of masts and rigging. The smaller boats and tubs of the water-beggars lay against the bank just beneath him, expectantly awaiting the Shanghai steamer. Out in the stream several stately junks lay at anchor; and near them a tiny river gunboat, her low free-board glistening white in the warm spring sunshine, a wisp of smoke trailing lazily from her funnel, the British ensign hanging ir folds astern.

Down and up the water steps were moving continuously the innumerable water bearers whose business it was to supply the city of near a million yellow folk that lay just behind the commercial buildings and the pyramid-like godowns of the Bund.

To Doane the picture, every detail of which had a place in the environment of his entire adult life, seemed unreal. The consul general, too, had been unreal. His talk, mostly of remembered if partly mellowed political grievances back home, of the great days when a certain "easy boss" was in power, and later of the mutterings of revolution up and down the Yangtse Valley, sounded in Doane's ears like quaint idle chatter of another planet.... His own talk, it seemed now, had been as unreal as the rest of it.

Of the compliment men of affairs usually paid him, despite his calling, in speaking out as man to man, Doane had never thought and did not think now. He was not self-conscious.

The hours of sober thought that followed his talk with Henry Withery had deepened the furrow between his brows.

In an odd way he was dating from that talk. It had been extraordinarily futile. It had to come, some sort of outbreak. For two or three years he had rather vaguely recognized this fact, and as vaguely dreaded it. Now it had happened. It was like a line drawn squarely across his life. He was different now; perhaps more honest, certainly franker with himself, but different... It had shaken him. Sleep left him for a night or two. Getting away for this trip to Hankow seemed a good thing. He had to be alone, walking it off, and thinking... thinking.... He walked the two hundred and ninety *li* to M. Pourmont's compound, at Ping Yang, the railhead that spring of the new meterguage line into Hans' Province in two days. The mule teams took three.

He dwelt much with memories of his daughter. She had been a winning little thing. Until the terrible Boxer year, that ended, for him, in the death of his wife, she had brought continuous happiness into their life.

She would be six years older now. He couldn't picture that. She had sent an occasional snapshot photograph; but these could not replace his vivid memories of the child she had been.

He was tremulously eager to see her. There would be little problems of adjustment. Over and over he told himself that he mustn't be stern with her; he must watch that.

He felt some uncertainty regarding her training. It was his hope that she would fit into the work of the mission. It seemed, indeed, necessary. She would be contributing eager young life. Her dutiful, rather perfunctory letters had made that much about her clear. They needed that.

During the talk with Withery—it kept coming, up—he had heard his own voice saying—in curiously deliberate tones—astonishing things. He had sent his friend away in a state of deepest concern. He thought of writing him. A letter might catch him at Shanghai. There would be time in the morning, during the long early hours before this household down here would be awaking and gathering for breakfast. It would help, he felt impulsively, to explain fully... But what? What was it that was to be so easily explained? Could he erase, with a few strokes of a pen, the unhappy impression he had made that night on Henry's brain?

The suggestion of marriage, with its implication of a rather cynical worldly wisdom, had come oddly from the devout Henry. Henry was older, too. But Doane winced at the mere recollection. He was almost excitedly sensitive on the topic. He had put women out of his mind, and was determined to keep them out. But at times thoughts of them slipped in.

On the walk to Ping Yang, the second afternoon, he was swinging down a valley where the road was no more than the stony bed of an anciently-diverted stream. The caravan of a mandarin passed, bound doubtless from Peking to a far western province. That it was a great mandarin was indicated by his richly decorated sedan chair borne by sixteen footmen with squadrons of cavalry before and behind. Five mule litters followed, each with a brightly painted, young face pressed against the tiny square window, the wives or concubines of the great one. Each demurely studied him through slanting eyes. And the last one smiled; quickly, brightly. It was death to be caught at that, yet life was too strong for her. He walked feverishly after that. He had said one thing to Henry... something never before formulated, even in his own thinking. What was it? Oh, this! — "Henry, I'm full of a fire and energy that no longer find an outlet in my work. I want to turn to new fields. If I don't, before it's too late, I may find myself on the rocks."

There was something bitterly, if almost boyishly true in that statement. The vital, vigorous adult that was developing within him, now, in the forties, seemed almost unrelated to the young man he had been. He felt life, strength, power. In spirit he was younger than ever. All he had done, during more than twenty years, seemed but a practising for something real, a schooling. Now, standing there, a stern figure, on the Hankow Bund, he was aware of a developed, flowering instinct for the main currents of the mighty social stream, for rough, fresh contacts, large enterprises. His religion had been steadily widening out from the creed of his youth, gradually including all living things, all growth, far outspreading the set boundaries of churchly thought. This development of his spirit had immensely widened his spiritual influence among the Chinese of the province while at the same time making it increasingly different to talk frankly with fellow churchmen.

He had come to find more of the bread of life in Emerson and Montaigne, Chaucer and Shakespeare; less in Milton and Peter. He could consider Burns now with a new pity, without moral condescension, with simple love. He could feel profoundly the moral triumph of Hester Prynne, while wondering at what seemed his own logic. He struggled against a weakening faith in the authenticity of divine revelation, as against a deepening perception that the Confucian precepts might well be a healthy and even sufficient outgrowth of fundamental Chinese characteristics.

He thought, at times rather grimly, of the trials for heresy that now and then rocked the church; and wondered, as grimly, how soon the heresy hunters would be getting around to him. The smallest incident might, sooner or later would, set them after him.

Henry Withery was certain, in spite of his personal loyalty, out of his very concern, to drop a word. And there was literally no word he could drop, after their talk, but would indicate potential heresy in his friend, James Griggsby Doane.

Or it might come from within the compound. Or from a passing stranger. Or from remarks of his own at the annual conference. Or from letters.

There were moments when he could have invited exposure as a relief from doubt and torment of soul. There was nothing of the hypocrite in him. But in soberer moments he felt certain that it was letter to wait until he could find, if not divine guidance, at least an intelligent earthly plan.

All he could do, as it stood, was to work harder and harder with body and mind. And to shoulder more and more responsibility. Without that he would be like a wild engine, charging to destruction.

His daughter would be, for a time certainly, one more burden. He was glad. Anything that would bring life real again! Work above all; every waking moment, if possible, filled; his mental and physical powers taxed to their uttermost; that was the thing; crowd out the brooding, the mere feeling. Action, all the time, and hard, objective thought. The difficulty was that his powers were so great; he seemed never to tire any more; his thoughts could dwell on many planes at once; he actually needed but a few hours' sleep.... And so Betty would be a young woman now, mysteriously as old as her mother on her wedding day: a young woman of unknown interests and sympathies, of a world he himself had all but ceased to know. And it came upon him suddenly, then with tremendous emotional force, that he had no heritage to leave her but a good name.

He stood gripping the railing, head back, gazing up out of misty eyes at a white-flecked blue sky. A prayer arose from his heart and, a whisper, passed his lips: "O God, show me Thy truth, that it may set me."

In the intensity of his brooding he had forgotten to watch for the steamer. But now he became aware of a stir of life along the river-front. The beggars were paddling out into the stream, making ready their little baskets at the ends of bamboo poles.

Over the cliffs, down-stream, hung a long film of smoke. The steamer had rounded the bend and was plowing rapidly up toward the twin cities. He could make out the two white stripes on the funnel, and the cluster of ventilators about it, and the new canvas across the front of the bridge. A moment later he could see the tiny figures crowding the rail.

The steamer warped in alongside a new wharf.

Doane stood near the gangway, all emotion, nearly out of control.

From below hundreds of coolies, countrymen and ragged soldiers swarmed up, to be herded off at one side of the wharf. The local coolies went aboard and promptly started unloading freight, handling crates and bales of half a ton weight with the quick, half grunted, half sung chanteys, intricately rhythmical, with which all heavy labor is accompanied in the Yangtse Valley.

Two spectacled Chinese merchants in shimmering silk robes came down the gangway. A tall American, in civilian dress and overcoat but carrying a leather sword case, followed. Two missionaries came, one in Chinese dress with a cue attached to his skull-cap, bowing to the stern giant as they passed. Then a French father in black robe and shovel hat; a group of Englishmen; a number of families, American, British, French; and finally, coming along the shaded deck, the familiar kindly face and silvery heard of Doctor Hasmer—he was distinctly growing older, Hasmer—then his wife, and, emerging from the cabin, a slim little figure, rather smartly dressed, extraordinarily pretty, radiating a quick charm as she hurried to the gangway, there pausing a moment to search the wharf.

Her eyes met his. She smiled.

It was Betty. He felt her charm, but his heart was sinking.

She kissed him. She seemed all enthusiasm, even very happy. But a moment later, walking along the wharf toward the Bund, her soft little face was sad. He wondered, as his thoughts whirled around, about that.

Her clothes, her beauty, her bright manner, indicating a girlish eagerness to be admired, wouldn't do at the mission. And she couldn't wear those trim little shoes with heels half an inch higher than a man's.

She had, definitely, the gift and the thought of adorning herself. She was a good girl; there was stuff in her. But it wouldn't do; not out there in T'ainan. And she looked like anything in the world but a teacher.

She fascinated him. She was the lovely creature his own little girl had become. Walking beside her up the Bund, chatting with the Hasmers, making a fair show of calm, his heart swelled with love and pride. She was delicate, shyly adorable, gently feminine.

It was going to be difficult to speak about her costume and her charming ways. It wouldn't do to crush her. She was quick enough; very likely she would pick up the tone of the compound very quickly and adapt herself to it.

Young Li Hsien, of T'ainan had come up on the boat. Doans talked a moment with him on the wharf. He was taking the Peking Express in the morning, traveling first-class. The boy's father was a wealthy banker and had always been generous with his firstborn son.

Li appeared in the dining-car at noon, calmly smiling, and, at Doane's imitation, sat with him and Betty. He carried a copy of *Thus Spake Zarathustra*, in English, with a large number of protruding paper bookmarks.

Doane glanced in some surprise at the volume lying rather ostentatiously on the table, and then at the pigtailed young man who ate foreign food with an eagerness and a relish that indicated an excited interest in novel experiment not commonly found among his race.

They talked in Chinese. Li had much to say of the Japanese. He admired them for adopting and adapting to their own purposes the material achievements of the Western world. He had evidently heard something of Theodore Roosevelt and rather less of Lloyd George and Karl Marx. Doane was of the opinion, later, that during the tiffin hour the lad had told all he had learned in six months at Tokio. When asked why he was not finishing out his college year he smiled enigmatically and spoke of duties at home. He knew, of course, that Doane would instantly dismiss the reason as meaningless; it was his Chinese way of suggesting that he preferred not to answer the question.

Twenty-four hours later they transferred their luggage to the Hansi Line, and headed westward into the red hills; passing, within an hour, through the southern extension of the Great Wall, now a ruin. The night was passed in M. Pourmont's compound at Ping Yang. After this there were two other nights in ancient, unpleasant village inns.

Duane made every effort to lessen the discomforts of the journey. Outwardly kind, inwardly emotions fought with one another. He felt now that he should never have sent for Betty; never in the world She seemed to have had no practical training. She grew quiet and wistful as the journey proceeded. The little outbreaks of enthusiasm over this or that half-remembered glimpse of native life came less frequently from day to day.

There were a number of young men at Ping Yang; one French engineer who spoke excellent English; an Australian; others, and two or three young matrons who had adventurously accompanied their husbands into the interior. They all called in the evening. The hospitable Pourmont took up rugs and turned on the talking-machine, and the young people danced.

Doane sat apart, watched the gracefully gliding couples; tried to smile. The dance was on, Betty in the thick of it, before he realized what was meant. He couldn't have spoken without others hearing. It was plain enough that she entered into it without a thought; though as the evening wore on he thought she glanced at him, now and then, rather thoughtfully. And he found himself, at these moments, smiling with greater determination and nodding at her.

The incident plunged him, curiously, swiftly, into the heart of his own dilemma. He rested an elbow on a table and shaded his eyes, trying, as he had been trying all these years, to think.

What a joyous little thing she was! What a fairy! And dancing seemed, now, a means of expression for her youth and her gift of charm. And there was an exquisite delight, he found, in watching her skill with the young men. She was gay, quick, tactful. Clearly young men had, before this, admired her. He wondered what sort of men.

She interrupted this brooding with one of those slightly perturbed glances. Quickly he lowered his hand in order that she might see him smile; but she had whirled away.

Joy!... Not before this moment, not in all the years of puzzled, sometimes bitter thinking, had he realized the degree in which mission life—for that matter, the very religion of his denominational variety—shut joy out. They were afraid of it. They fought it. In their hearts they associated it with vice It was of this world; their eyes were turned wholly to another.

His teeth grated together. The muscles of his strong jaws moved; bunched on his cheeks. He knew now that he believed in joy as an expression of life.

Had he known where to turn for the money he would gladly have planned, at this moment, to send Betty back to the States, give her more of an education, even arrange for her to study drawing and painting. For on the train, during their silences, she had sketched the French conductor, the French-speaking Chinese porter, the sleepy, gray-brown, walled villages, the wide, desert-like flats of the Hoang-Ho, the tumbling hills. He was struck by her persistence at it; the girlish energy she put into it.

That night, late, long after the music had stopped and the last guests had left for their dwellings about the large compound, she came across the corridor and tapped at his door. She wore a kimono of Japan; her abundant brown hair rippled about her shoulders.

"Just one more good night, Daddy," she murmured.

And then, turning away, she added this, softly:

"I never thought about the dancing until—well, we'd started..."

He stood a long moment in silence, then said:

"I'm glad you had a pleasant evening, dear. We—we're rather quiet at T'ainan."

4

Pao Ting Chuan was a man of great shrewdness and considerable distinction of appearance, skilled in ceremonial intercourse, a master of the intricate courses a prominent official must steer between beautifully phrased moral and ethical maxims on the one hand and complicated political trickery on the other. But, as Doane had said, he knew the cost of indemnities. It was on his shrewdness, his really great intelligence, and on his firm control of the "gentry and people" of the province that Doane relied to prevent any such frightful slaughter of whites and destruction of their property as had occurred in 1900. Pao, unlike most of the higher mandarins, was Chinese, not Manchu.

The tao-tai of the city of T'ainan-fu, Chang Chih Ting, was an older man than Pao, less vigorous of body and mind, simpler and franker. He was of those who bewail the backwardness of China.

From the tao-tai's yamen, on the first day of the great April fair, set forth His Excellency in full panoply of state—a green official chair with many bearers, an escort of twenty footmen, with runners on ahead.

Behind this caravan, hidden from view in the depths of a blue Peking cart, with the conventional extra servant dangling his heels over the foreboard, rode Griggsby Doane.

The principal feature of the opening day was a theatrical performance. The play, naturally, was an historical satire, shouted and occasionally sung by the heavily-costumed actors, to a continuous accompaniment of wailing strings. The stage was a platform in the open air, under a tree hung with bannerets inscribed to the particular spirit supposed to dwell within its encircling bark.

His Excellency stood, with Doane, on a knoll, looking out over the heads of the vast audience toward the stage. Doane estimated the attendance at near ten thousand.

The play, begun in the early morning, was now well advanced. At its conclusion, the audience was beginning to break up when a slim blue-clad figure mounted the platform and began a hurried speech.

Chang and Doane looked at each other; then as one man moved forward down the knoll with the throng. The tao-tai's attendants followed, in scattered formation.

The speaker was Li Hsien.

Slowly the magistrate and the missionary made their way toward the stage.

At first the crowd, at sight of the magistrate's button and embroidered insignia, made way as well as they could. But as the impassioned phrases of Li Hsien sank into their minds resistance developed. From here and there in the crowd came phrases expressing a vile contempt for foreigners such as Doane had not heard for years.

Li was lashing himself up, crying out more and more vigorously against the Ho Shan Company, the barbarous white governments from which it derived force, foreign pigs everywhere. The crowds closed, solidly, before the two advancing men.

The magistrate waved his arms; shouted a command that Li leave the platform. Li, hearing only a voice of opposition in the crowd, poured out voluble scorn on his head. The crowd jostled Duane. A stick struck his cheek. He whirled and caught the stick, but the wielder of it escaped in the crowd.

Chang tried to reason, then, with the few hundred within ear-shot.

The sense of violence seemed to be increasing. A few of the magistrate's escort were struggling through. These formed a circle about him and Doane.

Li shouted out charge after charge against the company. He begged his hearers to be brave, as he was brave; to destroy all the works of the company with dynamite; to wreck all the grounds of the foreign engineer at Ping Yang and kill all the occupants; to kill foreigners everywhere and assert the ancient integrity and superiority of China. "Be brave!" he cried again. "See, I am brave. I die for Hansi. Can not you, too, die for Hansi? Can not you think of me, of how I died for our cause, and yourself, in memory of my act, fight for your beloved country, that it may again be the proud queen of the earth?"

He drew a revolver from his sleeve; shot twice; fell to the stage in a widening pool of blood.

At once the vast crowd went wild. Those near the white man turned on him as if to kill him. His clothes were torn, his head cut. Man after man he knocked down with his powerful fists. Before many moments he was exulting in the struggle, in his strength and the full use of it.

The magistrate, struggled beside him. For the people. In their frenzy, forgot or ignored his rank and overwhelmed him.

The runners fought as well as they could. Two or three of them fell. Then a body of horsemen came charging into the crowd, soldiers from the judge's yamen, all on shaggy little Manchu ponies, swinging clubbed carbines as they rode. Right and left, men and boys fell. The crowd broke and scattered.

Chang, bleeding from several small wounds, his exquisitely embroidered silken garments torn nearly off his body, made his way back to the green chair.

Doane was escorted by soldiers to the mission compound. He slipped in to wash off the blood and change his clothes without being seen by Betty or any of the whites.

Shortly came two runners of His Excellency, Pao Ting Chuan, bearing trays of gifts. And a Chinese note expressing deepest regret and pledging complete protection in the future.

Doane dismissed the runners with a Mexican dollar each, and thoughtfully considered the situation. Pao was strong, very strong. Yet the self-destruction of Li Hsien would act as a flaming signal to the people It was the one appeal that might rouse them beyond control.

CHAPTER V
IN T'AINAN

1

THE Boatwrights were at this time in the thirties; he perhaps thirty-six or seven, she thirty-three or four. As has already been noted through the observing eyes of Mr. Withery, Elmer Boatwright had lost the fresh enthusiasm of his first years in the province. And he had by no means attained the mellow wisdom that seldom so much as begins to appear in a man before forty. His was a daily routine of innumerable petty tasks and responsibilities. He had come to be a washed-out little man, whose unceasing activity was somehow unconvincing. He had stopped having opinions, even views. He taught, he kept accounts and records, he conducted meetings, he prayed and sometimes preached at meetings of the students and the native Christians, he was kind in a routine way, his rather patient smile was liked about the compound, but the gift of personality was not his. Even his religion seemed at times to have settled into routine....

He was small in stature, not plump, with light thin hair and a light thin mustache.

His wife was taller than he, more vigorous, more positive, with something of an executive gift. The domestic management of the compound was her province, with teaching in spare hours. Her husband, with fewer petty activities to absorb his energy until his life settled into a mold, might have exhibited some of the interesting emotional quality that is rather loosely called temperament; for that matter it was still a possibility during the soul-shaking changes of middle life; certainly his odd, early taste for taxidermy had carried him to the borders of a sort of artistry; but her own gift was distinctly that of activity. She seemed a wholly objective person. She was physically strong, inclined to sternness, or at least to rigidity of view, yet was by no means unkind. The servants respected her. She was troubled by no doubts. Her religious faith, like her housekeeping practise, was a settled thing. Apparently her thinking was all of the literal things about her. Of humor she had never shown a trace. Without the strong proselyting impetus that had directed and colored her life she might have become a rather hard, sharp-tongued village housewife. But at whatever cost to herself she had brought her tongue under control. As a result, having no mental lightness or grace, she talked hardly at all. When she disapproved, which was not seldom, she became silent.

The relation between this couple and Griggsby Doane had grown subtly complicated through the years that followed the death of Mrs. Doane. Doane, up in his simply furnished attic room, living wholly alone, never interfered in the slightest detail of Mrs. Boatwright's management. Like her, when he disapproved, he kept still. But he might as well have spoken out, for she knew, nearly always, what he was thinking. The deepest blunder she made during this period was to believe, as she firmly did, that she knew all, instead of nearly all his thoughts. The side of him that she was incapable of understanding, the intensely, warmly human side, appeared to her merely as a curiously inexplicable strain of weakness in him that might, some day, crop out and make trouble. She felt a strain of something disastrous in his nature. She regarded his growing passion for solitude as a form of self-indulgence. She knew that he was given more and more to brooding; and brooding—all independent thought, in fact—alarmed her. Her own deepest faith was in what she thought of as submission to divine will and in self-suppression. But she respected him profoundly. And he respected her. Each knew something of the strength in the other's nature. And so they lived on from day to day and year to year in a practised avoidance of conflict or controversy. And between them her busy little husband acted as a buffer without ever becoming aware that a buffer was necessary in this quiet, well-ordered, industrious compound.

Regarding the change of tone for the more severe and the worse that had impressed and disturbed Withery, none of the three but Duane had formulated a conscious thought. Probably the less kindly air was really more congenial to Mrs. Boatwright. Her husband was not a man ever to survey himself and his environment with detachment. And both were much older and more severe at this time than they were to be at fifty.

The introduction of Betty Doane into this delicately balanced household precipitated a crisis. Breakfast was served in the mission house at a quarter to eight. Not once in a month was it five minutes late. A delay of half an hour would have thrown Mrs. Boatwright out of her stride for the day.

During the first few days after her arrival Betty appeared on time. It was clearly necessary. Mrs. Boatwright was hostile. Her father was busy and preoccupied. She herself was moved deeply by a girlish determination to find some small niche for herself in this driving little community. The place was strange to her. There seemed little or no companionship.

Even Miss Hemphill, the head teacher, whom she remembered from her girlhood, and Dr. Mary Cassin, who was in charge of the dispensary and who had a pleasant, almost pretty face, seemed as preoccupied as Griggsby Doane. During her mother's lifetime there had been an air of friendliness, of kindness, about the compound that was gone now. Perhaps less work had been accomplished then than now under the firm rule of Mrs. Boatwright, but it had been a happier little community.

From the moment she rode in through the great oak, nail-studded gates of the compound, and the mules lurched to their knees, and her father helped her out through the little side door of the red and blue litter, Betty knew that she was exciting disapproval. The way they looked at her neat traveling suit, her becoming turban, her shoes, worked sharply on her sensitive young nerves. She was aware even of the prim way they walked, these women—of their extremely modest self-control—and of the puzzling contrast set up with the free activity of her own slim body; developed by dancing and basketball and healthy romping into a grace that had hitherto been unconscious.

And almost from that first moment, herself hardly aware of what she was about but feeling that she must be wrong, struggling bravely against an increasing hurt, her unrooted, nervously responsive young nature struggled to adapt itself to the new environment. A pucker appeared between her brows; her voice became hushed and faintly, shyly earnest in tone. Mrs. Boatwright at once gave her some classes of young girls. Betty went to Miss Hemphill for detailed advice, and earnestly that first evening read into a work on pedagogics that the older teacher, after a kindly enough talk, lent her.

She went up to her father's study, just before bedtime on the first evening, in a spirit of determined good humor. She wanted him to see how well she was taking hold.... But she came down in a state of depression that kept her awake for a long time lying in her narrow iron bed, gazing out into the starlit Chinese heavens. She felt his grave kindness, but found that she didn't know him. Here in the compound, with all his burden of responsibility settled on his broad shoulders, he had receded from her. He would sit and look at her, with sadness in his eyes, not catching all she said; then would start a little, and smile, and take her hand.

She found that she couldn't unpack all her things; not for days. There were snapshots of boy and girl members of "the crowd," away off there, beyond the brown hills, beyond the ruined wall, beyond the yellow plains, and the Pacific Ocean and the wide United States, off in a little New Jersey town, on the other side of the world. There were parcels of dance programs, with little white pencils dangling from silken white cords. There were programs of plays, with cryptic pencilings, and copies of a high-school paper, and packets of letters. She couldn't trust herself to look at these treasures. And she put her drawing things away.

And other more serious difficulties arose to provoke sober thoughts. One occurred the first time she played tennis with her father; the day before Li Hsien's suicide. The court had been laid out on open ground adjoining the compound. Small school buildings and a wall shut it off from the front street, and a Chinese house-wall blocked the other end; but the farther side lay open to a narrow footway. Here a number of Chinese youths gathered and watched the play. It happened that none of the white women attached to the mission at this time was a tennis player; and the spectacle of a radiant girl darting about with grace and zest and considerable athletic skill was plainly an experience to the onlookers. At first they were respectful enough; but as their numbers grew voices were raised, first in laughter, then in unpleasant comment. Finally all the voices seemed to burst out at once in chorus of ribaldry and invective. Betty stopped short in her play, alarmed and confused.

These shouted remarks grew in insolence. All through her girlhood Betty had grown accustomed to occasional small outbreaks from the riff-raff of T'ainan. She recalled that her father had always chosen to ignore them. But there was a new boldness evident in the present group, as the numbers increased and more and more voices joined in. And it was evident, from an embroidered robe here and there, that not all were riff-raff.

Her father lowered his racket and walked to the net.

"I'm sorry, dear," he said; "but this won't do."

Obediently she returned to the mission house; while Doane went over to the fence. But before he could reach it the youths, jeering, hurried away. That evening he told Betty he would have a wall built along the footway.

2

Within less than a week Betty found herself fighting off a heart-sickness that was to prove, for the time, irresistible. On the sixth evening, after the house had became still and her big, kind father had said good night—in some ways, at moments, he seemed almost close to her; at other moments, especially now, at night, in the solitude, he was hopelessly far away, a dim figure on the farther shore of the gulf that lies, bottomless, between every two human souls—she locked herself in her little room and sat, very still, with drooping face and wet eyes, by the open window.

The big Oriental city was silent, asleep, except for the distant sound of a watchman banging his gong and shouting musically on his rounds. The spring air, soft, moistly warm, brought to her nostrils the smell of China; and brought with it, queerly disjointed, hauntlike memories of her childhood in the earlier mission house that had stood on this same bit of ground. She closed her eyes, and saw her mother walking in quiet dignity about the compound, the same compound in which Luella Brenty, a girl of hardly more than her-own present age, was, in 1900, burned at the stake. Down there where the ghostly tablet stood, by the chapel steps.

She shivered. There was trouble now. They were talking about it among themselves, if not in her presence. That would doubtless explain her father's preoccupation.... She must hurry to bed. She knew she was tired; and it wouldn't do to be late for breakfast. And she had a class in English at 8:45.

But instead she got out the bottom tray of her trunk and mournfully staring long at each, went through her photographs. She had been a nice girl, there in the comfortable American town. Here she seemed less nice. As if, in some way, over there in the States, her nature had changed for the worse. They looked at her so. They were not friendly. No, not that. Yet this was home, her only home. The other had seemed to be home, but it was now a dream... gone. She could never again pick up her place in the old crowd. It would be changing. That, she thought, in the brooding reverie known to every imaginative, sensitive boy and girl, was the sad thing about life. It slipped away from you; you could nowhere put your feet down solidly. If, another year, she could return, the crowd would be changed. New friendships would be formed. The boys who had been fond of her would now be fond of others. Some of the girls might be married... She herself was changed. A man—an older man, who had been married, was, in a way, married at the time—-had taken her in his arms and kissed her. It w'as a shock. It hurt now. She couldn't think how it had happened, how it had ever begun. She couldn't even visualize the man, now, with her eyes closed. She couldn't be sure even that she liked him. He was a strange being. He had interested her by startling her. Romance had seized them. He said that. He said it would be different at Shanghai. It was different; very puzzling, saddening. There was no doubt as to what Mrs. Boatwright would say about it, if she knew. Or Miss Hemphill. Any of them.... She wondered what her father would say. She couldn't tel! him. It had to be secret. There were things in life that had to be; but she wondered what he would say.

But she was, with herself, here in her solitude, honest about it. It had happened. She didn't blame the man. In his strange way, he was real. He had meant it. She had read his letter over and over, on the steamer, and here in T'ainan. It was moving, exciting to her that odd letter. And he had gone without a further word because he felt it to be the best way. She was sure of that.... She didn't blame herself, though it hurt. No, she couldn't blame him. Yet it was now, as it had been at the time, a sort of blinding, almost an unnerving shock.... Probably they would never meet again. It was a large world, after all; you couldn't go back and pick up dropped threads. But if they should meet, by some queer chance, what would they do, what could they say? For he lingered vividly with her; his rough blunt phrases came up, at lonely moments, in her mind. He had stirred and, queerly, bewilderingly, humbled her.... She wondered, all nerves, what his wife was like. How she looked.

Perhaps it was this change in her that these severe women noticed. Perhaps her inner life lay open to their experienced eyes. She could do nothing about it, just set her teeth and live through somehow.... Though it couldn't be wholly that, because she had worn the clothes they didn't like before it happened, and had danced, and played like a child. And they didn't seem to care much for her drawing; though Miss Hemphill had, she knew, suggested to Mr. Boatwright that he let her try teaching a small class of the Chinese girls.... No, it wasn't that. It must, then, be something in her nature.

She had read, back home—or in the States—in a woman's magazine, that every woman has two men in her life, the one she loves, or who has stirred her, and the one she marries. The girls, in some excitement, had discussed it. There had been confidences.

She might marry. It was possible. And even now she saw clearly enough, as every girl sees when life presses, that marriage might, at any moment, present itself as a way out. The thought was not stimulating. The pictures it raised lacked the glowing color of her younger and more romantic dreams.... That mining engineer was writing her, from Korea. His name was Apgar, Harold B. Apgar; he was stocky, strong, with an attractive square face and quiet gray eyes. She liked him. But his letters were going to be hard to answer.

The soft air that fanned her softer cheek brought utter melancholy. She felt, as only the young can feel, that her life, with her merry youth, was over. Grim doors had closed on it. Joy lay behind those doors. Ahead lay duties, discipline, the somber routine of womanhood.

She shivered and stirred. This brooding wouldn't do.

She got out a pad of paper and a pencil, and sitting there in the dim light, sketched with deft fingers the roofs and trees of T'ainan, as they appeared in the moonlight of spring, with a great faint gate tower bulking high above a battlemented wall. Until far into the morning she drew, forgetful of the hours, finding a degree of melancholy pleasure in the exercise of the expressive faculty that had become second nature to her.

She slept, then, like a child, until mid-forenoon. It was nearly eleven o'clock when she hurried, ready to smile quickly to cover her confusion, down to the dining-room.

The breakfast things had been cleared away more than two hours earlier. The table boy (so said the cook) had gone to market. She ate, rather shamefaced, a little bread and butter (she was finding it difficult to get used to this tinned butter from New Zealand).

In the parlor Mrs. Boatwright sat at her desk. She heard Betty at the door, lifted her head for a cool bow, then resumed her work. Not a word did she speak or invite. There was an apology trembling on the tip of Betty's tongue, but she had to hold it back and turn away.

3

The day after the suicide of Li Hsien rumors began to drift into the compound. News travels swiftly in China. The table "boy" (a man of fifty-odd) brought interesting bits from the market, always a center for gossip of the city and the mid-provincial region about it. The old gate-keeper, Sun Shao-i, picked up much of the roadside talk. And the several other men helpers about the compound each contributed his bit. The act of the fanatical student had, at the start, as Doane anticipated, an electrical effect on public sentiment. Suicide is by no means generally regarded in China as a sign of failure. It is employed, at times of great stress, as a form of deliberate protest; and is then taken as heroism.

So reports came that the always existent hatred of foreigners was rising, and might get out of control. A French priest was murdered on the Kalgan highway, after protracted torture during which his eyes and tongue were fed to village dogs. This, doubtless, as retaliation for similar practises commonly attributed to the white missionaries. The fact that the local Shen magistrate promptly caught and beheaded a few of the ringleaders appeared to have small deterrent effect on public feeling.

Detachments of strange-appearing soldiers, wearing curious insignia, were marching into the province over the Western Mountains. A native worker at one of the mission outposts wrote that they broke into his compound and robbed him of food, but made little further trouble.

Reports bearing on the activities of the new Great Eye Society—already known along the wayside as "The Lookers"—were coming in daily. The Lookers were initiating many young men into their strange magic, which appeared to differ from the incantations of the Boxers of 1900 more in detail than in spirit.

And in the western, villages this element was welcoming the new soldiers.

Here in T'ainan disorder was increasing. An old native, helper of Dr. Cassin in the dispensary, was mobbed on the street and given a beating during which his arm was broken. He managed to walk to the compound, and was now about with the arm in a sling, working quietly as usual. But it was evident that native Christians must, as usual in times of trouble, suffer for their faith.

On the following afternoon the tao-tai called, in state, with bearers, runners, soldiers and secretaries. The main courtyard of the compound was filled with the richly colored chairs and the silks and satins and plumed ceremonial hats of his entourage. For more than an hour he was closeted with Griggsby Doane, while the Chinese schoolgirls, very demure, stole glances from curtained windows at the beautiful young men in the courtyard.

By this impressive visit, and by his long stay, Chang Chih Ting clearly meant to impress on the whole city his friendship for these foreign devils. For the whole city would know of it within an hour; all middle Hansi would know by nightfall.

He brought disturbing news. It had been obvious to Doane that the menacing new society could hardly spread and thrive without some sort of secret official backing. He was inclined to trust Chang. He believed, after days of balancing the subtle pros and cons in his mind, that Pao Ting Chuan would keep order. And he knew that the official who was responsible for the province—as Pao virtually was—could keep order if he chose.

Chang, always naively open with Doane, supported him in this view. But it was strongly rumored at the tao-tai's yamen that the treasurer, Kang Hsu, old as he was, weakened by opium, for the past two or three years an inconsiderable figure in the province, had lately been in correspondence with the Western soldiers. And officers from his yamen had been recognized as among the drill masters of the Looker bands. Chang had reported these proceedings to His Excellency, he said ("His Excellency," during this period, meant always Pao, though Kang Hsu, as treasurer, ranked him) and had been graciously thanked. It was also said that Kang had cured himself of opium smoking by locking himself in a room and throwing pipe, rods, lamp and all his supply of the drug out of a window. For two weeks he had suffered painfully, and had nearly died of a diarrhea; but now had recovered and was even gaining in weight, though still a skeleton.

Doane caught himself shaking his head, with Chang, over this remarkable self-cure. It would apparently be better for the whites were Kang to resume his evil ways. It was clear to these deeply experienced men that Kang's motives would be mixed. Doubtless he had been stirred to jealousy by Pao. It seemed unlikely that he, or any prominent mandarin, could afford to run the great risks involved in setting the province afire so soon after 1900. Perhaps he knew a way to lay the fresh troubles at Pao's gate. Or perhaps he had come to believe, with his befuddled old brain, in the Looker incantations. Only seven years earlier the belief of ruling Manchus in Boxer magic had led to the siege of the legations and something near the ruin of China. Come to think of it, Kang, unlike Pao and Chang, was a Manchu.

Chang also brought with him a copy of the Memorial left by Li Hsien, which it appeared was being widely circulated in the province. The document gave an interesting picture of the young man's complicated mind. His death had been theatrical and, in manner, Western, modern. Suicides of protest were traditionally managed in private. But the memorial was utterly Chinese, written with all the customary indirection, dwelling on his devotion to his parents and his native land, as on his own worthlessness; quoting apt phrases from Confucius, Mencius and Tseng Tzu; quite, indeed, in the best traditional manner. And he left a letter to his elder brother, couched in language humble and tender, giving exact directions for his funeral, down to the arrangement of his clothing and the precise amount to be paid to the Taoist priest, together with instructions as to the disposition of his small personal estate. Doane pointed out that these documents were designed to impress on the gentry his loyal conformity to ancient tradition, while his motives were revolutionary and his final act was designed to excite the mob at the fair and folk of their class throughout the province. Chang believed he had scholarly help in preparing the documents. And both men felt it of sober significance that the memorial was addressed to "His Excellency, Kang Hsu, Provincial Treasurer."

That Li Hsien's inflammatory denunciation of "the foreign engineer at Ping Yang" had an almost immediate effect was indicated by the news from that village at the railhead. M. Puurmont wrote, in French, that an Australian stake-boy had been shot through the lungs while helping an instrument man in the hills. He was alive, but barely so, at the time of writing. As a result of this and certain lesser difficulties, M. Pourmont was calling in his engineers and mine employees, and putting them to work improvising a fort about his compound, and had telegraphed Peking for a large shipment of tinned food. He added that there would be plenty of room in case Doane later should decide to gather in his outpost workers and fall back toward the railroad.

Doane translated this letter into Chinese for Chang's benefit.

"Has he firearms?" asked the tao-tai.

Doane inclined his head. "More than the treaty permits," he replied. "He told me last winter that he thought it necessary."

"It is as well," said Chang. "Though it is not necessary for you to leave yet. To do that would be to invite misunderstanding."

"It would invite attack," said Doane.

It was on the morning after Chang's call that the telegram came from Jen Ling Pu. Doane was crossing the courtyard when he heard voices in the gate house; then Sun Shao-i came down the steps and gave him the message. He at once sent a chit to Pao, writing it in pencil against a wall; then ordered a cart brought around. Within an hour the boy was back. Pao had written on the margin of the note: "Will see you immediately."

For once the great mandarin did not keep him waiting. The two inner gates of the yamen opened for him one after the other, and his cart was driven across the tiled inner court to the yamen porch. It was an unheard-of honor. Plainly, Pao, like the lesser Chang, purposed standing by his guns, and meant that the city should know. By way of emphasis, Pao himself, tall, stately, magnificent in his richly embroidered robe, the peacock emblem of a civil mandarin of the third-class embroidered on the breast, the girdle clasp of worked gold, wearing the round hat of office crowned with a large round ruby—Pao, deep and musical of voice, met him in the shadowy porch and conducted him to the reception room. Instantly the tea appeared, and they could talk.

"Your Excellency," said Doane, "a Christian worker in So T'ung, one Jen Ling Pu, telegraphs me that strange soldiers, helped by members of the Great Eye Society, last night attacked his compound. They have burned the gate house, but have no firearms. At eight this morning, with the aid of the engineer for the Ho Shan Company in that region, and with only two revolvers, he was defending the compound. I am going there. I will leave this noon."

"I hear your alarming words with profound regret," Pao's deep voice rolled about the large high room. "My people are suffering under an excitement which causes them to forget their responsibility as neighbors and their duty to their fellow men. I will send soldiers with you."

"Soldiers should be sent, Your Excellency, and at once. Well-armed men. But I shall not wait."

"You are not going alone? And not in your usual manner, on foot?"

"Yes, Your Excellency."

"But that may be unsafe.".

"My safety is of little consequence."

"It is of great consequence to me."

"For that I thank you. But it is to So T'ung a hundred and eighty *li*. The best mules or horses will need two days. I can walk there in less than one day. I have walked there in twenty hours."

"You are a man of courage. I will order the soldiers to start by noon."

Back at the compound, Doane assembled his staff in one of the schoolrooms. Mr. and Mrs. Boatwright were there, Miss Hemphill and Dr. Cassin. He laid the telegram before them, and repeated his conversation with the provincial judge.

They listened soberly. For a brief time one spoke. Then Mrs. Boatwright asked, bluntly:

"You are sure you ought to go?"

Doane inclined his head.

"If things are as bad as this, how about our safety here?"

"You will be protected. Both Pao and Chang will see to that. And in case of serious danger—something unforeseen, you must demand an escort to Ping Yang. You will be safe there with Monsieur Pourmont."

"How about your own safety?"

"I have put the responsibility squarely on Pao's shoulders. He knows what I am going to do. He is sending soldiers after me. He will undoubtedly telegraph ahead; he'll have to do that."

4

Betty was in his study, standing by the window. She turned quickly when he came in. He closed the door, and affecting a casual manner passed her with a smile and went into the bedroom for the light bag with a shoulder strap, the blanket roll and the ingenious light folding cot that he always carried on these expeditions if there was likelihood of his being caught overnight at native inns. He put on his walking boots and leggings, picked up his thin raincoat and the heavy stick that was his only weapon, and returned to the study.

He felt Betty's eyes on him, and tried to speak in an offhand manner.

"I'm off to So T'ung, Betty. Be back within two or three days."

She came over, slowly, hesitating, and lingered the blanket roll.

"Will there he danger at So T'ung, Dad?" she asked gently.

"Very little, I think."

He saw that neither his words nor his manner answered the questions in her hind. Patting her shoulder, he added:

"Kiss me good-by, child. You've been listening to the chatter of the compound. The worst place for gossip in the world."

But she laid a light finger on the court-plaster that covered a cut on his cheek-bone.

"You never said a word about that, Dad. It was the riot at the fair. I know. You had to fight with them. And Li Hsien killed himself."

"But His Excellency put down the trouble at once. That is over."

She sank slowly into the swivel chair before the desk; dropped her cheek on her hand; said, in a low uneven voice:

"No one talks to me... tells me..."

He looked down at her, standing motionless. His eyes filled. Then, deliberately, he put his park aside, and seated himself at the other side of the desk.

She looked up, with a wistful smile.

"I'm not afraid, Dad."

"You wouldn't be," said he gravely.

"No. But there is trouble, of course."

"Yes. There is trouble."

"Do you think it will be as—as bad as—nineteen hundred?"

"No... no, I'm sure it won't. The officials simply can't afford to let that awful thing happen again."

"It would be... well, discouraging," said she thoughtfully. "Wouldn't it? To have all your work undone again."

He found himself startled by her impersonal manner. He saw her, abruptly then, as a mature being. He didn't know how to talk to her. This thoughtful young woman was, curiously, a stranger.... And this was the first moment in which it had occurred to him that she might already have had beginning adult experience. She was an individual; had a life of her own to manage. There would have been men. She was old enough to have thought about marriage, even. It seemed incredible.... He sighed.

"You're worried about me," she said.

"I shouldn't have brought you out here, dear."

"I don't fit in."

"It is a great change for you."

"I... I'm no good."

"Betty, dear—that is not true. I can't let you say that, or think it."

"But it's the truth. I'm no good. I've tried. I have, Dad. You know, to put everything behind me and make myself take hold.... And then I draw half the night, and miss my classes in the morning. It seems to go against my nature, some way. No matter how hard I try, it doesn't work. The worst of it is, in my heart I know it isn't going to work."

"I shouldn't have brought you out here."

"But you couldn't help that, Dad."

"It did seem so.... I'm planning now to send you back as soon as we can manage it."

"But, Dad... the expense...!"

"I know. I am thinking about that. There will surely be a way to manage it, a little later. I mean to find a way."

"But I can't go back to Uncle Frank's."

"I must work it out so that it won't be a burden to him."

"You mean... pay board?"

"Yes."

"But think, Dad! I've cost you so much already!"

"I am glad you have, dear. I think I've needed that. And I want you to go back to the Art League. You have a real talent. We must make the most of it." Betty's gaze strayed out the window. Her father was a dear man. She hadn't dreamed he could see into her problems like this. She was afraid she might cry, so she spoke quickly.

"But that means making me still more a burden!"

"It is the sort of burden 1 would love, Betty. But don't misunderstand me—I can't do all this now."

"Oh, I know!"

"You may have to be patient for a time. Tell me, dear, first though... is it what you want most?"

"Oh... why..."

"Answer me if you can. If you know what you want most."

"I wonder if I do know. It's when I try to think that out clearly that it seems to me I'm no good."

"I recognize, of course, that you are reaching the age when many girls think of marrying."

"I... oh..."

"I don't want to intrude into your intimate thoughts, dear. But in so far as we can plan together... it may help if..."

She spoke with a touch of reserve that might have been, probably was, shyness.

"There have been men, of course, who—-well, wanted to marry me. This last year. There was one in New York. He used to come out and take me riding in his automobile. I—I always made some of the other girls come with us."

Doane found it impossible to visualize this picture. When he was last in the States there were no automobiles on the streets. It suggested a condition of which he knew literally nothing, a wholly new set of influences in the life of young people. The thought was alarming; he had to close his eyes on it for a moment. Much as his daughter had seemed like a visitor from another planet, she had never seemed so far off as now. And he fell to thinking, along with this new picture, of the terribly hard struggle they had had out here, since 1900, in rebuilding the mission organization, in training new workers and creating a new morale. He felt tired.... His brain was tired. It would help to get out on the road again, swinging gradually into the rhythm of his forty-inch stride. Once more he would walk himself off, even as he hastened on an errand of rescue.

Betty was speaking again.

"And there's one now. He's in Korea, a mining engineer. He's awfully nice. But I—I don't think I could marry him."

"Do you love him, Betty?"

"N—no. No, I don't. Though I've wondered, sometimes, about these things...." The person she was wondering about, as she said this, was Jonathan Brachey. Suddenly, with her mind's eye, she saw this clearly. And it was startling. She couldn't so much as mention his name; certainly not to her father, kind and human as he seemed. But she would never hear from him again; not now. If he could live through those first few weeks without so much as writing, he could let the years go. That would have been the test for her sort of nature, and she could understand no other sort.

She compressed her lips. She didn't know that her face showed something of the trouble in her mind. She spoke, bravely, with an abruptness that surprised herself a little, as it surprised him.

"No, Dad, I shan't marry. Not for years, if ever. I'd rather work. I'd rather work hard, if only I could fit in somewhere."

"I'm seeing it a little more clearly, Betty."' He arose. "On the way out I'll tell Mrs. Boatwright and Miss Hemphill both that I don't want you to do any more work about the compound.... No, dear, please! Let me finish!... When you're a few years older, you'll learn as I have learned, that the important thing is to find your own work, and find it early. So many lives take the wrong direction, through mistaken judgment, or a mistaken sense of duty. And nothing—nothing—can so mislead us as a sense of duty."

He said this with an emphasis that puzzled Betty.

"The thing for you," he went on, "is to draw. And dream. The dreaming will work out in more drawing, I imagine. For you have the nature of the artist. Your mother had it. You are like her, with something of my energy added. Don't let the atmosphere of the compound pull you down. It mustn't do that. Live within yourself. Let your energy go into honest expression of yourself. You see what I'm getting at—*be* yourself. Don't try to be some one else.... You happen to be here in an interesting time. There's a possibility that the drawings you could make out here, now, would have a value later on. So try to make a record of your life here with your pencil. And don't be afraid of happiness, dear." He pointed to a row of jonquils in a window-box. "Happiness is great a contribution to life as duty. Think how those flowers contribute! And remember that you are like them to me."

She clung to him, in impulsive affection, as she kissed him good-by. And it wasn't until late that night, as she lay in her white bed, such a glow did he leave in her warm little heart, that the odd nature of his talk caught her attention. She had never, never, heard him say such things. It was as if he, her great strong dad, were himself starved for happiness. As if he wanted her to have all the rich beauty of life that had passed him grimly by.

She fell to wondering, sleepily, what he meant by finding a way to get the money. There was no way. Though it was dear of him even to think of it.

She fell asleep then.

CHAPTER VI
CATASTROPHE

1

DOANE left the compound a little before noon, and arrived at So T'ung at six the following morning. The distance, a hundred and eighty *li*, was just short of sixty-five English miles. The road was little more than a footpath, so narrow that in the mountains, where the grinding of ages of traffic and the drainage from eroded slopes had long ago worn it down into a series of deep, narrow canyons, the came! trains, with their wide panniers, always found passing a matter of difficulty and confusion. Here it skirted a precipice, or twisted up and up to surmount the Pass of the Flighting Geese, just west of the sacred mountain; there it wandered along the lower hillsides above a spring torrent that would be, a few months later, a trickling rivulet. His gait averaged, over all conditions of road and of gradient, about five miles an hour. He followed, on this occasion, the principle of walking an hour, then resting fifteen minutes. And toward midnight he set up his cot by the roadside, in the shelter of a tree by a memorial arch, and gave himself two hours of sleep.

The little hill city of So T'ung was awake and astir, with gates open and traffic already flowing forth. There were no signs of disorder. But Doane noted that the anti-foreign mutterings and sneers along the roadside (to which he had grown accustomed twenty years earlier) were louder and more frequent than common. For himself he had not the slightest fear. His great height, his enormous strength, his commanding eye, had always, except on the one recent occasion of the riot at the T'ainan fair, been enough to cow any native who was near enough to do him injury. And added to this moral and physical strength he had lately felt a somewhat surprising recklessness. He felt this now. He didn't care what happened, so long as he might be busy in the thick of it. His personal safety took on importance only when he kept Betty in mind. He must save himself to provide for her. And, of course, in the absence of any other strong personality, the mission workers needed him; they had no one else, just now, on whom to lean. And then there were the hundreds of native Christians; they needed him, for they would be slaughtered first... if it should come to that. They would be loyal, and would die, at the last, for their faith.

During the long hours of walking through the still mountain night, his thoughts ranged far. He considered talking over his problems with M. Pourmont. There should be work for a strong, well-trained man somewhere in the railroad development that was going on all over the yellow kingdom. Preferably in some other region, where he wouldn't be known. Starting fresh, that was the thing!

Over and over the rather blank thought came around, that a man has no right to bring into the world a child for whom he can not properly, fully, care. And it came down to money, to some money; not as wealth, but as the one usable medium of human exchange. A little of it, honestly earned, meant that a man was productive, was paying his way. A saying of Emerson's shot in among his racing thoughts—something about clergymen always demanding a handicap. It was wrong, he felt. It was—he went as far as this, toward dawn—parasitic. A man, to live soundly, healthily, must shoulder his way among his fellows, prove himself squarely.

And he dwelt for hours at a time on the ethical basis of all this missionary activity. It was what he came around to all night. There was an assumption— it was, really, the assumption on which his present life was based—that the so-called Christian civilization, Western Europe and America—owed its superiority to what he thought of as the Christian consciousness. That superiority was always implied. It was the motive power back of this persistent proselytizing. But to-night, as increasingly of late years, he found himself whittling away the implications of a spiritual and even ethical quality in that superiority of the White over the Yellow. More and more clearly it seemed to come down to the physical. It was the amazing discoveries in what men call modern science, and the wide application in industry of these discoveries, that made much of the difference. Then there were the accidents of climate and soil and of certain happy mixtures of blood through conquests... these things made a people great or weak. And lesser accidents, such as a simple alphabet, making it easy and cheap to print ideas; the Chinese alphabet and the lack of easy transportation had held China back, he believed.... Back of all these matters lay, of course, a more powerful determinant; the genius that might be waxing or waning in a people. The genius of America was waxing, clearly; and the genius of China had been waning for six hundred years. But in her turn, China had waxed, as had Rome, and Greece, and Egypt. None of these had known the Christian consciousness, yet each had run her course. And Greece and Rome, without it, had risen high. Rome, indeed, whatever the reason, had begun to wane from the very dawn of Christianity; and had finally succumbed, not to that, but to barbarians who had in them crude physical health and enterprise.

The more deeply he pondered, the more was he inclined to question the importance of Christianity in the Western scheme. For Western civilization, to his burning eyes, walking at night, alone, over the hills of ancient Hansi, looked of a profoundly materialistic nature. You felt that, out here, where oil and cigarettes and foreign-made opium and merchandise of all sorts were pushing in, all the time, about and beyond the missionaries. And with bayonets always bristling in the background. The West hadn't the finely great gift of Greece or the splendid unity of Rome. Its art was little more than a confusion of copies, a library of historical essays. And art seemed, now, important. And as for religion... Doane had moments of real bitterness, that night, about religion. And he thought around and around a circle. The one strongest, best organized church of the West—the one that made itself felt most effectively in China—seemed to him not only opposed to the scientific enterprise that was, if anything, peculiarly the genius of the West, but insistent on superstitions (for so they looked, out here) beside which the quiet rationalism of the Confucian drift seemed very reality. And the period of the greatest power and glory of that church had been, to all European civilization, the Dark Ages. The Reformation and the modern free political spirit appeared to be cognates, yet the evangelical churches fought science, in their turn, from their firm base of divine revelation. It was difficult, to-night, to see the miracles and mysteries of Christianity as other than legendary superstitions handed down by primitive, credulous peoples. It was difficult to see them as greatly different from the incantations of the Boxers or of these newer Lookers.

And then, of all those great peoples that had waxed and waned, China alone remained.... There was a thought! She might wax again. For there she was, as always. Without the Christian consciousness, the Chinese, of all the great peoples, alone had endured.

A fact slightly puzzling to Doane was that he thought all this under a driving nervous pressure. Now and then his mind rushed him, got a little out of control. And at these times he walked too fast.

2

The mission station was situated in the northern suburbs of So T'ung-fu, outside the wall. Duane went directly there.

The mission compound lay a smoking ruin. Not a building of the five or six that had stood in the walled acre, was now more than a heap of bricks, with a Ft of wall or a chimney standing. The compound wall had been battered down at a number of points, apparently with a heavy timber that now lay outside one of the breaches. There was no sign of life.

He walked in among the ruins. They were still too hot for close examination. But he found the body of a white man lying in an open space, clad in flannel shirt and riding breeches, with knee-high laced boots of the sort commonly worn by engineers. The face was unrecognizable. The top of the head, too, had been beaten in. But on the back of the head grew' curly yellow' hair. From the figure evidently a young man; one of Pourmont's adventurous crew; probably one of the Australians or New Zealanders. A revolver lay near the outstretched hand. Doane picked it up and examined it. Every chamber was empty. And here and there along the path were empty cartridges; as if he had retreated stubbornly, loading and firing as he could. Not far off lay an empty cartridge box. That would be where he had filled for the last time. He must have sent some of the bullets home; but the attackers had removed their dead. Yes, closer scrutiny discovered a number of blood-soaked areas along the path.

A young Chinese joined him, announcing himself as a helper at the station. Jen Ling Pu had sent him out over the rear wall, he said, with the telegram to Mr. Doa ne.

Together they carried the body of the white man to a clear space near the wall and buried him in a shallow grave. Duane repeated the burial service in brief form.

The boy, whose name was Wen, explained that on his return from the telegraph station he had found it impossible to get into the compound, as it was then surrounded, and accordingly hid in the neighborhood. By that time, he said, Jen, with the three or four helpers and servants who had not perished in the other buildings, one or two native Bible-women, a few children of native Christians and the white man were all in the main house, and were firing through the windows. They had all undoubtedly been burned to death, as only the white man had come out. He himself could not get close enough to see much of what happened, though he slipped in among the curious crowd outside and picked up what information he could. The attacking parlies were by no means of one mind or of settled purpose. The Lookers among them were for a quick and complete massacre, as were the young rowdies who had joined in the attack for the fun of it. But there were more moderate councils. And so many were injured or killed by the accurate marksmanship of the young foreign devil, that for a time they all seemed to lose heart. The Lookers were subjected to ridicule by the crowd because by their incantations they were supposed to render themselves invisible to foreign eyes, and it was difficult to explain the high percentage of casualties among them on the grounds of accidental contact with flying bullets. Finally a ruse was decided on. The white man was to come out for a parley. A student, recently attached to the yamen of the local magistrate as an interpreter volunteered—in good faith, Wen believed—to act in that capacity on this occasion.

The meeting took place by one of the breaches in the wall. The engineer demanded that the three principal leaders of the Lookers Le surrendered to him on the spot, and held until the arrival of troops from T'ainan. While they were pretending to listen, a party crept around behind the wall. He heard them, stepped back in time to avoid being clubbed to death, in a moment shot two of them dead, and shot also the captain of the Lookers, who had been conducting the parley. Then, evidently, he had backed tow ard the main house and had nearly reached it when his cartridges gave out.

Doane was busy, what with the improvised burial and with noting down Wen's narrative, until nearly noon. By this time he was very sleepy. There was nothing more he could do. The ruins of the main house would not be cool before morning. Nor would the soldiers arrive. He decided to call at once on the magistrate and arrange for a guard to be left in charge of the compound; then to set up his cot in a cell in one of the local caravansaries. He had brought a little food, and the magistrate would give him what else he needed. The innkeeper would brew him tea.... Before two o'clock he was asleep.

3

He was awakened by a persistent light tapping at the door. Lying there in the dusky room, fully clad, gazing out under heavy lids at the dingy wall with its dingier banners hung about lettered with the Chinese characters for happiness and prosperity, and at the tattered gray paper squares through which came soft evening sounds of mules and asses munching their fodder at the long open manger, of children talking, of a carter singing to himself in quavering falsetto, it seemed to him that the knocking had been going on for a very long time. His thoughts, slowly coming awake, were of tragic stuff. Death stalked again the hills of Hansi. Friends had been butchered. The blood of his race had been spilled again. Life was a grim thing....

A voice called, in pidgin-English.

He replied gruffly; sat up; struck a match and lighted the rush-light on the table. It was just after eight.

He went to the door; opened it. A small, soft, yellow Chinaman stood there.

"What do you want?" Doane asked in Chinese.

The yellow man looked blank.

"My no savvy," he said.

"What side you belong?" The familiar pidgin-English phrases sounded grotesquely in Doane's ears, even as they fell from his own lips.

"My belong Shanghai side," explained the man. He was apparently a servant. Some one would have brought him out here. Though to what end it would be hard to guess, for a servant who can not make himself understood has small value. And no Shanghai man can do that in Hansi.

"What pidgin belong you this side?"

"My missy wanchee chin-chin."

Thus the man. His mistress wished a word. It was odd. Who, what, would his mistress be!

Doane always made it a rule, in these caravansaries, to engage the "number one" room if it was to be had. A countryside inn, in China, is usually a walled rectangle of something less or more than a halfacre in extent. Across the front stands the innkeeper's house, and the immense, roofed, swinging gates, built of strong timbers and planks. Along one side wall extend the stables, where the animals stand a row, looking over the manger into the courtyard. Along the other side are cell-like rooms, usually on the same level as the ground, with floors of dirt or worn old tile, with a table, a narrow chair or two of bent wood, and the inevitable brick *kang*, or platform bed with a tiny charcoal stove built into it and a thickness or two of matting thrown over the dirt and insect life of the crumbling surface. At the end of the court opposite' the gate stands, nearly always, a small separate building, the floor raised two or three steps from the ground. This is, in the pidgin vernacular, the "number one" room. Usually, however, it is large enough for division into two or three rooms. In the present instance there were two rather large rooms on either side of an entrance hall. Doane had been ushered into one of these rooms with no thought for the possible occupant of the other, beyond sleepily noting that the door was closed.

Hastily brushing his hair and smoothing the wrinkles out of his coat he stepped across the hall. That other door was ajar now. He tapped; and a woman's voice, a voice not unpleasing in quality, cried, in English, "Come in!"

4

She rose, as he pushed open the door, from the chair. She was young—certainly in the twenties—and unexpectedly, curiously beautiful. Her voice was Western American. Her abundant hair wras a vivid yellow. She was clad in a rather elaborate negligee robe that looked odd in the dingy room. Her cot stood by the paper windows, on a square of new white matting. Two suit-cases stood on bricks nearer the *kang*. And a garment was tacked up across the broken paper squares.

"I'm sorry to trouble you," she said breathlessly. "But it's getting unbearable. I've waited here ever since yesterday for some word. I know there was trouble. I heard so much shooting. And they made such a racket yelling. They got into the compound here. I had to cover my windows, you see. It was awful. All night I thought they'd murder me. And this morning I slept a little in the chair. And then you came in... I saw you... and I was wild to ask you the news. I thought perhaps you'd help me. I've sat here for hours, trying to keep from disturbing you. I knew you were sleeping."

She ran on in an ungoverned, oddly intimate way.

"I'm glad to be of what service I—" He found himself saying something or other; wondering with a strangely cold mind what he could possibly do and why on earth she was here. His own long pent-up emotional nature was answering hers with profoundly disturbing force.

"I ought to ask you to sit down," she was saying. She caught his arm and almost forced him into the chair. She even stroked his shoulder, nervously yet casually. He coldly told himself that he must keep steady, impersonal; it was the unexpectedness of this queer situation, the shock of it...

"It's all right," said she. "I'll sit on the cot. It's a pig-sty here. But sometimes you can't help these things.... please tell me what dreadful thing has happened!"

She had large brown eyes... odd, with that hair!... and they met his, hung on them.

In a low measured voice he explained:

"The natives attacked a mission station here—"

"Oh, just a mission!"

"They burned it down, and killed all but one of the workers there."

"Were they white?"

"The workers were Chinese, Christian Chinese. But—"

"Oh, I see! I couldn't imagine what it was all about. It's been frightful. Sitting here, without a word. But if it was just among the Chinese, then where's—I've got to tell you part of it—where's Harley Beggins? He brought me out here. He isn't the kind that skips out without a word. I've known him two years. He's a good fellow. You see, this thing—whatever it is—leaves me in a hole. I can't just sit here."

"I am trying to tell you. Please listen as calmly as you can. First tell me something about this Harley Beggins."

"He's with the Ho Shan Company. An engineer. But say—you don't mean—you're not going to—"

"He was a young man?"

"Yes. Tall. Curly hair. A fine-looking young man. And very refined. His family... but, my God, you—"

"You must keep quiet!"

"Keep quiet! I'd like to know how, when you keep me in suspense like this!" She was on her feet now.

"I am going to tell you. But you must control yourself. Mr. Beggins must be the young engineer who tried to help the people in the compound."

"He was killed?"

"Quiet! Yes, he was killed. I buried him this morning."

Then the young woman's nerves gave way utterly, Doane found his mind divided between the cold thought of leaving her, perhaps asking the magistrate to give her an escort down to Ting Yang or up through the wall to Peking, and the other terribly strong impulse to stay. It was clear that she was not—well, a good woman; excitingly clear. She said odd things. "Well, see where this mess leaves *me*!" for one. And, "What's to become of me? Do I just stay out here? Die here? Is this all?"... When, daring a lull in the scene she was making he undertook to go, she clung to him and sobbed on his shoulder. The young engineer had meant little in her life. Her present emotion was almost wholly fright.

He knew, then, that he couldn't go. He was being swept toward destruction. It seemed like that. He could think coolly about it during the swift moments. He could watch his own case. One by one, in quick-flashing thoughts, he brought up all the arguments for morality, for duty, for common decency, and one by one they failed him. Something in life was too strong for him. Something in his nature.... This, then was the natural end of all his brooding, speculating, struggling with the demon of unbelief.... And even then he felt the hideously tragic quality of this hour.

5

She was, it came out, a notorious woman of Soo-chow Road, Shanghai; one of the so-called "American girls" that have brought a good name to local disgrace. The new American judge, at that time engaged in driving out the disreputable women and the gamblers from the quasi protection of the consular courts, had issued a warrant for her arrest, whereupon young Beggins, who had been numbered among her "friends," had undertaken to protect her, out here in the interior, until the little wave of reform should have passed.

Despite her vulgarity, and despite the chill of spiritual death in his heart, he wished to be kind to her. Something of the long-frustrated emotional quality of the man overflowed toward her. He did what he could; laid her case before the magistrate, and left enough money to buy her a ticket to Peking from the northern railroad near Kalgan. This in the morning.

One other thing he did in the morning was to write to Hidderleigh, at Shanghai, telling enough of the truth about his fall, and asking that his successor be sent out at the earliest moment possible. And he sent off the letter, early, at the Chinese post-office. At least he needn't play the hypocrite. The worst imaginable disaster had come upon him. His real life, it seemed, was over As for telling the truth at the mission, his mind would shape a course. The easiest thing would be to tell Boatwright, straight. Though in any case it would come around to them from Shanghai. He had sealed his fate when he posted the letter. They would surely know, all of them. Henry Withery would know. It would reach the congregations back there in the States. At the consulates and up and down the coast—where men drank and gambled and carved fortunes out of great inert China and loved as they liked—they would be laughing at him within a fortnight.

And then he thought of Betty.

That night, on the march back to T'ainan, he stood, a solitary figure on the Pass of the Flighting Geese, looking up, arms outstretched, toward the mountain that for thousands of years has been to the sons of Han a sacred eminence; and the old prayer, handed down from another Oriental race as uttered by a greater sinner than he, burst from his lips:

"I will lift mine eyes to the hills, from whence cometh my help!"

But no help came to Griggsby Duane that night. With tears lying warm on his cheeks he strode down the long slope toward Tainan.

CHAPTER VII
LOVE IS A TROUBLE

1

IT WAS early morning—the first day of April—when the Pacific liner that carried Betty Doane and Jonathan Brachey out of Yokohama dropped anchor in the river below Shanghai and there discharged passengers and freight for all central and northern China.

Brachey, on that occasion, watched from his cabin porthole while Betty and the Hasmers descended the accommodation ladder and boarded the company's launch. Then, not before, he drank coffee and nibbled a roll. His long face was gray and deeply lined. He had not slept.

He went up to Shanghai on the next launch, walked directly across the Bund to the row of steamship offices, and engaged passage on a north-bound coasting steamer. That evening he dined alone, out on the Yellow Sea, steaming toward Tsingtau, Chefu and (within the five days) Tientsin. He hadn't meant to take in the northern ports at this time; his planned itinerary covered the Yangtse Valley, where the disorderly young shoots of revolution were ripening slowly into red flower. But he was a shaken man. As he saw the problem of his romance, there were two persons to be saved, Betty and himself. He had behaved, on the one occasion, outrageously. He could see his action now as nothing other than weakness, curiously despicable, in the light of the pitiless facts. Reason had left him. Gusts of emotion lashed him. He now regarded the experience as a storm that must be somehow weathered. He couldn't weather it in Shanghai. Not with Betty there. He would surely seek her; find her. With his disordered soul he would cry out to her. In this alarming mood no subterfuge would appear too mean—sending clandestine notes by yellow hands, arranging furtive meetings.

He was, of course, running away from her, from his task, from himself. It was expensive business. But he had meant to work up as far as Tientsin and Peking before the year ran out. He was, after all, but taking that part of it first. To this bit of justification he clung. He passed but one night at Tientsin, in the curiously British hotel, on an out-and-out British street, where one saw little more to suggest the East than the Chinese policeman at the corner, an occasional passing amah or mafoo, and the blue-robed, soft-footed hotel servants; then on to Peking by train, an easy four-hour run, lounging in a European dining-car where the allied troops had fought their way foot by foot only seven years earlier.

Brachey, though regarded by critical reviewers as a rising authority on the Far East, had never seen Peking. India he knew; the Straits Settlements—at Singapore and Penang he was a person of modest but real standing; Borneo, Java, Celebes and the rest of the vast archipelago, where flying fish skim a burnished sea and green islands float above a shimmering horizon against white clouds; the Philippines, Siam, Cochin China and Hongkong; but the swarming Middle Kingdom and its Tartar capital were fresh fuel to his coldly eager mind. He stopped, of course, at the almost Parisian hotel of the International Sleeping Car Company, just off Legation Street.

Peking, in the spring of 1907, presented a far from unpleasant aspect to the eye of the traveler. The siege of the legations was already history and half-forgotten; the quarter itself had been wholly rebuilt. The clearing away of the crowded Chinese houses about the legations left *à glacis* of level ground that gave dignity to the walled enclosure. Legation Street, paved, bordered by stone walks and gray compound-walls, dotted with lounging figures of Chinese gatekeepers and alert sentries of this or that or another nation—British, American, Italian, Austrian, Japanese, French, Belgian, Dutch, German—offered a pleasant stroll of a late afternoon when the sun was low. Through gateways there were glimpses to be caught of open-air tea parties, of soldiers drilling, or even of children playing. Tourists wandered afoot or rolled by in rickshaws drawn by tattered blue and brown coolies.

From the western end of the street beyond the American *glacis*, one might see the traffic through the Chien Gate, with now and then a nose-led train of camels humped above the throng; and beyond, the vast brick walls and the shining yellow palace roofs of the Imperial City. Around to the north, across the Japanese *glacis*, one could stroll, in the early evening, to the motion-picture show, where one-reel films from Paris were run off before an audience of many colors and more nations and costumes, while a placid Chinaman manipulated a mechanical piano.

2

Brachey had letters to various persons of importance along the street. With the etiquette of remote colonial capitals, he had long since trained himself to a mechanical conformity. Accordingly he devoted his first afternoon to a round of calls, by rickshaw; leaving cards in the box provided for the purpose at the gate house of each compound. Before another day had gone he found return cards in his box at the hotel; and thus was he established as *persona grata* on Legation Street. Invitations followed. The American minister had him for tiffin. There were pleasant meals at the legation barracks. Tourist groups at the hotel made the inevitable advances, which he met with austere dignity. Meantime he busied himself discussing with experts the vast problems confronting the Chinese in adjusting their racial life to the modern world, and within a few days was jotting down notes and preparing tentative outlines for his book.

This activity brought him, at first, some relief from the emotional storm through which he had been passing. Work, he told himself, was the thing; work, and a deliberate avoidance of further entanglements.

If, in taking this course, he was dealing severely with the girl whose brightly pretty face and gently charming ways had for a time disarmed him, he was dealing quite as severely with himself; for beneath his crust of self-sufficiency existed shy but turbulent springs of feeling. That was the trouble; that had always been the trouble; he dared not let himself feel, lie had let go once before, just once, only to skim the very border of tragedy. The color of that one bitter experience of his earlier manhood ran through every subsequent act of his life. Month by month, through the years, he had winced as he drew a check to the hard, handsome, strange woman who had been, it appeared, his wife; who was, incredibly, his wife yet. With a set face he had read and courteously answered letters from this stranger. A woman of worldly wants, all of which came, in the end, to money. The business of his life had settled down to a systematic meeting of those wants. That, and industriously employing his talent for travel and solitude.

No, the thing was to think, not feel. To logic and will he pinned his faith. Impulses rose every day, here in Peking, to write Betty. It wouldn't be hard to trace her father's address. For that matter he knew the city. He found it impossible to forget a word of hers. Vivid memories of her round pretty face, of the quick humorous expression about her brown eyes, the movements of her trim little head and slim body, recurred with, if anything, a growing vigor They would leap into his mind at unexpected, awkward moments, cutting the thread of sober conversations. At such moments he felt strongly that impulse to explain himself further. But his clear mind told him that there would be no good in it. None. She might respond; that would involve them the more deeply. He had gone too far. He had (this in the bitter hours) transgressed. The thing was to let her forget; it would, he sincerely tried to hope, be easier for her to forget than for himself He had to try to hope that.

But on an evening the American military attaché dined with him. They sat comfortably over the coffee and cigars at one side of the large hotel dining-room. Brachey liked the attaché. His military training, his strong practical instinct for fact, his absorption in his work, made him the sort with whom Brachey, who had no small talk, really no social grace, could let himself go. And the attaché knew China. He had traversed the interior from Manchuria and Mongolia to the borders of Thibet and the Loto country of Yunnan, and could talk, to sober ears, interestingly. On this occasion, after dwelling long on the activity of secret revolutionary societies in the southern provinces and in the Yangtse Valley, he suddenly threw out the following remark:

"But of course, Brachey, there's an excellent chance, right now, to study a revolution in the making out here in Hansi. You can get into the heart of it in less than a week's travel. And if you don't mind a certain element of danger..."

The very name of the province thrilled Brachey. He sat, fingering his cigar, his face a mask of casual attention, fighting to control the uprush of feeling. The attache was talking on. Brachey caught bits here and there; "You've seen this crowd of banker persons from Europe around the hotel? Came out over the Trans Siberian with their families. A committee representing the Directorate of the Ho Shan Company. The story is that they've been asked to keep out of Hansi for the present for fear of violence.... You'd get the whole thing, out there—officials with a stake 'n the local mines shrewdly stirring up trouble while pretending to put it down; rich young students agitating, the Chinese equivalent of our soap-box Socialists; and queer Oriental motives and twists that you and I can't expect to understand.... The significant thing though, the big fact for you, I should say—is that if the Hansi agitators succeed in turning this little rumpus over the mining company into something of a revolution against the Imperial Government, it'll bring them into an understanding with the southern provinces. It may yet prove the deciding factor in the big row. Something as if Ohio should go democratic this year, back home. You see?... There are queer complications. Our Chinese secretary says that a personal quarrel between two mandarins is a prominent item in the mix-up.... That's the place for you, all right— Hansi! They've got the narrow-gauge railway nearly through to T'ainan-fu, I believe. You can pick up a guide here at the hotel. He'll engage a cook. You won't drink the water, of course; better carry a few cases of Tan San. And don't eat the green vegetables. Take some beef and mutton and potatoes and rice. You can buy chickens and eggs. Get a money belt and carry all the Mexican dollars you can stagger under. Provincial money's no good a hundred miles away. Take some English gold for a reserve. That's good everywhere. And you'll want your overcoat."

Five minutes later Brachey heard this:

"A. P. Browning, the Agent General of the Ho Shan Company, is stopping here now, along with the committee. Talk with him, first. Get the company's view of it. He'll talk freely. Then go out there and have a look—see for yourself. Say the word, and I'll give you a card to Browning."

Now Brachey looked up. It seemed to him, so momentous was the hour, that his pulse had stopped. He sat very still, looking at his guest, obviously about to speak.

The attaché, to whom this man's deliberate cold manner was becoming a friendly enough matter of course, waited.

"Thanks," Brachey finally said. "Be glad to have it."

But the particular card, scribbled by the attaché, there across the table, was never presented. For late that night, in a bitter revulsion of feeling, Brachey tore it up.

4

In the morning, however, when he stopped at the desk, the Belgian clerk handed him a thick letter from his attorney in New York, forwarded from his bank in Shanghai. He read and reread it, while his breakfast turned cold; studied it with an unresponsive brain.

It seemed that his wife's attorney had approached his with a fresh proposal. Her plan had been to divorce him on grounds of desertion and non-support; this after his refusal to supply what is euphemistically termed "statutory evidence." But the fact that she had from month to month through the years accepted money from him, and not infrequently had demanded extra sums by letter and telegram, made it necessary that he enter into collusion with her to the extent of keeping silent and permitting her suit to go through unopposed. His own instructions to his lawyer stood flatly to the contrary.

But a new element had entered the situation. She wished to marry again. The man of her new choice had means enough to care for her comfortably. And in her eagerness to be free she proposed to release him from payment of alimony beyond an adjustment to cover the bare cost of her suit, on condition that he withdraw his opposition.

It was the old maneuvering and bargaining. At first thought it disgusted and hurt him. The woman's life had never come into contact with his, since the first few days of their married life, without hurting him. He had been harsh, bitter, unforgiving. He had believed himself throughout in the right. She had shown (in his view) no willingness to take marriage seriously, give him and herself a fair trial, make a job of it. She had exhibited no trait that he could accept as character. It had seemed to him just that she should suffer as well as he.

But now, as the meaning of the letter penetrated his mind, his spirits began to rise. It was a tendency he resisted; but he was helpless. From moment to moment his heart, swelled. Not once before in four years had the thought of freedom occurred to him as a desirable possibility. But now he knew that he would accept it, even at the cost of collusion and subterfuge. He saw nothing of the humor in the situation; that he, who had judged the woman so harshly, should find his code of ethics, his very philosophy, dashed to the ground by a look from a pair of brown eyes, meant little. It was simply that up to the present time an ethical attitude had been the important thing, whereas now the important thing was Betty. That was all there seemed to be to it. But then there had been almost as little of humor as of love in the queerly solitary life of Jonathan Brachey.

He cabled his attorney, directly after breakfast, to agree to the divorce. Before noon he had engaged a guide and arranged with him to take the morning train southward to the junction whence that narrow-gauge Hansi Line was pushing westward toward the ancient provincial capital.

In all this there was no plan. Brachey, confused, aware that the instinctive pressures of life were too much for him, that he was beaten, was soberly, breathlessly, driving toward the girl who had touched and tortured his encrusted heart. He was not even honest with himself; he couldn't be. He dwelt on the importance of studying the Hansi problem at close range He decided, among other things, that he wouldn't permit himself to see Betty, that he would merely stay secretly near her, certainly until a cablegram from New York should announce his positive freedom. In accordance with this decision he tore up his letters to her as fast as they were written. If the fact that he was now writing such letters indicated an alarming condition in his emotional nature, at least his will was still intact. He proved that by tearing them up. He even found this thought encouraging.

But, of course, he had taken his real beating when he gave up his plans and caught the coasting steamer at Shanghai. He was to learn now that rushing away from Betty and rushing toward her were irradiations of the same emotion.

He left Peking on that early morning way-train of passenger and freight cars, without calling again at the legation; merely sent a chit to the Commandant of Marines to say that he was off. He had not heard of the requirement that a white traveler into the interior carry a consular passport countersigned by Chinese authorities, and also, for purposes of identification, a supply of cards with the Chinese equivalent of his name; so he set forth without either, and (as a matter of fixed principle) without firearms.

CHAPTER VIII
THE WAYFARER

1

PASSENGER traffic on the Hansi Line ended at this time at a village called Shau T'ing, in the heart of the red mountains. Brachey spent the night in a native caravansary, his folding cot set up on the earthen floor. The room was dirty, dilapidated, alive with insects and thick with ancient odors. A charcoal fire in the crumbling brick *kang* gave forth fumes of gas that suggested the possibility of asphyxiation before morning. Brachey sent his guide, a fifty-year-old Tientsin Chinese of corpulent figure, known, for convenience, as "John," for water and extinguished the fire. The upper half of the inner wall was a wooden lattice covered with paper; and by breaking all the paper squares within his reach, Brachey contrived to secure a circulation of air. Next he sent John for a piece of new yellow matting, and by spreading this under the cot created a mild sensation of cleanliness, which, though it belied the facts, made the situation a thought more bearable. For Brachey, though a veteran traveler, was an extremely fastidious man. He bore dirt and squalor, had borne them at intervals for years, without ever losing his squeamish discomfort at the mere thought of them. But the stern will that was during these, years the man's outstanding trait, and his intense absorption in his work, had kept him driving ahead through all petty difficulties. The only outward sign of the strain it put him to was an increased irritability.

He traveled from Shau T'ing to Ping Yang, the next day in an unroofed freight ear without a seat, crowded in with thirty-odd Chinese and their luggage. During the entire day he spoke hardly a word. His two servants guarded him from contact with the other natives; but he ignored even his own men. At a way station, where the engine waited half an hour for water and coal, a lonely division engineer from Lombardy called out a greeting in bad French. Brachey coldly snubbed the man.

He planned to pick up either a riding animal or a mule litter at Ping Yang. As it turned out, the best John could secure was a freight cart; springless, of course. T'ainan was less than a hundred miles away, yet he was doomed to three days of travel in a creaking, hard-riding cart through the sunken roads, where dust as fine as flour sifts through the clothing and rubs into the pores of the skin, and to two more nights at native inns—with little hope of better accommodation at T'ainan.

By this time Brachey was in a state of nerves that alarmed even himself. Neither will nor imagination was proving equal to this new sort of strain. The confusion of motives that had driven him out here provided no sound justification for the journey. When he tried to think work now, he found himself thinking Betty. And misgivings were creeping into his mind. It amounted to demoralization.

He walked out after the solitary dinner of soup and curried chicken and English strawberry jam. The little village was settling into evening calm. Men and boys, old women and very little girls, sat in the shop fronts—here merely rickety porticoes with open doorways giving on dingy courtyards— or played about the street. Carpenters were still working on the roof of the new railway station. Three young men, in an open field, were playing decorously with a shuttlecock of snake's skin and duck feathers, deftly kicking it from player to player. Farther along the street a middle-aged man of great dignity, clad in a silken robe and black skull-cap with the inevitable red knot, was flying a colored kite ... through all this, Jonathan Brachey, the expert observer, wandered about unseeing.

2

Farther up the hill, however, rounding a turn in the road, he stopped short, suddenly alive to the vivid outer world. A newly built wall of brick stood before him, enclosing an area of two acres or more, within which appeared the upper stories of European houses, as well as the familiar curving roofs of Chinese tile. And just outside the walls two young men and two young women, in outing clothes, white folk all, were playing tennis. To their courteous greeting he responded frigidly.

Later a somewhat baffled young Australian led him to the office of M. Pourmont and presented him.

The distinguished French engineer, looking up from his desk, beheld a tall man in homespun knickerbockers, a man with a strong if slightly forbidding face. He fingered the card.

"Ah, Monsieur Brashayee! Indeed, yes! It is ze *grand plaisir!* But it mus' not be true zat you go on all ze vay to T'ainan-fu."

"Yes," Brachey replied with icy courtesy, "I am going to T'ainan."

"But ze time, he is not vat you call—-ripe. One makes ze trouble. It is only a month zat zay t'row ze *pierre* at me, zay tear ze cart of me, zay destroy ze ear of me! *Choses affreuses!* I mus'not let you go!"

Brachey heard this without taking it in any degree to himself. He was looking at the left ear of this stout, bearded Parisian, from which, he observed, the lobe was gone.... Then, with a quickening pulse, he thought of Betty out there in T'ainan, in real danger.

"Come wiz me!" cried M. Pourmont. "I vill show you vat ve do—*nous ici.*" And snatching up a bunch of keys he led Brachey out about the compound. He opened one door upon what appeared to be a heap of old clothes.

"*Des sac à terres,*" he explained.

Brachey picked one up. "Ah," he remarked, coldly interested—"sand-bags!"

"Yes, it is zat. Sand-bag for ze vail. Ve have ze *femme Chinoise*—ze Chinese vimmen—sew zem all every day. And you vill look..." He led the way with this to a corner of the grounds where the firm loess had been turned up with a pick. "It is so, Monsieur Brashayee, *partout.* All is ready. In von night ve fill ze bag, ve are a fort, ve are ready.... See! An' see!"

He pointed out a low scaffolding built here and there along the compound wall for possible use as a firing step. Just outside the wall crowding native houses were being torn down. "I buy zem," explained M. Pourmont with a chuckle, "an' I clear avay. I make a *glacis, nest ce pas?*" On several of the flat roofs of supply sheds along the wall were heaps of the bags, ready filled, covered from outside eyes with old boards. In one building, under lock and key, were two machine guns and box on box of ammunition. Back in M. Pourmont's private study was a stand of modern rifles.

"You vill see by all zis vat is ze t'ought of myself," concluded the genial Frenchman. "Ze trouble he is real. It is not safe to-day in Hansi. Ze Société of ze Great Eye—ze Lookair—he grow, he *fait l'exercice,* he make ze t'reat. You vill not go to T'ainan, alone. It is not right!"

Brachey was growing impatient now.

"Oh, yes," he said, more shortly than he knew. "I will go on."

"You have ze arm—ze revolvair?"

Brachey shook his head.

"You vill, zen, allow me to give you zis."

But Brachey declined the weapon stiffly, said good night, and returned to the inn below.

The next morning a Chinese servant brought a note from M Pourmont. If he would go—thus that gentleman—and if he would not so much as carry arms for protection, at least he must be sure to get into touch with M. Griggsby Duane at once on arriving at T'ianan. M. Doane was a man of strength and address. He would be the only support that M. Brachey could look for in that turbulent corner of the world.

3

The lamp threw a flickering unearthly light, faintly yellow, on the tattered wall-hangings that bore the Chinese characters signifying happiness and hospitality and other genial virtues. The lamp was of early Biblical pattern, nor unlike a gravy boat of iron, full of oil or grease, in which the wick floated. It stood on the roughly-made table.

The inn compound was still, save for the stirring and the steady crunching of the horses and mules at their long manger across the courtyard.

Brachey, half undressed, sat on his cot, staring at the shadowy brick wall. His face was haggard. There were hollows under the eyes. His hands lay, listless, on his knees. The fire that had been for a fortnight consuming him was now, for the moment, burnt out.

But at least, he now felt, the particular storm was over. That there might be recurrences, he recognized. That girl had found her way, through all the crust, to his heart. The result had been nearly unbearable while it lasted. It had upset his reason; made a fool of him. Here he was—now—less than a day's journey from her. He couldn't go back; the thought stirred savagely what he thought of as the shreds of his self-respect. And yet to go on was, or seemed, unthinkable. The best solution seemed to be merely to make use of T'ainan as a stopping place for the night and pass on to some other inland city. But this thought carried with it the unnerving fear that he would fail to pass on, that he might even communicate with her.

His life, apparently, was a lie. He had believed since his boyhood that human companionship lay apart from the line of his development. Even his one or two boy friends he had driven off. The fact embittered his earlier life; but it was so. In each instance he had said harsh things that the other could not or would not overlook. His marriage had contributed further proof. Along with his pitilessly detached judgment of the woman went the sharp consciousness that he, too, had failed at it. He couldn't adapt his life to the lives of others. Since that experience—these four years—by living alone, keeping away, keeping clear out of his own land, even out of touch with the white race, and making something of a success of it, he had not only proved himself finally, he had even, in a measure, justified himself. Yet now, a chance meeting with a nineteen-year-old girl had, at a breath, destroyed the laborious structure of his life. It all came down to the fact that emotion had at last caught him as surely as it had caught the millions of other men—men he had despised. He couldn't live now without feeling again that magic touch of warmth in his breast. He couldn't go on alone.

He bowed his head over it. Round and round went his thoughts, cutting deeper and deeper into the tempered metal of his mind.

He said to her: "I am selfish."

He had supposed he was telling the simple truth. But clearly he wasn't. At this moment, as at every moment since that last night on the boat deck, he was as dependent on her as a helpless child. And now he wasn't even selfish. These two days since the little talk with M. Pourmont he had been stirred deeply by the thought that she was in danger.

Over and over, with his almost repelling detachment of mind, he reviewed the situation. She might not share his present emotion. Perhaps she had recovered quickly from the romantic drift that had caught them on the ship. She was a sensitive, expressive little thing; quite possibly the new environment had caught her up and changed her, filled her life with fresh interest or turned it in a new direction. With this thought was interwoven the old bitter belief that no woman could love him. It must have been that she was stirred merely by that romantic drift and had endowed him, the available man, with the charms that dwelt only in her own fancy. Young girls were impressionable; they did that.

But suppose—it was excitingly implausible—she hadn't swung away from him. What would her missionary folk say to him and his predicament? Sooner or later he would be free; but would that clear him with these dogmatic persons, with her father? Probably not. And if not, wouldn't the fact thrust unhappiness upon her? You could trust these professionally religious people, he believed, to make her as unhappy as they could—nag at her.

Suppose, finally, the unthinkable thing, that she—he could hardly formulate even the thought; he couldn't have uttered it—loved him. What did he know of her? Who was she? What did she know of adult life? What were her little day-by-day tastes and impulses, such as make or break any human companionship...? And who was he? What right had he to take on his shoulders the responsibility for a human life... a delicately joyous little life? For that was what it came down to. It came to him, now, like a ray of blipdirig light, that he who quickens the soul of a girl must carry the burden of that soul to his grave. At times during the night he thought wistfully of his freedom, of his pleasant, selfish solitude and the inexigent companionship of his work.

His suit-case lay on the one chair. He drew it over; got out the huge, linen-mounted map of the Chinese Empire that is published by the China Inland Mission, and studied the roads about T'ainan. That from the east— his present route—swung to the south on emerging from the hills, and approached the city nearly from that direction. Here, instead of turning up into the city, he could easily enough strike south on the valley road, perhaps reaching an apparently sizable village called Hung Chan by night.

He decided to do that, and afterward to push southwest. It should be possible to find a way out along the rivers tributary to the Yangtse, reaching that mighty stream at either Ichang or Hankow. And he would work diligently, budding up again the life that had been so quickly and lightly overset. At least, for the time. He must try himself out This riding his emotions wouldn't do. At some stage of the complicated experience it was going to be necessary to stop and think. Of course, if he should find after a reasonable time, say a few months, that the emotion persisted, why then, with his personal freedom established, he might write Betty, simply stating his case.

And after all this, on the following afternoon, dusty, tired of body and soul, Jonathan Brachey rode straight up to the East Gate of T'ainan-fu.

CHAPTER IX
KNOTTED LIVES

1

IF Brachey had approached that East Gate a year later he would have rolled comfortably into the city in a rickshaw (which has followed the white man into China) along a macadamized road bordered by curbing of concrete from the new railway station. But in the spring of 1907 there was no station, no pavement, not a rickshaw. The road was a deep-rutted way, dusty in dry weather, muddy in wet, bordered by the crumbling shops and dwellings found on the outskirts of every Chinese city. A high, bumpy little bridge of stone spanned the moat.

Over this bridge rode Brachey, in his humble cart, sitting fiat under a span of tattered matting, surrounded and backed by his boxes and bales of food and water and his personal baggage. John and the cook rode behind on mules. The muleteers walked.

Under the gate were lounging soldiers, coolies, beggars, and a money-changer or two with their bags of silver lumps, their strings of copper cash and their balanced scales. Two of the soldiers sprang forward and stopped the cart. Despite their ragged uniforms (of a dingy blue, of course, like all China, and capped with blue turbans) these were tall, alert men. Brachey was rapidly coming to recognize the Northern Chinese as a larger, browner, more vigorous type of being than the soft little yellow men of the South with whom he had long been familiar in the United States as well as in the East. A mure dangerous man, really, this northerner.

Brachey leaned back on his baggage and watched the little encounter between his John and the two soldiers. Any such conversation in China is likely to take up a good deal of time, with many gestures, much vehemence of speech and an 'ncreasing volume of interference from the inevitable curious crowd. The cook and the two muleteers joined the argument, Brachey had learned before the first evening that this interpreter of his had no English beyond the few pidgin phrases common to all speech along the coast. And since leaving Shau T'ing it had transpired that the man's Tientsin-Peking dialect sounded strange in the ears of Hansi John was now in the position of an interpreter who could make headway in neither of the languages in which he was supposed to deal. Brachey didn't mind. It kept the man still. And he had learned years earlier that the small affairs of routine traveling can be managed with but few spoken words. But just now, idly watching the little scene, he would have liked to know what it meant.

Finally John came to the cart, followed by shouts from the soldiers and the crowd.

"Card wanchee," he managed to say.

"Card? No savvy," said Brachey.

"Card," John nodded earnestly.

Brachey produced his personal card, bearing his name in English and the address of a New York club.

John studied it anxiously, and then passed it to one of the soldiers. That official fingered it; turned it over; discussed it with his fellow. Another discussion followed.

Brachey now lost interest. He filled and lighted his pipe; then drew from a pocket a small leather-bound copy of *The Bible in Spain*, opened at a bookmark, and began reading.

There was a wanderer after his own heart—George Borrow! An eager adventurer, at home in any city of any clime, at ease in any company, a fellow with gipsies, bandits, Arabs, Jews of Gibraltar and Greeks of Madrid, known from Mogadore to Moscow. Bor-row's missionary employment puzzled him as a curious inconsistency; his skill at making much of every human contact was, to the misanthropic Brachey, enviable; his genius for solitude, his self-sufficiency in every state, whether confined in prison at Madrid or traversing alone the dangerous wilderness of Galicia, were to Brachey points of fine fellowship. This man needed no wife, no friend. His enthusiasm for the new type of human creature or the unfamiliar tongue never weakened.

The cart jolted, creaking, forward, into the low tunnel that served as a gateway through the massive wall. A soldier walked on either hand. Two other soldiers walked in the rear. The crowd, increasing every moment, trailed off behind. Small boys jeered, even threw bits of dirt and stones, one of which struck a soldier and caused a brief diversion.

They creaked on through the narrow, crowded streets of the city. A murmur ran ahead from shop to shop and corner to corner. Porters, swaying under bending bamboo, shuffled along at a surprising pace and crowded past. Merchants stood in doorways and puffed at lung pipes with tiny nickel bowls as the strange parade went by.

Finally it stopped. Two great studded gates swung inward, and the cart lurched into the courtyard of an inn.

Brachey appropriated a room, sent John for hot water, and coolly shaved. Then he stretched out on the folding cot above its square of matting, refilled his pipe and resumed his Borrow.

2

Within half an hour fresh soldiers appeared, armed with carbines and revolvers, and settled themselves comfortably, two of them, by his door; two others taking up a position at the compound gate.

They brought a letter, in Chinese characters, on red paper in a buff and red envelope, which Brachey examined with curiosity.

"No savvy," he said.

But the faithful John, inarticulate from confusion and fright could not translate.

Between this hour in mid-afternoon and early evening, six of these documents were passed in through Brachey's door. With the last one, John appeared to see a little light.

"Number one policeman wanchee know pidgin belong you," he explained laboriously.

That would doubtless mean the police minister. So they wanted to know his business! But as matters stood, with no other medium of communication than John's patient but bewildered brain, explanation would be difficult. Brachey reached for his book and read on. Something would have to happen, of course. It really hardly mattered what. He even felt a little relief. The authorities might settle his business for him. Pack him off. It would be better. M. Pourmont's letter to Griggsby Doane had burned in his pocket for two days. It had seemed to press him, like the hand of fate, to Betty's very roof. Now, since he had become—the simile rose—a passive shuttlecock, a counterplay of fate might prove a way out of his dilemma.

He had chicken fried in oil for his dinner. And John ransacked the boxes for dainties; as if the occasion demanded indulgence.

At eight John knocked with shaking hands at his door. It was dark in the courtyard, and a soft April rain was falling. Two fresh soldiers stood there, each with carbine on back and a lighted paper lantern in band. A boy from the inn held two closed umbrellas of oiled paper.

"Go now," said John, out of a dry throat.

"Go what side?" asked Brachey, surveying the little group.

John could not answer.

Brachey compressed his lips; stood there, knocking his pipe against the door-post. Then, finally, he put on overcoat and rubber overshoes, took one of the umbrellas, and set forth.

<h1 style="text-align:center">3</h1>

They walked a long way through twisting, shadowy streets, first a soldier with the boy from the inn, then Brachey under his umbrella, then John under another, then the second soldier. Dim figures finished past them. Once the quaint waihng of stringed instruments floated out over a compound wall. They passed through a dark tunnel that must have been one of the city gates; then on through other streets.

They stopped at a gate house. A door opened, and yellow lamplight fell warmly across the way. Brachey found himself stepping up into a structure that was and yet was not Chinese. A smiling old gate-keeper received him with striking courtesy, and, to his surprise, in English.

"Will you come with me, sir?"

John and the soldiers waited in the gate house.

Brachey followed the old man across a paved court. His pulse quickened. Where were they bringing him?

Through a window he saw a white woman sitting at a desk, under an American lamp.

He mounted stone steps, left his coat and hat in a homelike front hall. The servant led the way up a flight of carpeted stairs.

On the top step, Brachey paused. At the end of the corridor, where a chair or two, a table, bookcase, and lamp made a pleasant little lounge, a young woman sat quietly reading. She looked up; sat very still, gazing straight at him out of a white face. It was Betty. His heart seemed to stop.

Then a man stood before him. A little, dusty blond man. They were clasping hands. He was ushered rather abruptly into a study. The door closed.

The little man said something twice. It proved to be, "I am Mr. Boatwright," and he was looking down at the much-thumbed card; Brachey's own card.

Brachey was fighting to gather his wits. Why hadn't he spoken to Betty, or she to him? Would she wait there to see him? If not, how could he reach her?... He must reach her, of course. He knew now that through all his confusion of mind and spirit he had come straight to her.

4

The little man was nervous, Brachey observed; even jumpy. He hurried about, drawing down the window-shades. Then he sat at a desk and with twitching fingers rolled a pencil about. He cleared his throat.

"You've come in from the railroad?" he asked.... "Yes? Do you bring news?"

"No," said Brachey coldly.

"What gossip have your boys picked up along the road, may I ask?"

Back and forth, back and forth, his fingers twitched the pencil. Bradley's eyes narrowly followed the movement. After a little, he replied:

"I have no information from my boys."

"Seven years ago" — thus Mr. Boatwright, huskily, "they killed all but a few of us. Now the trouble has started again — a similar trouble They attacked our station up at So T'ung yesterday. Mr. Doane is on his way there now. He left this noon. That is why they referred your case to me. Oh. yes, I should have told you — the tao-tai, Chang Chili Ting, has asked me to get from you an explanation of your appearance here without a passport. But perhaps your card explains. You come simply as a journalist?"

Brachey bowed.

"You have no connection w ith the Ho Shan Company?"

"None"

"Chang is taking up your case this evening with the provincial judge, Pao Ting Chuan. Pao is to give you an audience to-morrow, I believe, at noon. I will act as your interpreter." Mr. Boatwright paused, and sighed. "I am very busy."

"I regret this intrusion on your time," said Brachey. It was impossible for him to be more than barely courteous to such a man as this.

"Oh, that's all right," Boatwright replied vaguely. "The audience will probably be at noon. Then you will come back here with me for tiffin." He sighed again; then went on. "They shot one of Pourmont's white men. Through the lungs.... You must have seen Pourmont at Ping Yang, as you came through."

"I called on him."

"Didn't he tell you?"

"No. He advised against my coming on."

"Of course. It's really very difficult. He wants us all to get out, as far as his compound. But, you see, our predicament is delicate. Already they've attacked one of our outposts. But the trouble may not spread. We can't draw in our people and leave at the first sign of difficulty. It would be interpreted as weakness not only on our part but on the part of all the white governments as well. Mr. Doane, I know"—he said this rather regretfully—"would never consent to that.... Mr. Doane is a strong man. We shall all breathe a little more easily when he is safely back. If he should not get back—well, you will see that I must face this situation—-the decision would fall on me. That's why I asked you for news. I have to consider the problem from every angle. We have other stations about the province and we must plan to draw all our people in before we can even consider a general retreat."

Brachey heard part of this. He wished the man would keep still: His own racing thoughts were with that pale girl in the hall. Was she still there? He must plan. He must be prepared with something to say, if they should meet face to face.

As it turned out, they met on the stairs. Betty was coming up. She paused; looked up, then down. The color stole back into her face; flooded it. She raised her hand, hesitatingly.

The color stole back into her face

Brachey heard and felt the surprise of Boatwright, behind him. The little man said:

"Oh!"

Brachey felt the warm little hand in his. It should have been, easy to explain their acquaintance; to speak of the ship, ask after the Hasmers. In the event, however, it proved impossible, all he could say—he heard the dry hard tones issuing from his own lips:

"Oh, how do you do! How have you been?"

Betty said, after too long a pause, glancing up momentarily at Mr. Boatwright:

"Mr. Brachey was on the steamer."

It was odd, that little situation. It might so easily have escaped being a situation, had not their own turbulent hearts made it so. But now, of course, neither could explain why they hadn't spoke before he went into the study. And little, distrait Mr. Boatwright was wide-eyed.

The situation passed from mildly bad to a little worse. Betty went on up the stairs; and Brachey went down.

The casual parting came upon Brachey like a tragedy. It was unthinkable. Something personal he must say. On the morrow it might be worse, with a whole household crowding about. It was a question if he could face her at all, that way. He got to the bottom step; then, with an apparently offhand, "I beg your pardon!" brushed past the now openly astonished Boatwright and bolted back up the stairs.

Betty moved a little way along the upper hall; hesitated; glanced back.

He spoke, low, in her ear. "I must see you!"

Her head inclined a little.

"Once! I must see you once. I can't leave it this way. Then I will go. To-morrow—at tiffin—if we can't talk together—you must give me some word. A note, perhaps, telling me how I can see you alone. There is one thing I must tell you."

"Please!" she murmured. There were tears in her eyes. They scalded his own high-beating heart, those tears.

"You will plan it? I am helpless. But I must see you—tell you!"

He thought her head inclined again.

"You will? You'll give me a note? Oh, promise!"

"Yes," she whispered; and slipped away into another room.

So this is why he had to come to T'ainan-fu—to tell her the tremendous news that he would one day be free! And she had promised to arrange a meeting!

Never in all his cold life had Jonathan Brachey experienced such a thrill as followed that soft "Yes."

Not a word passed between him and Boatwright until they stood in the gate house. Then, for an instant, their eyes met. He had to fight back the burning triumph that was in his own. But the little man seemed glad to look away; he was even evasive.

"You'd better be around about half past eleven in the morning," said he. "We'll go to the yamen from here. We must have blue carts and the extra servants. Good night." And again he sighed.

That was all. Boatwright let him go like that, back to the dirty, dangerous native inn.

He fell in behind the leading soldier, holding his umbrella high and marching stiffly, like a conqueror, through the sucking mud.

CHAPTER X
GRANITE

1

BETTY did not get down for breakfast in the morning. And Mrs. Boatwright sent nothing up.

It was close upon noon when Betty, sketching portfolio under arm, came slowly down the stairs. Mrs. Boatwright, at her desk in the front room, glanced up, called:

"Oh, Betty—just a moment!"

The girl stood in the doorway. She looked so slim and small and, even, childlike, that the older woman, to whom responsibility for all things and persons about her was a habit, knit her heavy brows slightly. What on earth were you to do with the child? What had Griggsby Doane been thinking of in bringing her out here? Anything, almost, would have been better. And just now, of all times!

"Would you mind coming in? There's a question or two I'd like to ask you."

Betty paused by a rocking chair of black walnut that was upholstered in crimson plush; fingered the crimson fringe. Mrs. Boatwright was marking out a geometrical pattern on the back of an envelope; frowning down at it. The silence grew heavy.

Finally Mrs. Boatwright, never light of hand, rame out with:

"This Mr. Brachey—who is he?"

Betty's fringed lids moved swiftly up; dropped again. "He—he's a writer, a journalist."

"You knew him on the ship?"

"Yes."

"You knew him pretty well?"

"I—saw something of him."

"Do you know why he came out here?"

Betty was silent.

"Do you know?"

"I should think you would ask him."

Mrs. Boatwright considered this. The girl was selfconscious, a little. And quietly—very quietly—hostile. Or perhaps merely on the defensive.

"Then you do know?"

"No," replied Betty, with that same very quiet gravity, "I can't say that I do. He is studying China, of course. He came from America to do that, I understand."

"Did you know he was coming out here?"

Betty slowly shook her head.

"Have you been corresponding with him?"

Another silence. Then this from Betty, without heat:

"I don't understand why you are asking these questions."

"Are you unwilling to answer them?"

"Such personal questions as that last one—yes."

"Why?"

"You have no right to ask it."

"Oh!" Mrs. Boatwright considered. "Hmm!" She controlled her temper and framed her next remark with care. This slip of a girl was unexpectedly in fiber like Griggsby Doane. There was no weakness in her quiet resistance, no yielding. Perhaps she was strong, after all. Though she looked soft enough; gentle like her mother. Perhaps, even, she was a person, of herself. This was a new thought. Mrs. Boatwright drew a parallelogram, then painstakingly shaded the lines.

"We mustn't misunderstand each other, Betty," she said. "In your father's absence, I am responsible for you. This man has appeared rather mysteriously. His business is not clear. The tao-tai asked Mr. Boatwright to look him up, for it seems he hasn't even an interpreter. He has just been here. They've gone for an audience with the provincial judge. Mr. Boatwright has asked him to come back here for tiffin. Which was rather impulsive, I'm afraid...." She paused; started outlining an octagon. "I may as well come out with it. Mr. Boatwright told me a little of what happened last evening—"

"Of what happened But nothing—"

"If you please! Mr. Boatwright is not a particularly observant man in these matters, but he couldn't help seeing that there is something between you and this Mr. Brachey.... Now, since you see what is in my mind, will you tell me why he is here?"

During this speech Betty stopped fingering the crimson fringe. She stood motionless, holding the portfolio still against her side. A slow color crept into her cheeks. She wouldn't, or couldn't, speak.

"Very well, if you won't answer that question, will you at least tell me something of what you do know about him?"

"I know very little about him," said Betty now, in a low but clear voice, without emphasis.

"I must try to make you understand this, my dear. Here the man is. Within the hour we are to sit down at tiffin with him. It is growing clearer every minute that Mr. Boatwright's suspicion was correct—

"You have no right to use that word!"

"Well, then, his surmise, say. There *is* something between you and this man. Don't you think you'd better tell me what it is?"

"There is nothing—nothing at all—that I need tell you."

"Is there nothing that you ought to tell your father?"

"You can not speak for him."

"I stand in his place, while he's away It is a responsibility I must accept. You say you know very little about the man?"

Betty bowed.

"You met him on the ship, by chance?"

"Yes."

"Do you know any of his friends?"

"No."

"Anything of his past?"

Betty hesitated. Then, as the woman glanced keenly up, she replied:

"Only what he has told me."

"Do you know, even, whether he is a married man?"

Another long silence fell. Betty stood as quietly as before, looking out of frank brown eyes at the sunlit courtyard and the gate house beyond where old Sun Shao-i, seated on a stool, was having the inside of his eyelids scraped by an itinerant barber.

"Yes," Betty replied.

"You mean—?"

"I know that he *is* married."

2

Betty, as she threw out this bit of uncompromising truth, was stirred with a thrill of wilder adventure than had hitherto entered her somewhat untrammeled young life. The situation had outrun her experience; she was acting on instinct. There was a sense of shock, too; and of hurt—hurt that Mrs. Boatwright could look, feel, so forbidding. Her firm face, now pressed together from chin to forehead, wrinkled across, squinting unutterable suspicions, stirred a resistance in Betty's breast that for a little time flared into anger.

There was no telling what Mrs. Boatwright felt. Her frown even relaxed, after a moment. The outbreak of moral superiority that Betty looked for didn't come. Instead she said:

"How did you learn this?"

"He told me."

"Oh, he told you?"

"Well, he wrote a letter before he—went away."

"Oh. he went away!"

"Yes. He went. Without a word. I didn't know where he was."

"When was that?"

"When we landed at Shanghai."

"Hardly three weeks ago. He's here now. Tell me—he wouldn't have gone off like that, of course, leaving such an intimate letter, unless a pretty definite situation had arisen."

Betty was silent.

"Will you tell me what it was?"

"No."

"Then—I really have a right to ask this of you—will you give me your word not to see him until your father returns, and then not until you have laid it before him?"

Silence again. The fringed lids fluttered. A small hand reached for the crimson fringe, slim fingers clung there.

Betty's thoughts were running away. She felt the situation now as a form of torture. That grim experienced woman must be partly right, of course; Betty was still so young as to defer mechanically to her elders, and she had no great opinion of herself, of her strength of character or her judgment. She thought of the boys at home, who had been fond of her. ... She thought of Harold Apgar, over there in Korea. He was clean, likable, prosperous; and he wanted to marry her. It really would solve her problems, could she only feel toward him so much as a faint reflection of the glow that Jonathan Brachey had aroused in her. But nothing in her nature answered Harold Apgar. For that matter—and this was the deeply confusing thing—she could not formulate her feeling for Brachey. She couldn't admit that she loved him. The thought of giving her life into his keeping—one day, should he come to her with clean hands; should he ask—was not to be entertained at all. But she couldn't think of him without excitement; and that excitement, last night and to-day, was the dominant fact in her life. She had no plans in which he figured. She was vaguely bent on forgetting him. During the night she had regretted her promise to meet him once more alone. Yet she had given that promise. Given the same situation she would—she knew with a touch of bewilderment that this was so—promise again.

Betty looked appealingly at Mr. Boatwright. Then, meeting with no sympathy, she drew up her little figure.

"You said he was coming here for tiffin, Mrs. Boatwright?"

"Yes." The woman glanced out at the courtyard. "Any moment."

"Then I shan't come into the dining-room." And Betty turned to leave the room.

"Just a moment! Am I to take that as an answer? Are you promising?"

Hetty turned; hesitated; then, suddenly, impulsively, came across the room.

"Mrs. Boatwright," she said unsteadily—her eyes were filling—"would it do any good for me to talk right out with you? Probably I do need advice." She faltered momentarily, shocked by the expression on that nearly square face. "Oh, it isn't a terribly serious situation. It really isn't. But that man is honest. He has led an unhappy, solitary life..."

Her voice died out.

"But you said he was *married!*" cried Mrs. Boatwright explosively.

"Yes, but—"

"'But! But!' Child, what are you talking about?"

There was nothing in Betty's experience of life that could interpret to her mind such a point of view as that really held by the woman before her. She had no means of knowing that they were speaking across a gulf wider and deeper perhaps than has ever before existed between two generations; and that each of them, quite unconsciously, was an extreme example of her type. She turned again.

It was a commotion out at the gate house that arrested her this time. She felt that curious excitement rising up in her heart and brain. Old Sun was springing up from the barber's stool, with his always great dignity brushing that public servitor aside. Then Brachey appeared, followed by Mr. Boatwright.

The wife of that little man now caught the look on Betty's face, the sudden light in her eyes, and rose, alarmed, to her feet. Taking in the situation, she said:

"I shall send something up to your room."

Betty moved her head wanly in the negative. It was no use explaining to this woman that she couldn't think of food. She moved slowly toward the door. She was unexpectedly tired.

"Where are you going?" asked the older woman shortly.

"I've got to be by myself," said Betty, apparently less resentful now. It was more a rather faint statement of fact. And she went on out, not so much as answering Mrs. Boatwright's final "But you will not promise?" It wasn't even certain that she heard.

3

Mrs. Boatwright stood thinking. Betty had run up the stairs. The two men were coming slowly across the courtyard, talking. Or her husband was talking; she could hear his light voice. The other man was silent; a gloomy figure in knickerbockers. She studied him. Already he was catalogued in her mind, and permanently. For nothing that might happen to present Brachey in another light could ever, now, shake her judgment of him. No new evidence of ability or integrity in the man or of genuine misfortune in marriage, would influence her. No play of sympathy, no tolerant reflectiveness, would for a moment occupy her mind. She was a New Englander, with the old non-conformist British insistence on conduct and duty bred in her bone. Her emotional nature was almost the granite of her native lulls. And she was strong as that granite. She feared nothing, shrank from nothing, that could be classified as duty. No Latin flexibility ever softened her vigorous expression of independent thought. Her duty, now, was clear.

She went out into the hall and opened the door.

The two men were just mounting the steps.

"My dear," began her husband, sensing her mood, glancing up apprehensively, "this is Mr. Brachey. He—

"Yes," said she, standing squarely in the doorway, "I understand. Mr. Brachey, I can not receive you in this house. You, of course, know why. I must ask you to go at once."

Then she simply waited; commandingly. From her eyes blazed honest, invincible anger.

Mr. Boatwright caught his breath; stood motionless, very white; finally murmured:

"But, my dear, I'm sure you..."

His wife merely glanced at him.

Brachey stood as she had caught him, on the steps, one foot above the other. His face was expressionless. His eyes fastened on the woman a gaze that might have meant no more than cold curiosity, growing slowly into contempt. Then, after a moment, as quietly, he turned and descended the steps.

Boatwright caught his arm.

"Really, Mr. Brachey—"

"Elmer!" cried his wife shortly. "Let him go!"

But Brachey had already shaken off the detaining hand. He marched straight across the court, stepped into the gate house, and disappeared.

Betty, all hurt confusion, had lingered in the second floor hall. At the first sound of Mrs. Boatwright's firm voice, she stepped, her brain a tangle of little indecisions, to the stair rail.

She ran lightly to the front window and watched Jonathan Brachey as he walked away. Then she shut herself in her own room, telling herself that the time had come to think it all out. But she couldn't think.

Against the granite in Mrs. Boatwright Betty, who understood herself not at all, had to set a quick strong impulsiveness that was certain, given a little time, to work out in positive act. Very little time indeed now intervened between impulse and act. She scribbled a note, in pencil:

"Dear Mr. Brachey—I am going out to sketch in the tennis court. You can reach it by the little side street just beyond our gate house as you come from the city. Please do come!—Betty D."

She went down the stairs again, portfolio under arm, and on to the gate house. Sun, as she had thought, knew at which inn the white gentleman was stopping, and at Miss Doane's request sent a boy with the chit.

CHAPTER XI
EMOTION

BRACHEY came suddenly into view, around the corner of the wall from the little side street.

He was dressed almost stiffly—not in knickerbockers now, but in what would be called at home a business suit, with stiff white collar and a soft but correct hat; and he carried a stick—like an Englishman, Betty thought, careful to the last of appearances. As if there were no such thing as danger; only stability. She might have been back in the comfortable New Jersey town and he a casual caller. And then, after taking him in, in a quick conflict of moods that left her breathless, she glanced hurriedly about. But only the blank compound wall met her gaze, and tile roofs, with the chimneys of the higher mission house peeping above foliage. The gate was but a narrow opening, near the farther end of the tennis court. No one could see. For that matter, it was to be doubted that any one in the compound knew she was here. And beyond the little street stood another blank wall.... And he had come!

She could not know that she seemed very composed as she laid her portfolio on the camp stool and rose. Then her hand was in his. Her voice said:

"It was nice of you to come. But—"

"When I asked for a meeting—for one meeting...." Her eyes were down; he was set, as for a formal speech.... "It was, as you may imagine, because a matter has arisen that seems to me of the greatest importance."

She wondered what made him talk like that. As if determined to appeal to her mind. She couldn't listen; not with her mind; she was all feeling. He was a stranger, this man. Yet she had thought tenderly of him. It was difficult.

"You didn't come alone?" she asked, unaware that her manner, too, was formal.

"Yes. Oh, yes! I know the way."

"But it isn't safe. When I wrote... I heard what Mrs. Boatwright said. I was angry."

"She was very rude."

"It seemed as if I ought to get word to you—after that. I promised, of course."

"But your note surprised me."

"You thought I wouldn't keep my promise?"

"I wasn't sure that you could."

"If you hadn't heard from me, what would you have done?"

"I should have left T'ainan this afternoon."

"But how could you? Where could you go?"

"The provincial judge has assigned four soldiers to me. He was most courteous. He wants me to publish articles in America and England against the Ho Shan Company. He seems a very astute man. And he sent runners to the inn just now with presents."

"Oh—what were they?"

"Some old tins of sauerkraut. A German traveler must have left them here."

Betty smiled. Then, sober again, said:

"But you should have brought the soldiers with, you."

"Oh, no. I preferred being alone."

"But I don't think you understand. It isn't safe to go about alone now. Not if you're a white man. I don't like to think that I've put you in danger."

"You haven't. It doesn't matter. As I was about to tell you... you must understand that I assume no interest on your part—I can't do that, of course—but after what happened, that night on the ship..." He was ha\ ing difficulty with this set speech of his. Betty averted her face to hide the warm color that came. Why on earth need he come out with it so heavily! Whatever had happened had happened, that was all!... His voice was going on. Something about a divorce. He was to be free shortly. He said that. He sounded almost cold about it, deliberate. And he had come clear out here to T'ainan just to say that. He *was* assuming, of course. To a painful degree. He seemed to feel that he owed it to her to make some sort of payment... for kissing her... and the payment, apparently, was to be himself. She was moved by a little wave of anger. She managed to say:

"We won't talk about that."

"I felt that I must tell you. I'll go now, of course."

"But..."

"As soon as I am free I shall write you. I will ask you, then, to be my wife."

He drew himself up, at this, stiffly.

Betty's blush was a flush now. She gathered up her drawing tilings; deliberately arranged the sheets of paper in the portfolio.

"I shall say good-by...

"Wait," said Betty, rather shortly, not looking up "You mustn't go like this."

There was a long silence. Then, abruptly, he broke out:

"There is no way that I can stay. I would bring you only trouble. And it will be easier for me to go. Of course, I should never have come. It has been very upsetting, I haven't faced it honestly. I wanted to forget you. I've been tortured. And then I learned that you were in danger. I—can't talk about it!" And he clamped his lips shut.

Betty opened her portfolio and slowly fingered the sheets of drawing paper. Her eyes filled; she had to keep them down.

"Where are you going?" Her voice was no more than a murmur. She said it again, a little louder: "Where are you going?"

"Back to the inn. And then, perhaps—"

"You mustn't leave T'ainan."

"That is the difficulty. I couldn't save myself and leave you here."

"On your account, I mean. We're safe enough; I've heard them talking at the house. Pao will protect us. And Chang, the tao-tai. But if you were to go out alone—on the highway—"

"Oh, that is nothing. I have soldiers."

"You said four soldiers. Father was attacked right here in the city, with Chang and his body-guard defending him. They even tore Chang's clothes."

"I don't care about myself," said he.

She glanced up at him. She knew he spoke the truth, however bitter his spirit. He was talking on: "Don't misunderstand me...."

"I don't."

"This journey has been a time of painful self-revelation. I used to think myself strong. That was absurd, of course. I am very weak. In this new trouble my will seems to have broken down. Yes, it has broken down; I may as well admit it. I had no right to fall in love with you. Already I have injured the life of one woman. Now, by merely coming out here in this ill-considered way, I am injuring yours.... The worst of it is these moments of terrible feeling. They make it impossible for me to reason. At one time I can really believe that a fatal accident out here—an accident to myself—would be the best thing that could happen for everybody concerned: but then, in a moment, I become inflamed with feeling, and desire, and a perfectly unreasonable hope."

"I wonder," mused Betty, moved now by something near a thrill of power—a disturbing sort of power—"if love is like that."

"I don't know. I don't even know if this is love Part of the time I resent you."

"Oh!... Well—yes, I can understand that."

"Then you resent me?"

"Sometimes."

"In my lucid moments I sec the thing clearly enough. It is simply an impossible situation. And I have added the final touch by coming out here." He seated himself on a block of stone, and rested his chin moodily on his two hands. "That is what disturbs me—it frightens me. I have watched other men and women going through this queer confusion we call falling in love. I've pitied them. They were weak, helpless, surrendering the reasoning faculty to sheer emotion. Sometimes, I've thought of them as creatures caught in a net."

"Oh!" Betty breathed softly, "I've never thought.. I wonder if it is like that." ⁻

"It is with me. I see no happiness in it. I hope you will never have to live through what I've lived through these past few weeks. And now I sit here——weakly—knowing I ought to go at once and never disturb you again. But the thought of going—of saying good-by—is terrible. It's one more thing I seem unable to face."

Betty was struggling now against tumultuous thoughts. And without overcoming them, without even making headway against them, she spoke:

"I can't let you take all this on yourself. I must have—well made it hard for you, there on the ship. I enjoyed being with you."

This was all she could say about that.

There was a long, long silence.

Suddenly, with an inarticulate exclamation, he sprang up.

Startled, all impulses, she caught his hand. His fingers tightened about hers.

"What?" she asked, breathless.

"I'll go."

"Not away from T'ainan?"

"Yes. It's the only thing. After all, it doesn't matter much what happens to any individual. We've got to take that chance. When my—when I'm—free, if I'm alive, and you're alive. I'll write you. I won't come—I'll write. Meanwhile, you can make up your mind. All I'll ask of you then is a decision. I'll accept it."

Her fingers were twisting around his. She couldn't look up at him, nor he down at her.

"When shall you leave T'ainan?"

"Now—this afternoon."

"No."

"But... don't you see?..

"I don't know what to say."

He knelt beside her.

"You dear child!" he murmured unsteadily, "can't you see what a trouble we're in? It's my fault—"

"It's no more your fault than mine."

"Oh, but it is! I'm an experienced man. You're a girl. They're right in blaming me."

"People can't help their feelings."

"God, if they could! Don't you see, child, that I can't stay near you? I can't look at you—you're so little, so pretty, so charming! When I'm with you, all this feeling, all the warm feminine quality, all the beautiful magic that's been shut out of my life comes to me through you. It drives me crazy.... Betty, God forgive me! I can't help it—this once! It's good-by." He took her lightly, reverently, in his arms, and brushed his lips against her forehead. Then he arose.

"Good-by, Betty!"

"It's too late to start to-day. You can't travel Chinese roads at night."

"I'll start early in the morning."

"I'll—if you—I'll come out here this evening. I think I can."

"Oh—Betty!..."

"It may be a little late. Perhaps about half past eight. They'll all be busy then.... Just for a little while."

He considered this. "It's wrong," he said. "But what's the good of my deciding not to come. Of course I will."

"You came clear to T'ainan."

"I know...."

"And how about me!" she broke out. "I'm shut in a prison here. You're the only friend that's come—the only person I can talk with. Father is wonderful, but he's busy and worried, and I'm his daughter, and we can't talk much. And you and I—if you're going in the morning—we can't leave things—our very lives"—her voice wavered—"like this."

"I'll come," he said.

"And keep the soldiers with you."

"I'll come."

"I wonder if it is like a net," said she.

CHAPTER XII
STORM CENTER

1

CHINA, in its vastness, its mystery, its permanence, its ceaseless ebb and flow of myriad, uncounted life, suggests the ocean. The surface is restless, ripped by universal family discord, whipped by gusts of passion from tong or tribe, upheaved by political storms, but everywhere in the unsounded depths lies the peace of submissiveness. Within its boundaries breathes sufficient power to overwhelm the world, yet only on the self-conscious surface is this power sensed and slightly used. Chinese life, in city and village, as in the teeming countryside, moves in disorganized poverty about its laborious daily tasks, little more aware of the surface political currents than are Crustacea at the bottom of the sea of ships passing overhead; while to these patient minds the mighty adventure of the Western World is no more than a breath upon the waters.

This simile found a place among the darker thoughts of Griggsby Doane as he tramped down into the fertile valley of the Han. Behind him lay tragedy; yet on every hand the farmers were at work upon the narrow holdings that terraced the red hills to their summits. At each countryside well the half-naked coolies—two, three, or four of them—were turning windlasses and emptying buckets of water into stone troughs from which trickled little painstakingly measured streams to the sunbaked furrow of this or that or another field. The trains of asses anil camels wound ceaselessly up and down the road that led from the northern hills to T'ainan. The roadside vendors and beggars chanted their wares and their grievances. The villages, always indolent, lived on exactly as always, stirred only by noisy bargains or other trivial excitement. The naked children tumbled about. It w as hard to believe that here could be—had so lately been—violence and cruelty. It was simply one of the occasions, evidently, when no Lookers or hostile young men happened to be about to shout their familiar taunts at the white devil. Though the fighting of 1900, for that matter, had passed like a wave, leaving hardly more trace. Still more, at dusk, the outskirts of the great city stirred perplexing thoughts. The quiet of a Chinese evening was settling on shops and homes. Children's voices carried brightly over compound walls. Kites flew overhead. The music of stringed instalments floated pleasantly, faintly, to the ear.

And every quaint sight and sound was registered with a fresh vividness on Doane's highly strung nerves. He was tired; might easily, too easily, become irritable; a fact he sensed and struggled to guard against. Now, of all occasions in his life, he must exercise self-control. Difficult tasks lay directly ahead. One would be the talk with Pao Ting Chuan about the So T'ung massacre. Pao was, in his Oriental way, friendly; but his way was Oriental. It would be necessary to meet him at every evasive turn; necessary to read behind every courteous speech of a cultivated and charming gentleman the complex motivation of a mandarin skilled in the intricate relationships of the Court of Peking. Helping avert trouble was one matter; Pao could doubtless, or apparently, be counted on to that extent; but assuming full responsibility for the taking of white life and the destruction of white man's property, was a vastly more complicated matter. No other sort of human creature is so skilful at evading responsibility as the Chinaman; this, perhaps, because responsibility, once accepted, is, under the Chinese tradition and system, inescapable.... Another task, of course, would be the telling Boatwright of his personal disaster. It still seemed better to do this before the news could drift around in some vulgar, disruptive way from Shanghai. He couldn't plan this talk, not yet; but a way would doubtless present itself. He stood before his God, in his own strong heart, convicted of sin. There had been moments, during the tramp southward, when he found himself welcoming this nearly public self-arraignment with a bitter eagerness. But at such moments pictures of Betty rose in his mind, and of the gentle beautiful wife of his youth—wistful, delicately traced pictures.

His face would change then; the lines would deepen and a look of torment, of wild hurt animal strength that was new, would appear in and about his deep-shaded eyes.

2

As he drew near the mission compound his stride shortened and slowed. Once he stopped, and for a brief bme stood motionless, not heeding the curious Chinese who passed (dim figures with soft-padded shoes), his lips drawn tightly together over nervous mutterings that nearly, once or twice, came out as sounds. He was not a man who talks out overwrought feelings on the public way. The tendency alarmed him.

He came deliberately into the gate house. Here, talking in some excitement with old Sun, were four or five of the servants.

He paused to ask what was the matter. To take hold again, to step so quickly into his position as head of the compound, brought a sense of relief. That would be habit functioning. A moment later, his confusion was deeper than before; in one of those quick flashes that can illuminate and occupy the inner mind while the outer is engaged with the brisk affairs of life, he was wondering how soon these men would know what he was, what pitiful sort he had overnight become; and what they would think of him, they who now obeyed and loved him.

'They told him the gossip of the streets. Those strange soldiers, Lookers, from beyond the western mountains, had been coming of late to the yamen of old Kang Hsu. Kang, so ran the local story, had reviewed these troops within the twelve hours, witnessing their incantations, giving them his approval.

Doane said what little he could to quiet their fears; he even managed a rather austere smile; then passed on into the courtyard.

Dr. Cassin came slowly down the steps from the dispensary, her keys jingling in her hand. She was a spare, competent woman, deeply consecrated to her work, but not lacking in kindliness.

"Oh, Mr. Doane!" she said. Then, "How did you find things at So T'ung?"

He stood a moment, looking at her.

"Very bad," he said.

"Not—well—"

Doane inclined his head. "Yes, Jen is gone—and twelve to fifteen others. Shot or burned. One helper escaped. I could get word of no others. One of Monsieur Pourmont's engineers helped very bravely in the defense, but was finally clubbed to death."

Dr. Cassin stood silent; then drew in her breath sharply. The keys jingled.

"Oh!" she murmured in a broken voice, "That is bad!"

"It couldn't be worse. How is it here?"

"Well"—she pursed her lips—"I'm afraid we've all been getting a little nervous. It's well you're back. We need you. The servants are jumpy...."

"I gathered that, in the gate house."

"I wonder... in the fighting at So T'ung there must have been a good many wounded...

"Among the attackers, yes; the Lookers themselves, and village rowdies."

"I was wondering... mightn't it be a good thing for me to go up there and take charge?"

"No."

"For the effect it might have on the people, I mean. Wouldn't it help restore their confidence in us?"

"No, Doctor. The people—except the young men—haven't changed. Trouble will come wherever the Lookers go. No, your place is here."

Once in the mission residence, Doane hurried up the two flights of stairs to his own rooms. He met no one; the door of Boatwright's study was closed.

So they needed him. The strain was shaking their monde a little. It was really not surprising, after 1900. But if they needed him it was no time to indulge his own emotions. He would have to take hold again, that was all; perhaps keep hold, letting the news that was to be to him so evil come up as it might. He sighed as he closed his door. Some sort of a scene there must be; at least a talk with the Boatwrights about So T'ung and about the local problem.... One thing he could do; remove his dusty clothing, wash, put on fresh things. It would help a little, just the physical refreshment. He went back to the door and locked it..... Boatwright would be up, almost certainly.

Very shortly came the familiar hesitant tapping. For years the little man had made his presence known in that same faintly timid way. It was irritating.... Doane called out that he would be down soon.

"Oh... all right... thank you!" Thus Boatwright, outside the door. And then he moved slowly, uncertainly, down the stairs.

3

Boatwright was sitting idle at his desk, rolling a pencil about. It was an old roll-top desk from Michigan via Shanghai. Doane closed the door, quietly, and drew up a chair.

"You'd better read this." Boatwright spread a telegram on the desk. "I haven't told the others. It came late this afternoon."

The message was from Mrs. Nacy, acting dean of the little college at Hung Chan.

"Several hundred Lookers"—it ran—"broke into compound this noon and took all our food, slightly injuring cook and helper who resisted; they order us to send all girl students home; remain at present carousing near compound; very threatening; commander forbids any communication with you as they seem to fear you and your influence at Judge's yamen, though boasting that Treasurer now rules province and that Judge will be fortunate to escape with his life; wish greatly you could be here."

Doane, sitting very quietly, shading his eyes with a powerful hand, read the message twice; then asked, calmly:

"Have you notified Pao?"

"Not yet. Your message came several hours earlier. It seemed wise to wait for yuu."

Doane considered the matter; then reached for red paper, ink pot and brush, and wrote, in Chinese, the equivalent of the following note:

"I beg to report that a band of Lookers at So T'ung, assisted by local young men, killed Jen Ling Pu and about fourteen others, including white engineer named Beggins from compound of Monsieur Pourmont at Ping Yang. Considerable property destroyed. Several buildings burned to ground. Further, to-day, comes a report of attack on the Mission College at Hung Chan, with urgent appeal for help. I am going to Hung Chan at once, to-night, and must beg of Your Excellency immediate support from local officials and troops. I must further beg to advise Your Excellency that I am reporting these unfortunate events to the American Minister at Peking by telegraph to-night and to suggest that only the greatest promptness and firmness on your part can now avert widespread trouble which threatens to bow the head of China once more with shame in the dust.

"James Griggsby Doane."

He struck a bell then, and to the servant who entered gave instructions regarding the etiquette to be observed in promptly delivering the note at the yamen of the provincial judge.

"I am worried, I'll admit, about Kang," observed Boatwright, when the servant had gone. He said this without looking up, rolling the pencil back and forth, back and forth. His voice was light and husky.

Deane, watching him, felt now that his own task was to forget self utterly. It was beginning, even, to seem the pleasantly selfish course. The trip down to Hung Chan he welcomed. He would drive himself mercilessly; it would be an escaping from his thoughts. Moments had come, during the walk from So T'ung, when for the first time in his life he understood suicide. So many men fell back on it during the tragic disillusionments of middle life. The trouble with suicide, of course, this sort, was the element of cowardice. He wasn't beaten. Not yet. At least, he had strength left, and physical courage. No, action was the thing. It was the sort of contribution he was best fitted to give these helpless, frightened people here. As to Betty, he would give to the limits of his great strength.

And so he answered Boatwright with a manner of calm confidence.

"Kang is putting up a fight, of course, but Pao will prove too strong for him. At least, there's no good in believing anything else, Elmer. It's the position we've got to take. I'll get into my walking clothes again."

"You're not going to Hung Chan alone, to-night?"

"Yes. It's the quickest way."

"Don't you need sleep—a few hours, at least?"

"No, I was too late at So T'ung."

"That was not your fault."

"No. Still... I'll go right along." Doane got up.

"If you could give me a few minutes more there's another matter. I'm afraid you'll regard it as rather important. It's—difficult...." And then, instead of continuing, he fell to rolling the pencil, and gazing at it. His color rose a little.

There was a light knock at the door. Neither man responded. After a moment the door opened a little way, and Mrs. Boatwright looked in.

"Oh!..." she exclaimed, then: "How do you do, Mr. Doane!... Elmer, have you spoken of that matter?"

"I was just beginning to, my dear."

Mrs. Boatwright, after a silence, came in and closed the door softly behind her.

"Mr. Doane hasn't much time." Boatwright's voice was low, tremulous. "Matters at So Thing are as bad as they could be. And he is going down to Hung Chan now."

"To-night?" asked the wife, rather sharply.

Doane inclined his head.

"Then what are we to do?"

"Mr Doane," put in the husband, "has given instructions that we are to stay here."

"Oh—instructions?"

"Yes," said Doane gravely. And he courteously explained: "The situation is developing too rapidly for us to get all the others in to T'ainan.

And we can't desert them. Not yet. You will certainly be safer here than you would be on the road. Hung Chan is only eighteen miles. I shall be back within twenty-four hours, probably to-morrow evening. Then we will hold a conference and decide finally on a course. We may be reduced to demanding an escort to Ping Yang, telegraphing the others to save themselves as best they can."

Mrs. Boatwright soberly considered the problem.

"It looks like nineteen hundred all over again," Boatwright muttered huskily, without looking up.

"No," said Doane, "it won't be the same. The only thing we positively know is that history never repeats itself. We'll take it as it comes." He didn't see Mrs. Boatwright's sharp eyes taking him in as he said this. "I'll leave you now."

"Just this other matter," said the wife, more briskly. "I won't keep you long. But I don't feel free to handle the situation in my own way, and—well, something must be done."

"You see," said the husband, "there's a man here—a queer American— he turned up—"

"Elmer!" the wife interrupted, "if you will let me.... It is a man your daughter met on the ship coming out, Mr. Doane. Evidently a case of infatuation...."

"He is a journalist—has written works on British administration in India, I believe—"

"Elmer! Please! The fact is, the man has deliberately followed Betty out here. There is some understanding between them—something that should be got at. The man is married. Betty admits that—she seems to be intimately in his confidence. He came rushing out here without so much as a passport. Elmer has had to give up a good deal of time to setting him right at Pao's yamen. I very properly refused to accept him here as a guest, whereupon Hetty got word to him secretly and they have been meeting—"

"Out in the tennis court!"

"Last night I found them there myself. I sent him away, and brought Betty in."

"Tell it all, dear!"

"I will. Mr. Doane must know the facts. The man was kissing her. He offered no apology. And Betty was defiant. She seemed then to fear the man would not appear again, but in some way she found him this afternoon out in the side street. They must have been there together for some time, walking back and forth, talking earnestly. I had other things to do, of course. I couldn't devote all my time to watching her. And it would seem, if she had any normal sense of... I secured a promise then from Betty that she would not meet him again until after your return. The man, however, would promise nothing."

On few occasions in her intensely busy life had Mrs. Boatwright been so voluble. But she was excited and perhaps a little prurient; for to such severe self-discipline as hers there are opposite and sometimes equal reactions.

"Something must be done, and at once." She appeared to be bringing her speech to a conclusion. "The man impressed me as persistent and quite shameless. He is unquestionably exerting a dangerous power over the girl. Even in times like these, I am sure that you, as her father, will feel that a strong effort must be made to save her. I needn't speak of the whispers that are already loose about the compound."

Through all this, Doane, his face wholly expressionless except for a stunned look about the eyes and perhaps a sad settling about the mouth, looked quietly from wife to husband and back again. They seemed utter strangers, these two. With disconcerting abruptness he discovered that he disliked them both.... Another thought that came was of the scene of desolation he had left at So T'ung. After that, what mattered, what little human thing! Then it occurred to his dazed mind that this wouldn't do. Suddenly he could see Betty—her charm and grace, her bright pretty ways, with his inner eye; and again his spirit was torn and tortured as all during the night, back there in the hills. If only he could recall the prayers that used to rise so easily and earnestly from his eager heart!

"Where is she now?" he asked, outwardly so calm as to stir resentment in the woman before him. She replied, acidly:

"In her room. If she hasn't slipped out again."

"She promised, I believe you said."

This was uttered so quietly that a slow moment passed before it reached home. Then Mrs. Boatwright replied, with less emphasis:

"Yes. She promised."

"And where is the man?"

"At an inn, somewhere inside the walls. Sun would know."

"What is his name?"

Boatwright fumbled among the papers on his desk, and found a card which he passed over.

Doane looked thoughtfully at it, then slipped it into a pocket; said, quiet, deathly sober, "You may look for me sometime to-morrow night. We will make our final arrangements then. Meantime you had all better get what rest you can." Then he left the room.

Husband and wife looked at each other. The man's lids drooped first. He began rolling the pencil. Finally he said, listlessly:

"Probably it would be wise to sort out these papers—get the letters and reports straight. If we should go, there wouldn't be much time for packing."

4

Doane went directly to Betty's door, and knocked. She came at once, in her pretty kimono; peeped out at him; cried softly:

"Oh, Dad! You're safe!"

"Yes, dear. I have one more trip, a short one. It will be all I can do. To-morrow night I'll be back for good. Take care of yourself, little girl."

"Yes—oh, yes! But I shall worry about you."

"No. Never worry. I'll be back."

That seemed to be all he could say. She, too, was still. The silence lengthened, grew into a conscious thing in his mind anti hers. Finally he took a hesitating backward step.

"I must be off, dear."

"Dad—wait!" She stood erect, her head drawn back, looking directly at him out of curiously bright eyes. Her abundant hair flowed down about her shoulders... But he thought of her eyes. They were frank, brave, and very young and eager and bright. Somewhere within her slim little frame she had a store of fine young courage; he knew it now, and felt a thrill that was at once hope and pain. He had to fight back tears.... She was going to tell him. Yes, she was plunging wonderfully into it:

"There's one thing, Dad! I'm sorry—I oughtn't to make you think of other things now. But if we could only have a little talk...."

He managed to say:

"Only a day more, dear."

"Yes. I suppose we should wait... though..." He stepped forward, drew her to him, and in an uprush of exquisite tenderness kissed her forehead;

then, with an odd little sound that might almost have been a sob, he rushed off, descended the stairs, and went out the front door.

From the window she saw his dim figure crossing the court. At the gate house he paused and called aloud.

Two of the servants came; she could see their quaintly colored paper lanterns bobbing about. One of them went into the gate house and came out again. He was struggling with something. She strained her eyes against the glass. Oh. yes—he was getting into his long coat; that was all. Apparently he went out, this man, with her father.... The other colored lantern bobbed back into the gate house, and the compound settled again into calm.

Doane, though he could not talk with his daughter, could talk directly and bluntly to the man named Brachey, who had rushed out here incontinent after her He knew this; was alive with a slow swelling anger that came to him as a perverse sort of blessing after the cumulative emotional torment of the past three days.

CHAPTER XIII
THE PLEDGE

1

ON the morning of that same day—while Griggsby Doane was striding down the mountain road from So T'ung to T'ainan-fu—Jonathan Brachey sat in his room at the inn trying to read, trying to write, counting the minutes until two o'clock at which hour Betty would be waiting in the tennis court, when John slipped in with a small white card bearing the printed legend, in English:

MR. PO

Interpreter and Secretary

Yamen of His Excellency the Provincial Judge T'ainan-fu

Mr. Po proved to be a tall, slim, rather elegant young man in conventional plain robe, black skull-cap and large spectacles, who met Brachey's stiff greeting with a broad smile and a wholly Western grip of the hand.

"How d' do!" he said eagerly: "How d' do!" Then he glanced about at the two worn old chairs, the crumbling walls of the sun-dried brick with their soiled, ragged motto scrolls, the dirty matting on the *kang*, and slowly shook his head. "You're not comfortable as all get-out."

If there was in Mr. Po's speech a softness of intonation and a faint difficulty with the *r*'s and *l*'s, the faults were not so marked as to demand changes of spelling in setting it down. He accepted a cigarette. Brachey lighted his pipe.

"You are quite at home in English," remarked Brachey.

"Oh, yes! English is my professional matter in hand."

"You have lived abroad?"

"Oh, no! But at Tientsin Anglo-Chinese College, I made consumption largely of midnight oil. And among English people society I have broken the ice."

Brachey settled back in the angular chair; pulled at his pipe; thought. The man was here for a purpose, of course. But from that slightly eager manner, it seemed reasonable to infer that among his motives was a desire to practise and exhibit his English, a curious mixture of book phrases and coast slang, with here and there the Chinese sentence-structure showing through. And he offered an opportunity to study the local problem that Brachey mentally leaped at.

So these two fell into chat, the smiling young Chinese gentleman and the austere Westerner. Mr. Po, speaking easily, without emphasis, his casual manner suggesting that nothing mattered much—not old or new, life or death—revealed, through the words he so lightly used, stirring enthusiasms. And Brachey observed him through narrowed eyes.

Here, thought the journalist, before him, smoking a cigarette, sat modern China; in robe and queue, speaking of the future but ridden by the past; using strong words but with no fire, no urge or glow in the voice; as if eager to hope without the substance of hope; at once age and youth, smiling down the weary centuries at himself.

"It has been expressed to me that you are literature man." Thus Mr. Po.

Brachey's head moved downward.

"That is quite wonderful. If you will tell me the names of certain of your books I will give myself great delight in reading them. I read English like the devil—all the time. I'm crazy about Emerson."

Brachey led him on. They talked of Russia and England, of the new railways in China, of truculent Japan, of Edison, much of Roosevelt. Mr. Po suggested a walk; and they mounted the city wall, sat on the parapet and talked on; the Chinaman always smiling, nerveless, his calm, easily flowing voice without body or emphasis. Brachey finally succeeded in guiding the man to his own topic, China.

"It puzzles and bewilders," said Mr. Po. "China must leap like grasshopper over the many centuries. To railways one may turn for beneficent assistance. And also to missionaries."

"I'm surprised to hear you say that. I supposed all China was opposed to the missionaries."

"I do not dwell at present time upon their religion practises. That may be all to the good—I can not say. But the domicile of each and every missionary may be termed civilization propaganda center. Here are found books, medicines, lamps. Your eyes have discerned enveloping gloom of Chinese cities by night. Think, I beg of you, what difference it will be when illumination brightens all. Our people do not like these things, it is true. They descend avidly into superstitions. They make a hell of a fuss. But that fuss is growing pain. China must grow, though suffering accumulate and dismay."

"Come to think of it," mused Brachey aloud, "superstition isn't stopping the railroads."

Mr. Po snapped his fingers, smilingly. "A fig and thistle for superstition!" he remarked. "Take good look at the railways! What happened? In every field of China, as you know, stand grave mounds of honorable ancestral worshiping. It will break heart of China to desecrate those grave mounds. It will bring down untold misery upon ancestors. But when they build Hankow-Peking Rahway, very slick speculator employed observation upon surveyors and purchased up claims against railway for bringing misery upon ancestors and sold them to railway company at handsome profit to himself. And, sir, do you know what it set back company to desecrate ancestors of China? It set back twelve dollars per ancestor. And that slick speculator he is now millionaire. He erects imposing house at Shanghai and elaborates dinners to white merchants. It is said that he will soon be compradore and partner in most pretentious English Hong.... No, the superstition will have to go. It will go like the chaff."

"But this big change will take a little time."

"Time? Oh, yes, of course! But what is time to China! A few centuries! They are nothing!"

"A few centuries are something to me," observed Brachey dryly.

"Oh, yes! And to me. That is different. There are times to come of running to and fro and hubbub. It is not easy to adjust."

"It is not," said Brachey.

"For myself, I would like to get away. I have observed with too great width customs of white peoples, I have perused with too diligent attention many English books as well as those of French and German authorship, to find contentment in Chinese habit ways. I would appreciate to voyage freely to America. If I might ask, is not there an exception made under so-called Chinese Exclusion Act in instance of attentive student and gentleman who finds himself by no means dependent upon finance arrangements of certain others?"

"I really don't know," said Brachey. "You'd have to talk with somebody up at the legation about that."

"But up at legation somebodies make always assumption never to know a darn thing about anything." Mr Po laughed easily.

"I have employed great thought concerning this topic," he went on, with mounting assurance. "It is here and now time of beginning upset in Hansi, as perhaps as well in all China. At topmost pinnacle of Old Order here stands Kang, the treasurer. It can not, indeed, be said that for ennobling ideas of New Order he cares much of a damn. And he is miserably jealous of His Excellency, Pao Ting Chuan. But Pao is very strong. Sooner or later he will pin upon Kang defeat humiliation."

"You feel sure Pao will be able to do that?"

"Oh, yes! Pao is cat, Kang is mouse."

"Hmm!"

"Yes indeed! But it is nothing to me. Nothing in world! I have laid before His Excellency desires of my heart. He expresses willing courtesy. If I may make voyage freely he will make best of it. And not unlike myself he has perceived half-notion that if I turn to you for wisdom advice you will not turn cold shoulder and throw me down." Catching the opposition behind Brachey's slightly knit brows, he added hastily, "I have no need. That is to say, I'm not broke. And — with this thought plan I have made transferrence of certain monies to Hongkong Bank at Shanghai where no revolution or hell of a row can snatch it from my outstretched hands. With but a nod from your head, sir, and also with permission of His Excellency, I could make sneak out of province as your servant."

Brachey, after some thought, said he would take the proposal under consideration.

During the walk back to the inn he contrived to hold the interpreter's chatter closely to the ferment in the province.

Kang, it appeared, was openly backing the Lookers now. His yamen enclosure swarmed with ragged soldiers from the West who foraged among the shops for food and trinkets, and beat or shot the inoffensive Chinese merchants by way of emphasizing rather casually their privileged status in the capital city. Down the river, near Hung Chan, a more considerable concentration of the strange troops was taking place. Hung Chan was also the rendezvous for the local young men who had been initiated into the Looker bands. Rumors were flying of a general massacre to come of the white and secondary (or native) Christians. There was even talk of a political alliance with the organizers of rebellion in the South against the Imperial Manchu Government and of a triumphant march to the coast. A phrase that might be translated as "China for the Chinese" had come into circulation.

Brachey grew more and more thoughtful as he listened.

"If Pao is so strong, why does he permit matters to go so far?" he asked.

Mr. Po laughed. "His Excellency will in his own good time get move on himself."

"Hmm!"

"Only yesterday I myself was pinched on street by Western soldiers."

"Pinched?"

"Seized and arrested. Taken up."

Brachey raised his eyebrows; but Mr Po smiled easily on.

"Oh, yes! They called me secondary Christian. They ran me in before low woman, a courtesan. They have told Kang that this courtesan is second-sighted."

"Clairvoyant?"

"Yes, that is now firm belief of Kang on mere say-so of cheap skates. This courtesan has been conveyed to treasurer's yamen where with eunuchs and concubines to attend and soldiers to stand sentry-go she now holds forth to beat the Dutch. All perfectly absurd!"

"And this creature sat in judgment over you?"

"Oh, yes! Not a day since."

"What was her decision?"

Again that easy laugh. "Oh, she decree that I am to kick bucket."

"Execute you, eh? You take it lightly."

"It is nothing. I will tell you. In companionship with me was my bosom friend, Chili T'ang, who is third son of well-known censor of Peking, Chili Chang Pu. It was Chih who got hustle on to yamen of His Excellency—"

"By His Excellency you mean Pao?"

"In every instance, if you please! Well, like a shot His Excellency acted in my behalf. In person and with full retinue grandeur panoply he set forth to pay visit to old rascal Kang, carrying as gift of utmost personal esteem ancient ring for thumb of jade that Kang had long made goo-goo eyes at. And he asked of Kang as favor mark to himself that he be let known instanter, right away, if any of soldiers from his yamen should behave with unpleasantness toward new soldiers of Kang, for new soldiers of Kang had come to T'ainan-fu out of far country and not unnaturally felt homesick and were not in each instance in step with customs of our city. And he made explanation as well that he would instruct his secretary, Po Sui-an, to bring news quicker than Johnny get your gun if his own soldiers should act up freshly or become stench in the nostrils.... Well, you see, sir?"

"Not quite."

"But I am Po Sui-an! It was rebuke like ton of brick, falling on all but face of old Kang. It has been insisted to me that Kang trembled like swaying aspen reed as he made high sign to attendant mandarins. And then His Excellency set forth that I had just stepped out on brief journey but would shortly be back and that he would then instruct me with determined vigor.... Such is His Excellency, a statesman of stiff upper lip. A most wise guy! Thus he served notice on that old reprobate that he will strike when iron is hot."

"They released you?"

"At once. On return of His Excellency, to his yamen. There was I, slick as whistle!",

"Very interesting. But if Kang continues to bring in soldiers from the West, how is Pao going to strike with any hope of success? Is he, too, marshaling an army?"

"Oh, no! But you see, I come to call upon you, with you I walk freely about streets. At Kang I thumb my nose and tell him go chase himself. Pao will protect myself and you."

"But as I understand it, Kang officially ranks Pao."

"Oh, yes! But that is nothing."

"It looks like a little something to me."

"Oh, no! I will ask you for brief moment to glance sidelong at Forbidden City of Peking. There during long devil of a while Eastern Empress officially ranked Western Empress, but I would call your attention to insignificant matter that it was not Western Empress—she whom you dub Empress Dowager—that turned up her toes most opportunely to daisies."

"Oh, I see! Then it is believed that the Empress Dowager had the Eastern Empress killed?"

"You could not ask that she neglect wholly her fences.".

"No.... no, I suppose you couldn't ask that."

"She is great woman. She will not permit that another person put her on the blink. It is so with His Excellency. A dam' big man! We shall see!"... He hesitated, smiling a thought more eagerly than before. They had reached the gate of the inn compound. His quick eye had caught increasing signs of preoccupation in Brachey's manner. Finally, laughing again, he said:

"'There is one other little bagatelle. An utter absurdity! I have made preparation for lecture in English about China. Name of it is 'Pigtail and Chop-stick.' When I read it at college I must say they held sides and shook like jelly bowl. On that occasion it was made plain to me by men of thought that it is peach of a lecture. It's a scream." His laugh indicated now an apologetic self-consciousness. "It was said that in America my lecture would be knockout, that Chinaman treading with humor the lyceum would make novelty excitement. Indeed, by gentleman of Customs Administration this was handed me...." He fumbled inside his gown, finally producing a frayed bit of ruled paper, evidently torn from a pocket note-book, on which was written in pencil: "Try the J. B. Pond Lyceum Bureau, New York City."

"Since it was expressed to me," he hurried to add, "that American journalist notability was in our midst, I have amused myself with fool thought that you would run eyes over it and let me have worst of it."

"It would be a pleasure," said Brachey, civilly enough but with considerable dismissive force, extending his hand.

So, Mr. Po, smiling but something crestfallen, sauntered away.

2

At ten o'clock that night Brachey sat in the angular chair, his *Bible in Spain* lying open on his knees, his weary face deeply shadowed and yellow-gray in the flickering light of the native lamp on the table beside him.

John tapped at the door; came softly in; stood, holding the door to behind him.

"Well?" cried Brachey irritably. "Well?"

"Man wanchee see you. Can do?"

"Man?... What man?"

"No savvy."

"China man?"

"No China man. White man. Too big."

Brachey sprang up; dropped his book on the table with a bang; brushed John aside and opened the door. The only light out there came slanting down from a brilliant moon. Dimly outlined as shadowy masses were the now familiar objects of the inn courtyard — the row of pack-saddles over by the stable, the darkly moving heads of the horses ami mules behind the long manger, the two millstones on their rough standard; above these the roofs of curving tile and a glimpse of young foliage. Then, after a moment, he sensed movement and peered across, beyond the stable, toward the street gates. A man was approaching; a huge figure of a man, six feet five or six inches in height, broad of shoulder, firm of tread; stood now before him. He carried something like a soldier's pack on his back.

"Why did you come here?"

Brachey on the door-step found his eyes level with those of his caller.

"Mr. Brachcy?" The voice had the ring of power in it. Brachey's nerves tightened.

"Yes."

"I am Mr. Doane."

"Will you please come in?"

John slipped away. Doane entered; moved to the table; turned. Brachey closed the door and faced him.

"You will perhaps wish to take off your pack," he said, with bare civility.

Doane disposed of this remark with a jerk of his head. "I have very little time to waste on you," he said bruskly. "What are you doing in T'ainan? Why did you come here?"

"Why did you come here?"

There was a long silence.

"Very well, if you won't answer."... Doane's voice rasped.

Brachey raised his hand. "I was considering your question," he broke in coldly. "While it is not the whole truth, it will probably save time to say that I came to see your daughter."

He would have liked to express in his voice some thing of the desperate tenderness that he felt. The experiences of the preceding evening and of the afternoon just past—the glimpses he had had into the heart of a girl, his little storms of anger against Mrs. Boatwright and all her kind, followed in each instance by other little storms of anger against himself—had finally swept him from the last rational mooring place out into the bottomless, boundless sea of emotion. He had found himself, already to-night, a storm-tossed soul without compass or bearings or rudder. He burned to see Betty again. It had taken all that was left of his will to keep from charging out once more across the city, out through the wall, to the mission compound. He was shaken, humbled, frightened. To such a nature as Brachey's—stubbornly aloof from human contacts, sensitively self-sufficient—this was really a terrible experience. It was the worst storm of his life. He felt—had felt at times during the evening, as he tried to brace himself for this scene that he knew had to come within the twenty-four hours—something near tenderness for the man who was Betty's father. There were even moments when he looked forward to the meeting with the hope that through the father's feelings he might be helped in finding his lost self.

He had tried, sitting among the shadows, to build up a picture of the man. Several of these he had constructed, to meet each of which he felt he could hold himself in a mental attitude of frankness and even sympathy. But each of these pictures was but an elaboration of familiar missionary types. All were what he considered—or once had considered—weak, or over-earnest to the borders of fanaticism, or cautious little men, or narrow formalists... men like Boatwright And without realizing, it, too, he had counted on either real or counterfeited Christian forbearance. The only thing he had feared might come up to disturb him was intolerance, like that of Boatwright's wife.

With that, of course, you couldn't reason, couldn't talk at all.... What he really wanted to do, burned to do, was to tell the exact truth. He had passed the point where he could give Betty up; he would have to fight for her now, whatever happened. His one great fear had been that Betty's father would be incapable of entertaining the truth dispassionately, fairly.

But the actual Doane cleared his over-charged brain as a mountain storm will clear murky air. Here was a giant of a man who meant business. Back of that strong face, back of the deep voice, Brachey felt a pressure of anger. It was not Christian forbearance; it was vigor and something more;

something that perhaps, probably, would come out before they were through with each other. There was a restless power in the man, a wild animal pacing there behind the slightly clouded eyes. Even in the blinding fire of his own love for Betty he could look out momentarily and see or feel that this giant was burning too. And what he saw or felt, turned his heart to ice and his brain to tempered metal. Sympathy would have reached Brachey this night; weakness, blundering, might have reached him. But now, of all occasions, he would not be intimidated.. .. He felt the change coming over him, dreaded it, even resisted it; but was powerless to check it. The man proposed to beat him down. No one had ever yet done that to Jonathan Brachey. And so, though he tried to speak with simple frankness in saying, "I came to see your daughter," the words came out coldly, tinged with defiance, between set lips.

It might easily mean a fight of some sort, Brachey reflected. This mountain of a man could crush him, of course. Primitive emotion charged the air as each deliberately stud'ed the other.... It would hardly matter if he should be crushed. There were no police in T'airan to protect white men from each other. His wife would be relieved; a queer, bitter sob rose part way in his throat at the thought. There was no one else... save Betty. Betty would care! And this man was her father! It was terrible.... He was struggling now to attain a humility his austere life had never known; if only he could trample down his savage pride, hear the man out, swallow every insult! But in this struggle, at first, he failed. Like a soldier he faced the huge fighting man with a pack on his back.

"You knew my daughter on the steamer?"

"Yes."

"Before that—in America?"

"No."

"There is something between you?"

"Yes."

"You are a married man?"

"Yes."

Doane, his face working a very little, his arms stiff and straight at his sides, came a step nearer. Brachey lifted his chin and stared up the more directly at him. "You seem to have a little honesty, at least."

"I am honest."

"How far has this gone?"

Brachey was silent.

Doane took another step.

"Why don't I kill you?" he breathed.

It was then that Brachey first caught the full force of Doane's emotional torment. To say that he did not flinch, inwardly, would be untrue; but all that Doane saw was a slight hesitation before the cold reply came: "I can not answer that question."

"You can answer the other. How far has this gone?"

Brachey again clamped his lips shut. The situation, to him, had become inexplicable.

"Will you answer?"

"No."

Doane's eyes blazed down wildly. And Doane's voice broke through the restraint he had put upon it as he cried:

"Have you harmed my little girl?"

Brachey was still.

"Answer me!" Doane's great hand came down on his shoulder. "Have you harmed her?"

Brachey's body trembled under that hand; he was fighting himself, fighting the impulse to strike with his fists, to seize the lamp, a chair, his walking stick; he held his breath; he could have tossed a coin for his life; but then, wandering like a little lost breeze among his bitter thoughts, came a beginning perception of the anguish in this father's heart. It confused him, softened him. His own voice was unsteady as he replied: "Not in the sense you mean."

"In what sense, then?"

Brachey broke away. Doane moved heavily after him, but stopped short when the slighter man dropped wearily into a chair.

"I'm not going to attack you," said Brachey, "but for God's sake sit down!"

"What did you mean by that?"

"Simply this." Brachey's head dropped on his hand; he stared at the floor of rough tiles. "I love her. She knows it. She even seems to return it. I have roused deep feelings in her. Perhaps in doing that I have harmed her. I can't say."

"Is that all? You are telling me everything?"

"Everything."

Doane walked across the room; came back; looked down at Brachey.

"You know how such men as you are regarded, of course?"

"No.... Oh, perhaps!"

"You will leave T'ainan, of course."

"Well..."

"There is no question about that. You will leave."

"There's one question—a man dislikes to leave the woman he loves in actual danger."

An expression of bewilderment passed across Duane's face.

"You admit that you are married?"

"Oh, yes!"

"Yet you speak as my daughter's lover. Does the fact of your marriage mean nothing to you?"

"Nothing whatever."

"Oh, you are planning to fall back on the divorce court, perhaps?"

"Yes." Brachey's head came up then. "Does love mean nothing to you?" he cried. "In your narrow, hard missionary heart is there no sympathy for the emotions that seize on a man and a woman and break their wills and shake them into submission?"

Looking up, he saw the color surge into Doane's face. Anger rose there again. The man seemed desperate, bitter. There was no way, apparently, to handle him; he was a new sort.

Doane crossed the room again; came back to the middle. He seemed to be biting his lip.

"I'll have no more words from you," he suddenly cried out. "You'll go in the morning! I'll have to take your word that you won't communicate with Betty."

"But, my God, I can't just save myself—"

"It may not be so safe for you or any of us. Will you go?"

"Oh... yes!"

"You will not try to see Betty?"

"Not to-morrow."

"Nor after."

Brachey sprang up; leaned against the table; pushed the lamp away.

"How do I know what I shall do?"

"I know."

"Oh, you do!"

"Yes. You will do as I say. You are never to communicate with her again."

Brachey thought. "I'll say this: I'll undertake not to. If I can't endure it, I'll tell you first."

"You can endure it."

"But you don't understand! It's a terrible thing! Do you think I wanted to come out here? I meant not to. But I couldn't stand it. I came. Is it nothing that I told her of my marriage with the deliberate purpose of frightening her away? But she is afraid of nothing."

"No—she is not afraid."

"I tell you, I've been torn all to pieces. Good God, if I hadn't been, and if you weren't her father, do you think I'd have stood here to-night and let you say these things to me! Oh, you would beat me; likely enough you'd kill me; but that's nothing. That would be easy—except for Betty."

"I have no time for heroics," said Doane. "Have I your promise that you will leave in the morning, without a word to her?"

"Yes."

"I am going to Hung Chan. There are more important issues now than your life or mine. I shall be back to-morrow night and shall know then if you have failed to keep your word."

"I shan't fail."

"Very well! A word more. You are not to stop at Ping Yang on your way cut."

"Oh?"

"For a night only. Then go on. Go out of the province. Go back to the coast. Is that understood?"

Brachey inclined his head.

"I have your promise?"

"Yes."

"Very well. Good night, sir."

"Good night."

Doane turned to the door. But then he hesitated, turned, hesitated again, finally came straight over and thrust out his hand.

Brachey, to his own amazement, took it.

CHAPTER XIV
DILEMMA

1

WHEN DOANE had gone Brachey called John and ordered a mule litter for eight n the morning. John found ont of the soldiers among the lounging group by the gate. The soldier slipped out.

Brachey busied himself until midnight in packing his bags. He felt that he couldn't sleep; most of the later night was spent in alternately walking the floor and trying to read. Before dawn the lamp burned out; and he lay down in his clothes and for a few hours dreamed wildly.

At eight the spike-studded gates swung open and an Oriental cavalcade filed into the court. There was the litter, like a sedan chair but much larger, swung on poles between two mules; the sides covered with red cloth, the small swinging doors in blue; bells jingling about the necks of the mules. There were five or six other mules and asses, each hearing a wooden pack-saddle. There was a shaggy Manchurian pony for Brachey to ride in clear weather. Three muleteers, two men and a boy, marched beside the animals; hardy ragged fellows, already, or perhaps always, caked with dirt.

At once the usual confusion and noise began. Men of the inn crowded about to help pack the boxes and bags of food and water and clothing on the saddles. The mules plunged and kicked. A rope broke and had to be elaborately repaired. The four soldiers brought out their white ponies, saddled them, slung their carbines over their shoulders; they were handsome men, not so ragged, in faded blue uniforms of baggy Chinese cut, blue half-leggings, blue turbans. Into the litter went Brachey's mattress and pillow. He tossed in after them camera, note-book, and *The Bible in Spain*; then mounted his savage little pony, which for a moment plunged about among the pack animals, starting the confusion anew.

The cook mounted one of the pack-saddles, perching himself high on a bale, his feet on the neck of the mule. John was about to mount another, when the leading soldier handed him a letter which he brought at once to his master.

Brachey with bounding pulse looked at the envelope. But the address, "Mister J. Brachey, Esquire," was not in Betty's brisk little hand.

He tore it open, and read as follows:

"My Dear Sir—Taking Time touch and go by the forelock it becomes privileged duty to advise you to wit:

"So-called Lookers and Western soldiers of that ilk have attacked mission college Hung Chan with crop up outcome that these unpleasant fellow's go the limit in violence. By telegraph officer of devotion to His Excellency this morning very early passes the tip that that mission college stands longer not a whit upon earth.

"Looker soldiers acting under thumb of man mentioned during our little chin-chin of yesterday forenoon plan within twenty-four hours advance on T'ain-an-fu cutting off city from Eastern access and then resting on oars, jolly well taking their time to destroy mission here and secondary Christians, making clean job of it.

"Officer of devotion reports further of old reprobate plan that larger army has become nearly ready to march full tilt and devil take the hindmost on Ping Yang engineer compound fort and lay axe to root of it. Railroad and bridges and all works of white hands will go way of wrack and ruin except telegraph, that being offspring of Imperial Government.

"And now, my dear sir, as Ping Yang is place of some strength and come on if you dare, I would respectfully recommend that you engage at once in forlorn hope and make journey post haste to Ping Yang, as we sit on kegs of gun powder with ground slipping out from under us as hour-glass runs.

"Regretting in great heaviness and sadness of heart that civilization sees no longer light of day in Hansi Province, I beg to remain, my Dear Sir,

"Yours most respectfully,

"Po Sui-an.

"P. S. In my busy as bee excitement I have neglected to kill two birds with one stone, and inform you that Rev. Doane of this city met death bravely at 3 a.m. to-day at Hung Chan Northern Gate.

"Po."

The cavalcade was ready now in line. At the head two soldiers sat their ponies. The gay litter came next, bells jingling as the mules stirred. Behind the litter stood the pack animals, with John and the cook mounted precariously on the first two. The other two soldiers brought up the rear.

The muleteers stood lazily by, waiting.... Brachey slipped Mr. Po's letter into a pocket and gazed up at the smoke that curled lazily from the chimney of the innkeeper's house. The pony, restless to be off, plunged a little; Brachey quieted him without so much as looking down.... After a brief time he lowered his eyes. A little girl with normal feet was trudging round and round the millstones, laboriously grinding out a double handful of flour; a skinny old woman, in trousers, her feet mere stumps, hobbled across the court with a stew pan, not so much as looking up at the caravan or at the haughty white stranger; ragged men moved about among the animals behind the manger. The huge gates had been swung open by coolies, who stood against them; outside was the narrow, deep-rutted roadway, with shops beyond.... Finally, brows knit as if he were at once hurt and puzzled, face white, Brachey took in the caravan—the calmly waiting soldiers, the muleteers, the grotesquely mounted cook and interpreter, the large, boxlike vehicle suspended in its richly dingy colors between two mules—and then, with tightly compressed lips and a settling frown, he rode out into the street ahead of the soldiers.

With a lively jingle of bells and creakings from the litter as it swayed into motion, the others followed. One of the soldiers promptly came up alongside Brachey; their two ponies nearly filled the street, crowding passers-by into doorways.

Brachey led the way out through the Northern Gate to the mission compound. Here he dismounted, handed his reins to a muleteer, and entered the gate house.

He led the way out through the northern gate

Old Sun Shao-i hurried from his chair and barred the inner door. Regarding this white man he had orders from Mrs. Boatwright. Brachey, however, brushed him carelessly aside and went on into the court.

It was the sort of thing, this walking coolly in, where he was not wanted, that he did well. He really cared nothing what they thought. He distrusted profoundly Mrs. Boatwright's judgment, and did not even consider sending in his name or a note. The hour had come for meeting her face to fare and by force of will defeating her. There was no time now for indulgence in personal eccentricities on the part of any of these few white persons set off in a vast, threatening world of yellow folk.

Within the spacious courtyard the sunlight lay in glowing patches on the red tile. Through open windows came the fresh school-room voices of girls. At the steps of a small building at his right stood or lounged a group of Chinese men and old women and children—Brachey had learned that only by occasional chance is a personable young or even middle-aged.

He led the way out through the northern gate aged woman visible to masculine eyes in China—each apparently with some ailment; one man had eczema; one boy a goitre that puffed out upon his breast, others with traces of the diseases that rage over China unchecked except to a tiny degree here and there in the immediate neighborhood of a medical mission.... It was a scene of peace and apparent security. The mission organization was functioning normally. Clearly they hadn't the news.

A thin thoughtful woman came out of a school building, and confronted him.

"I am Mr. Brachey," said he coldly; "Jonathan Brachey."

The woman drew herself up stiffly.

"What can I do for you, sir?"

She was stern; hostile.... How little it mattered!

"I must see you all together, at once," he said in the same coldly direct manner—"Mr. and Mrs. Boatwright, if you please, and any others."

"Can't you say what you have to say to me now? I am Miss Hemphill, the head teacher."

"No," he replied, not a muscle of his face relaxing. "May I ask why not?"

"It is not a matter of individual judgment."

"But Mrs. Boatwright will refuse to see you."

"I am sony, but Mrs. Boatwright will have to see me and at once. And not alone, if you please. I don't care to allow her to dismiss what I have to say without consideration."

Miss Hemphill considered; finally went up into the dispensary, past the waiting unfortunates on the steps. Brachev stood erect, motionless, like a military man. After a moment, Miss Hemphill came out, followed by another woman.

"This is Dr. Cassin," she said; adding with a slight hesitation as if she found the word unpalatable—"Mr. Brachey."

The physician at once took the matter in hand.

"You will please tell us what you have to say, Mr. Brachey. It will be better not to trouble Mrs. Boatwright."

Brachey made no reply to this speech; merely stood as if thinking the matter over. Then his eye caught' a glimpse of something pink and white that fluttered past an up-stairs window. Then, still without a word, he went on to the residence, mounted the steps and rang the bell.

The two women promptly followed.

"You will please not enter this house," said Dr. Cassin severely.

A Chinese servant opened the door.

"I wish to see Mr. and Mrs. Boatwright at once," said Brachey; then, as the servant was about to close the door, stepped within.

The two women pressed in after him.

"You are acting in a very high-handed manner," remarked Dr. Cassin with heat—"an insolent manner."

"I regret that it is necessary."

"It is *not* necessary!" This from Miss Hemphill.

He merely looked at her, then away; stood waiting.

Mrs. Boatwright appeared in a doorway.

"What does this mean?" was all she seemed able to say at the moment.

"Will you kindly send for the others"—thus Brachey—"Mr. Boatwright, any other whites who may be here, and—Miss Doane."

"Certainly not."

"It is necessary."

"It is not. Why are you here?"

"It is not a matter for you to decide. I must have everybody present."

There was a rustle from the stairs. Betty, very pale, her slim young person clad in a lacy négligée gown of Japanese workmanship, very quick and light and nervously alert, came down.

"Will you please go back to your room?" cried Mrs. Boatwright.

But the girl, coming on as far as the newel post, stopped there and replied, regretfully, even gently, but firmly:

"No, Mrs. Boatwright."

"Will you at least do us the courtesy to dress yourself properly?"

This, Betty, her eyes straining anxiously toward Brachey, ignored.

3

Dr. Casein then abruptly, speaking in Chinese, sent the servant for Mr. Boatwright, and deliberately led the way into the front room. The others followed, without a word, and stood about silently until the appearance of Mr. Boatwright, who came in rather breathless, mopping his small features.

"How do you do?" he said to Brachey; and for an instant seemed to be considering extending his hand; but after a brief survey of the grimly silent figures in the room, catching the general depression in the social atmosphere, he let the hand fall by his side.

"Now, Mr. Braehey," remarked Dr. Cassin, with an air of professional briskness, "every one is present. We are ready for the business that brought you here." Brachey looked about the room; his eyes rested longest on the physician. To her he handed the letter, saying simply:

"This was written within the hour, by Po Sui-an, secretary to His Excellency Pao Ting Chuan. Will you please read it aloud, Dr. Cassin?"

Then, as if through with the others, he went straight over to Betty, who stood by the windows. Quickly and softly he said:

"Brace up, little girl! It is bad news."

"Oh!" she breathed, "is it—is it—father?"

He bowed. She saw his tightened lips and the shine in his eyes; then she wavered, fought for breath, caught at his hand.

Mrs. Boatwright was calling out, apparently to Betty, something about taking a chair on the farther side of the room. There was a stir of confusion; but above it Brachey's voice rose sharply:

"Read, please, Dr. Cassin!"

Soberly they listened. After beginning the postscript, Dr. Cassin stopped short; then, slowly, with considerable effort, read the announcement of Griggsby Duane's death.

Then the room was still.

Mrs. Boatwright was the first to speak; gently for her, and unsteadily, though the strong will that never failed this vigorous woman carried her along without a sign of hesitation.

"Mary," she said, addressing Miss Hemphill, "you had better go upstairs with Betty."

Dr. Cassin, ignoring this, or perhaps only half-hearing it (her eyes were brimming) broke in with:

"Mr. Brachey, you must have come here with some definite plan or purpose. Will you please tell us what it is?"

"No!" cried Mrs. Boatwright — "no! If you please, Mary, this man must not stay here. Betty!... Betty, dear!"

Betty did not even turn. She was staring out the window into the peaceful sunflecked courtyard, the tears running unheeded down her cheeks, her hand twisted tightly in Brachey's. He spoke now, in the cold voice, very stiff and constrained, that masked his feelings.

"The death of Mr. Doane makes it clear that there is no safety here. There is a chance, to-day, for us all to get safely away. I have, at the gate, a litter and one riding horse, also a few pack animals. Most of my goods can be thrown aside — clothing, all that. The food I have, used sparingly, would serve for a number of us. We should be able to pick up a few carts. I suggest that we do so at once, and that we get away within an hour, if possible. We must keep together, of course. I suggest further, that any differences between us be set aside for the present."

They looked at one another. Miss Hemphill pursed her lips and knit her brows, as if unable to think with the speed required. Dr. Cassin, sad of face, soberly thinking, moved absently over to the silent girl by the window; gently put an arm about her shoulders. Mr. Boatwright, sunk deeply in his chair, was pulling with limp aimless fingers at the fringe on the chair-arm; once he glanced up at his wife.

"This may not be true," said Mrs. Boatwright abruptly.

"It is from Pao's yamen," said Miss Hemphill.

"But it may be no more than a rumor. Our first duty is to telegraph Mrs. Nacy at Hung Chan and ask for full particulars."

"Is"—this was Mr. Boatwright; he cleared his throat—"is there time?"

Mrs. Boatwright's mouth had clamped shut. No one had ever succeeded in stampeding or even hurrying her mind. She had, for the moment, dismissed the special problem of Betty and this man Brachey from that mind and was considering the general problem. That settled, she would again take up the Brachey matter.

"There is time," she said, after a moment. "There must be. Mr. Doane left positive instructions that we were to await his return. He will be here to-night or to-morrow morning, if he is alive."

"But—my dear"—it was her husband again—"Po is careful to explain that by to-morrow escape will be cut off."

"That," replied his wife, still intently thinking, "is only a rumor, after all. China is always full of rumors. Even if it is true, these soldiers are not likely to act so promptly, whatever Po may think. If they should, we shall be no safer on the highway than here in our own compound.... And how about our natives? How about our girls—all of them? Shall we leave them?... No!" She was thinking, tanking. "No, I shall not go. I am going to stay here. I shall keep my word to Mr. Doane."

Then she rose and approached the little group by the window. Her eyes, resting on the firmly clasped hands of the lovers, snapped fire. Her face, again, was granite. To Dr. Cassiri, very quietly, she remarked, "Take Betty up-stairs, please."

The physician, obeying, made a gentle effort to draw the girl away; but met with no success.

Mrs. Boatwright addressed herself to Brachey: "Will you please leave this compound at once!"

He said nothing. Betty's fingers were twisting within his.

"I can hardly make use of force," continued Mrs. Boatwright, "but I ask you to leave us. And we do not wish to see you again."

Brachey drew in a slow long breath: looked about the room, from one to another. Miss Hemphill and Boatwright had risen; both were watching him; the little man seemed to have found his courage, for his chin was up now.

And Brachey felt, knew, that they were a unit against him. The fellow-feeling, the community of faith and habit that had drawn them together through long, lonely years of service, was stronger now than any mere threat of danger, even of death. They felt with the indomitable woman who had grown into the leadership, and would stay with her.

Brachey surveyed them. These were the missionaries he had despised as weak, narrow little souls. Narrow they might be, but hardly weak. No, not weak. Even this curious little Boatwright; something that looked like strength had come to life in him. He wouldn't desert. He would stay. To certain and horrible death, apparently. The very certainty of the danger seemed to be clearing that wavering little mind of his. A thought that made it all the more puzzling was that these people knew, so much better, so much more deeply, than he, all that had happened in 1900. Their own friends and pupils—white and yellow—had been slaughtered. The heart-breaking task of reconstruction had been theirs.

And at the same time, seeming like a thought-strand in his brain, was the heart-breaking pressure of that soft, honest little hand in his.... Very likely it was the end for all of them.

"Very well," he said icily. "I am sorry I can't be of use. However, if any of you care to go I shall esteem it a privilege to share my caravan with you."

No one spoke, or moved. The iron face of Mrs. Boatwright confronted his.

Very gently, fighting his deepest desire, fighting, it seemed, life itself, he tried to disentangle his fingers from Betty's.

But hers gripped the more tightly. There was a silence.

Then Betty whispered—faintly, yet not caring who might hear:

"I can't let you go."

"You must, dear."

"Then I can't stay here. Will you take me with you?"

He found this impossible to answer.

"It won't take me long. Just a few things in a bag." And she started away.

Mrs. Boatwright made an effort to block her, but Betty, without another sound, slipped by and out of the room and ran up the stairs.

Then Mrs. Boatwright turned on the man.

"You will do this?" she said, in firm stinging tunes. "You will take this girl away?"

He looked at her out of an expressionless face. Behind that mask, his mind was swiftly surveying the situation from every angle. He knew that he couldn't, as it stood, leave Betty here. And they wouldn't let him stay. He must at least try to save her. Nothing else mattered.

"Yes," he replied.

Mrs. Boatwright turned away. Brachey moved out into the hall and stood there. To her "At least you will step outside this house?" he replied, simply, "No." Dr. Cassin, with a remark about the waiting queue at the dispensary, went quietly back to her routine work, as if there were no danger in the world. Mr Boatwright had turned to his wife's desk, and was making a show of looking over some papers there. Miss Hemphill sank into a chair and stared at the wall with the memory of horror in her eyes. Mrs. Boatwright stood within the doorway, waiting.

A little time passed. Then Betty came running down the stairs, in traveling suit, carrying a hand-bag.

Mrs. Boatwright stepped forward.

"You really mean to tell me that you will go—alone—with this man?"

Betty's lips slowlyy formed the word, "Yes."

"Then never come again to me. I can not help you. You are simply bad."

Betty turned to Brachey; gave him her bag.

Outside the gate house the little caravan waited.

The mules were brought to their knees. Betty stepped, without a word, into the litter. Brachey closed the side door, and mounted his pony. The mules were kicked and flogged to their feet. The two soldiers in the lead set off around the city wall to the corner by the eastern gate, whence the main highway mounted slowly into the hills toward Ping Yang. As they turned eastward, a fourth muleteer, ragged and dirty, bearing a small pack, as the others, joined the party; a fact not observed by the white man, who rode close beside the litter.

But when they had passed the last houses and were out where the road began to sink below the terraced grain-fields, the new muleteer stepped forward. For a little space he walked beside the white man's pony.

Brachey, at last aware of him, glanced down at the ragged figure.

"It's a deuce of a note," said the new muleteer, looking up and smiling, "that your courtesy should return like confounded boomerang on your head. I make thousands of apologies."

Brachey started; then said, merely:

"Oh!... You!"

"Indeed I have in my own canoe take French leave. That it is funny as the devil and intruding presumption I know full well. But I have thought to be of service and pay my shot if you offer second helping of courtesy and glad hand."

Brachey nodded. "Come along," said he.

CHAPTER XV
THE HILLS

1

MOST of the day, advised by Brachey. Betty kept closed the swinging litter doors. The little caravan settled into the routine of the highway, the muleteers trudging beside their animals. The gait was a steady three miles an hour. John rode his pack-saddle hour after hour, until six' o'clock in the evening, without a word. Just behind him, the cook, a thin young man with dreamy eyes, sang quietly a continuous narrative in a wailing, yodling minor key.

Before the end of the first hour they had lost sight of T'ainan-fu and buried themselves in the hills; buried themselves in a double sense, for wherever water runs in Northwestern China the roads are narrow canyons. At times, however, the way mounted high along the hillsides, on narrow footways of which the mules all instinctively trod the outer edge. Brachey found it alarming to watch the litter as it swayed over some nearly perpendicular precipice. For neither up here on the hillsides nor along the path nor in the depths below was there a sign of solid rock; it was all the red-brown earth known as loess, which is so fine that it may be ribbed into the pores like talc or flour and that packs down as firmly as chalk. Along the sunken ways were frequent caves, the dwelling-places of crippled, loathsome beggars, with rooms cut out square and symmetrical doors and windows.

In the high places one might look across a narrow chasm and see, decorating the opposite wall, strata of the loess in delicately varied tints of brown, red, Indian red and crimson, with blurred soft streaks of buff and yellow at times marking the divisions.

The hills themselves were steep and crowded in, as if a careless Oriental deity had scooped together great handfuls of brown dice and thrown them haphazard into heaps. Trees were so few—here and there one might be seen clinging desperately to a terrace-wall where the narrow fields of sprouting millet and early shoots of vegetables mounted tier on tier to the very summits of the hills—that the general effect was of utter barrenness, a tumbling red desert.

Much cf the time they were winding through the canyons or twisting about the hillsides with only an occasional outlook wider than a few hundred yards or perhaps a half-mile, but at intervals the crowded little peaks would separate, giving them a sweeping view over miles of shadowy red valleys.... At such times Betty would open one of her windows a little and lean forward; riding close behind, Brachey could see her face, usually so brightly alert, now sad, peeping out at the richly colored scene.

Frequently they passed trains of camels or asses or carts, often on a precipice where one caravan hugged the loess wall while the other flirted with death along the earthen edge. But though the Hansean or Chihlean muleteers shouted and screamed in an exciting confusion of voices and the Mongol camel drivers growled and the ponies plunged, no animal or man was lost.

Nearly always the air was heavy with fine red dust. It enveloped them like a fog, penetrating clothing, finding its way into packs and hand-bags. At times it softened and exquisitely tinted the view.

At long intervals the little caravan wound its slow way through villages that were usually built along a single narrow street. In the broader valleys the villages, gray brown and faintly red like the soil of which their bricks had once been moulded, clung compactly to hill-slopes safely above the torrents of spring and autumn, each little settlement with its brick or stone wall and its ornamental pagoda gates, and each with its cluster of trees about some consequential tomb rising above the low roofs in plumes of pale green April foliage.

Nowhere was there a sign of the disorder that was ravaging the province like a virulent disease. Brachey was aware of no glances of more than the usual passing curiosity from slanting eyes. He saw only the traditional peaceful countryside of the Chinese interior.

This sense of peace and calm had an effect on his moody self that increased as the day wore on. Life was turning unreal on his hands. His judgment wavered and played tricks with memory. Had it been so dangerous back there in T'ainan? Could it have been? He had to look steadily at the ragged, trudging figure of the erstwhile elegant Mr. Po to recapture a small degree of mental balance.... He had brought Betty away. He saw this now with a nervous, vivid clarity for what it was, an irrevocable act. It had come about naturally and simply; it had felt inevitable; yet now at moments, unable to visualize again the danger that had seemed terribly real in T'ainan he felt it only as the logical end of the emotional drift that had carried the two of them far out beyond the confines of reason. It was even possible that Mrs. Boatwright's judgment was the better.

But Betty couldn't go back now; they had turned her off; not unless her father should yet prove to be alive, and that was hardly thinkable. Anxiously during the day, he asked Mr. Po about that. But Mr. Po's confidence in the accuracy of his information was unshakable. So here he was, with a life on his hands, a life so dear to him that he could not control his mind in merely thinking of her there in the litter, traveling along without a question, for better or worse, with himself; a life that perhaps, despite this new spirit of consecration that was rising in his breast, he might succeed only in injuring. Brooding thus, he became grave and remote from her.

In his distant way he was very considerate, very kind. During the afternoon, as they moved up a long valley, skirting a broad watercourse where peach and pear trees foamed with blossoms against the lower slopes of the opposite hills, he persuaded her to descend from the litter and walk for a mile or two with him. He felt then her struggle to keep cheerful and make conversation, but himself lacked the experience with women that would have made it possible for him to overcome his own depression and brighten her, Once, when the caravan stopped to repack a slipping saddle, he asked her to sketch the view for him. It was his idea that she should be kept occupied when possible. He always corrected his own moods in that disciplinary manner. But just then his feelings were running so high, his tenderness toward her was so sensitively deep, that he spoke bruskly.

They rode on through the sunset into the dusk. The red hills turned slowly purple under the glowing western sky, swam mistily in a world-wide sea of soft dame.

Betty opened her windows wide now; gazed out at this scene of unearthly beauty with a sad deep light in her eyes.

2

They rode into another village. A soldier galloped on ahead to inspect the less objectionable inn. He reappeared soon, and the caravan jingled and creaked into a courtyard and stopped for the night. John dismounted and plunged into argument with the innkeeper. The cook set to work removing a pack-saddle. Coolies appeared. The mules were beaten to their knees. Brachey threw his bridle to a soldier and helped Betty out of the litter. Then they stood, he and she, amid the confusion, her hand resting lightly on his arm, her eyes on him.

Here they were! He felt now her loneliness, her sadness, her—the word rose—her helpless dependence upon himself. She was so helpless! His heart throbbed with feeling. He couldn't look down at her, standing there so close. He couldn't have spoken; not just then. He was struggling with the impractical thought that he might yet protect her from the savage tongues of the coast; from himself, even, when you came to it. The depression that had been pulling him down all day was turning now, rushing up and flooding his fired brain like a bitter tide. He shouldn't have let her come. It had been a beautiful impulse; her quiet determination to give her life into his hands had thrilled him beyond his deepest dreams of happiness, had lifted him to a plane of devotion that he remembered now, felt again, even in his bitterness, as utter beauty, intensified rather than darkened by the tragic quality of the hour. But he shouldn't have let her come. Mightn't she, after all, have been as safe hack there in the mission compound? What was the matter?... He hadn't thought of her coming on with him alone. That had simply happened. It was bewildering. Life had swept them out of commonplace safety, and now here they were! And nothing to do but go on, go through!

"Oh, I left my bag in there," he heard her saying, and himself got it quickly from the litter.

Then John came. The "number one" rooms were to be theirs, it seemed; Betty's and his.... If only he could talk to her! She needed him so ! Never, perhaps, again, would she need him as now, and he, it seemed, was failing her. Silently he led her up the steps of the little building at the end of the courtyard and into the corridor; peered into one dim room and then into the other; then curtly, roughly ordered John to spread for her his own square of new matting.

Her hand was still on his arm, resting there, oh, so lightly. She seemed very slim and small.

"It's a dreadful place," he made himself say. "But we'll have to make the best of it."

"I don't mind," he thought she replied.

"Perhaps we'd better have dinner in here, It's a little cleaner than my room."

She glanced up at him, then down: "I don't believe I can eat anything."

"But you must."

"I—I'll try."

"I'll ask Mr. Po to come in with us. He is a gentleman. And perhaps it would be better."

"Oh, yes," said she, "of course."

"Here's John with hot water. I'll leave you now."

"You'll—come back?"

"For dinner, yes."

With this he gently withdrew his arm. As she watched him go her eyes filled Then she closed her door.

Brachey found Mr. Po curled on the ground against a pack-saddle, smoking a Chinese pipe.

He rose at once, all smiles, and bowed half-way to the ground. But he thought it inadvisable to accept the invitation.

"I hate to be fly in ointments," he said, with his curiously dispassionate quickness and ease of speech, "but it's really no go. Our own men would play game of thick and thin blood brother, but to village gossip monger I must remain muleteer and down and out person of no account. It's a dam' sight safer for each and every one of us."

3

Betty tried to set the dingy room to rights. John had laid a white cloth over the table, and put out Brachey's tin plate and cup, his knife, fork and spoon, an English biscuit tin and a bright little porcelain jar of Scotch jam that was decorated with a red-and-green plaid. These things helped a little. She tidied herself as best she could; and then waited.

For a time she sat by the table, very still, hands folded in her lap; but this was difficult, for thoughts came—thoughts that spun around and around and bewildered her—and tears. The tears she would not permit. She got up; rearranged the things on the table; moved over to the window, and through a hole in one of the paper squares watched with half-seeing eyes the coolies and soldiers and animals in the courtyard. Her head ached. And that wheel of patchwork thoughts spun uncontrollably around.

For a little time then the tears came unhindered. That her father, that strong splendid man, could have been casually slain by vagabonds in a Chinese city seemed now, as it had seemed all day, incredible. His loss was only in part personal to her, so much of her life had been lived on the other side of the world; but childhood memories of him rose, and pictures of him as she had lately seen him, grave and kind and (since that moving little talk about beauty and its importance in the struggle of life) lovable. Her mother, too, had to-day become again a vivid memory. And then the sheer mystery of death twisted and tortured her sensitive Pagination, led her thoughts out into regions so grimly, darkly beautiful, so unbearably poignant, that her slender frame shook with sobs.

The sensation of rootlessness, too, was upon her. But now it was complete. There was no tie to hold her to life. Only this man on whom, moved by sheer emotion, without a thought of self, yet (she thought now) with utter unreasoning selfishness, she had fastened herself.

Mrs. Boatwright had called her bad. That couldn't be true. She couldn't picture herself as that. Even now, in this bitter crisis, she wasn't hard, wasn't even reckless; simply bewildered and terribly alone. Emotion had caught her. It *was* like a net. It had carried her finally out of herself. There was no way back; she was caught. Yet now the only thing that had justified this step—and how simple, how easy it had appeared in the morning!—the beautiful sober passion that had drawn her to the one mate, was clouded. For he had changed! He had drawn away. They were talking no more of love. She couldn't reach him; her desperately seeking heart groped in a dim wilderness and found no one, nothing. His formal kindness hurt her. Nothing could help her but love; and love, perhaps, was gone.

So the wheel spun on and on.

She saw him talking with the indomitably courteous Mr. Po. He came back then to the building they were to share that night. She heard him working at his door across the narrow corridor, trying to close it. He succeeded; then stirred about his room for a long time; a very long time, she thought.

Then John came across the court from the innkeeper's kitchen with covered dishes, steaming hot. She let him in; then, while he was setting out the meal, turned away and once more fought back the tears. Brachey must not see them. She was helped in this by a sudden mentally blinding excitement that came, an inexplicable nervous tension. He was coming; and alone, for she had seen Mr. Po shake his head and settle back contentedly with his pipe against the pack-saddle.... That was the strange fact about love; it kept rushing unexpectedly back whenever her unstable reason had for a little while disposed of it; an unexpected glimpse of him, a bit of his handwriting, a mere thought was often enough. Sorrow could not check it; at this moment her heart seemed broken by the weight of the tragic world, yet it thrilled at the sound of his step. And it couldn't be wholly selfish, for the quite overwhelming uprush of emotion brought with it a deeper tenderness toward her brave father, toward that pretty, happy mother of the long ago; she thought even of her school friends. She was suddenly stirred with the desire to face this strange struggle called living and conquer it. Her heart leaped. He was coming!

His door opened. He stepped across the corridor and tapped at hers. She hurried to open it. All impulse, she reached out a hand; then, chilled, caught again in the dishearteringly formal mood of the day, drew it back.

For he stood stiffly there, clad in black with smooth white shirt-front and collar and little black tie. He had dressed for dinner.

She turned quickly toward the table.

"John has everything ready," she said, now quite as formal as he. "We may as well sit right down."

4

For a time they barely spoke. John had lighted the native lamp, and it flickered gloomily in the swiftly gathering darkness, throwing a huge shadow of him on the walls, and even on the ceiling, as he moved softly in his padded shoes about the table and in and out at the door.

Betty's mood had sunk, now at last, into the unreal. She seemed to be living through a dream of nightmare quality—something she had—it was elusive, haunting—lived through before. She saw Jonathan Brachey distantly, as she had seen him at first, so bewilderingly long ago on a ship in the Inland Sea of Japan. She saw again his long bony nose, coldly reflective eyes, firmly modeled head.... And he was talking, when he spoke at all, as he had talked on the occasion of their first meeting, slowly, in somewhat stilted language, pausing interminably while he hunted about in his amazing mind for the word or phrase that would precisely express his meaning.

"There is a village a short distance this side of Ping Yang, Mr. Po tells me"... here a pause... "not an important place. Ordinarily we should pass through it about noon of the day after to-morrow. But he has picked up word that a Looker band has been organized there, and he thinks it may be best for us to..." and here a pause so long as to become nearly unbearable to Betty. For a time she moved her fork idly about her plate, waiting for that next word. At length she gave up, folded her hands in her lap, tried to compose her nerves. After that she glanced timidly at him, then looked up at the waveing shadows on the dim veils. It was almost as if he had forgotten she was there. He was interested, apparently, in nothing in life except those words he sought: "... to make a detour to the south."

Betty drew in a deep breath. She felt her color coming slowly back. The 'best thing to do, she decided, was to go on trying to eat. He had been right enough about that. She must try. It was, in a way, her part of it; to keep strong. Or she would be more hopelessly than ever fastened on him.... It seemed to her as never before a dreadful thing to be a woman. Tears came again, and she fought them back, even managed actually to eat a little. "It will mean still another...."

"Another what?" She waited and waited.

"Another night on the road, after tomorrow. I am sorry."

"It will mean another night on the road"

She had lately forgotten the slightly rasping quality in his voice, though it had been what she had first heard there. Now it seemed to her that she could hear nothing else.... What blind force was it that had thrust them so wide apart; after those ardent, tender, heart-breaking hours together at T'ainan; wonderful stolen hours, stirring her to a happiness so wildly beautiful that it touched creative springs in her sensitive young soul and released the strong eager woman there. This, the present situation, carried her so far beyond her experience, beyond her mental grasp, that, she could only sit very quiet and try to weather it. She could do that, of course, somehow. One did. It came down simply to the gift of character. And that, however undeveloped, she had.

Now and then, of course, clear thoughts flashed out for a moment; but only for a moment at a time. She sensed clearly enough that his whole being was centered on the need of protecting her. It was the fineness in him that made him hold himself so rigidly to the task. But it was a task to him; that was the thing. And his reticence! It was his attitude—or was it hers?—that had made frank talk impossible all day, ever since their moment of perfect silent understanding facing Mrs. Boatwright. He had felt then, with her, that she had to come, that it was their only way out; but now he, and therefore she, was clouded with afterthoughts. They had come to be frank enough about their dilemma, back there at T'ainan. But from the moment of leaving the city gate and striking tiff into the hills, they had lost something vital. And with every hour of this reticence, this talking about nothing, the situation was going to grow worse. She felt that, even now; struggled against it; but found herself moving deeper, minute by minute, into the gloom that had settled on them.... And back of her groping thoughts, giving them a puzzling sort of life, was excitement, energy, the sense of being borne swiftly along on a mighty wave of feeling—swiftly, swiftly, to a tragic, dim place where the withered shadows of youth and joy and careless laughter caught at one in hopeless weakness and slipped off unheeded into the unknown.

They came down at last to politeness. They even spoke of the food; and he reproved John for not keeping the curried mutton hot. And then, without one personal word, he rose to go. She rose, too, and stood beside her chair; she couldn't raise her eyes. She heard his voice saying, coldly she thought:

"I shall leave you now. You must..."

She waited, holding her breath.

"... you must get what sleep you can. I think we shall have no trouble here."

After this he stood for a long moment. She couldn't think why. Then he went out, softly closing the door after him. Then his door opened, and, with some creaking of rusty hinges and scraping on the tiles, closed. And then Betty dropped down by the table and let the tears come.

CHAPTER XVI
DESTINY

1

SHE heard little more for several hours; merely a muffled stirring about, at long intervals, as if he were walking the floor or trying to move a chair very quietly. The cot on which she now so restlessly lay was his. She couldn't sleep; he might as well have it, but would, of course, refuse.... She listened for a long time to the movements of the animals in the stable. Much later—the gong-clanging watchman had passed on his rounds twice at fewest; it must have been midnight—she heard him working very softly at his door. He was occupied some little time at this. She lay breathless. At length he got it open, and seemed to stand quietly in the corridor. Then, after a long silence, he opened as carefully the outer door, that had on it, she knew, a spring of bent steel, like a bow. After this he was still; standing outside, perhaps, or sitting on the top step.

For a moment she indulged herself in the wish that she might ha\e courage to call to him; to call him by name; to call him by the name, "John," she had no more than begun, that last day in the tennis court, timidly to utter. Her whole being yearned toward him She asked herself, lying there, why honesty should be impossible to a girl. Why shouldn't she call to him? She needed him so; not the strange stilted man of the day and evening, but the other, deeply tender lover that breathed still, she was almost sure, somewhere within the crust that encased him. And they had been honest, he and she; that had turned out to be the wonderful fact in their swift courtship.

But this was only a vivid moment. She made no sound. The warm tears lay on her cheeks.

After a little—it rose out of a jumble of wild thoughts, and then slowly came clear; she must have been dozing lightly—she heard his voice, very low; then another voice, a man's, that ran easily on in a soft nervelessness, doubtless the voice of Mr. Po. She thought of making a sound, even of lighting the little iron lamp; they must not be left thinking her safely asleep; but she did nothing; and the voices faded into dreams as a fitful sleep came to her. Nature is merciful to the young.

During those evening hours, Brachey sat for the most part staring at his wall. Finally, at the very edge of despair—for life, all that night, and the next day and the next night, offered Brachey nothing but a blank, black precipice over which he and Betty were apparently plunging—he gave up hope of falling asleep in his chair (important though he knew sleep to he, in the grisly light of what might yet have to be faced) and went out and sat on the steps; still in the grotesquely inappropriate dinner costume.

A shape detached itself from the shadows of the stable door and moved silently toward him.

Brachey welcomed the opportunity for a little man talk, if only because it might, for the time, take his mind in some degree out of the emotional whirlpool in which it was helplessly revolving.

"You've heard no more news?" he asked.

"Oh, no," replied Mr. Po, with his soft little laugh. "There is no more oil on fire of province discontent."

"From your letter I gathered that you are not so sure of Pao."

Mr. Po did not at once reply to this; seemed to be considering it, gazing out on the moonlit courtyard.

"It is no longer a case of cat and mouse," Brachey pressed on. "Something happened last night at the yamen. Am I right?"

"Oh, yes."

Brachey waited. After a long pause Mr. Po shifted his position, laughed a little, then spoke as follows:

"In afternoon yesterday old reprobate, Kang, sent to His Excellency letter which passed between my hands as secretary. He said that in days like these of great sorrow and humiliation agony of China it is best that those of responsible care and devotion to her welfare should draw together in friendship, and therefore he would in evening make call on His Excellency to express friendship and speak of measures that might lay dust of misunderstanding and what-not."

"Hmm!" Thus Brachey. "And what did *that* mean?"

"Oh, the devil to pay and all! It was insult of blackest nature."

"I don't quite see that."

"Oh, yes. He should not have written in arrogant put-in-your-place way. His Excellency most graciously gave orders to prepare ceremonial banquet and presents of highest value, but in his calm eye flashed light of battle to death. You see, sir, it was thought of Kang to show all T'ainan and near-by province who was who, taking bull by horns."

"Hmm! I don't know as I... well, go on."

"In particular His Excellency made prepare great bowl of sweet lotus soup, for in past years Kang had great weakness for such soup made by old cook of far-away Canton who attach to His Excellency a devil of a while ago."

"And so they had the banquet?"

"Oh, yes, and I was privileged to be in midst."

"You were there?"

"Oh, yes. Banquet was of great dignity and courteous good fellowship."

"I don't altogether understand the good fellowship."

"China custom habit differs no end from Western custom habit."

"Naturally. Yes. But what was Kang really up to?"

"I'm driving at that. After banquet all attendant retinue mandarins withdraw out of rooms except secretaries."

"Why didn't they go too?"

"Oh, well, it was felt by Kang that His Excellency might put it all over him with knives of armed men. And His Excellency had not forgotten tricky thought of Kang in eighteen-ninety-eight in Shantung when he asks disagreement but very strong mandarins to banquet and then sends out soldiers to remove heads in a wink while mandarins ride out to their homes when all good nights are said."

"You mean that Kang's men beheaded all his dinner guests, because they disagreed with him?"

"Oh, yes." Here Mr. Po grew reflective. "Kang is very queer old son of a gun—very tall, very thin, very old, with face all lines that come down so"— he drew down his smooth young face in excellent mimicry of an old man— "and he stoops so, and squints little sharp eyes like river rat, so. A mighty smart man, the reprobate! Regular old devil!" Mr. Po laughed a little. "My bosom friend Chih T'ang slipped himself in to me and explained in whisper talk that yamen of His Excellency was surrounded by Western soldiers of that old Manchu devil. And within yamen, up to third gate itself, swarmed a hell of a crowd of Manchu guard of Kang. It was no joke, by thunder!"

"I should say not," observed Brachey dryly. "You were going to tell me what Kang was really up to."

"Oh, yes! I will tell that post haste. When all had gone except four—"

"That is, Kang, and His Excellency, and two secretaries?"

"Yes, of whom it was my honor to be absurdly small part. Then Kang explained with utmost etiquette courtesy to His Excellency that letter had but yesterday come to him of most hellish import and very front rank. And his secretary handed cool as you please letter to me and I to Kis Excellency. It was letter of Prince Tuan to old Kang giving him power to have beheaded at once His Excellency."

"To behead Pao?"

"Oh, yes! And Kang said in neat speech then that no one could imagine his heartsick distress that one in power should wish great headless injury to dear old friend of long years and association government. To him he said it meant hell to pay. And he asked that His Excellency pass over from own hand infamous letter to be destroyed on spot by own hand of himself with firm resolve. But His Excellency smiled—a dam' big man!—and said for letter of Prince Tuan he felt only worshipful respect and obedience spirit, and he gave letter to me, and I delivered it to secretary of Kang, and secretary of Kang delivered it; to old Manchu himself. Then Kang, with own hands tore letter to bits and dropped bits in bowl, and his secretary asked me to have servant burn them, but I put on courteous look of attention to slightest wish of His Excellency and do not hear low word of secretary to old devil. And then Manchu reprobate with great courtesy makes farewell ceremony and goes out to his chair and altogether it's a hell of a note."

Bradley, in his deliberately reflective way, put the curious story together in his mind.

"Kang, of course, sent to Peking for that letter." he said.

"Oh, yes."

"It was, in a way, fair warning to Pao that the time had come for action and that Pao had better not try to meddle."

"Oh, yes—all of that. When he had gone Pao was sad. For he knew now that Kang had on his side heavy hand of Imperial Court at Peking. And then, late in night we have word from yamen of Kang and other word from observing officers of His Excellency that Western soldiers make attack at Hung Chan and that Reverend Doane is killed at city gate. Old Kang express great regret consideration and shed tears of many crocodiles, but they don't go."

"And Pao found himself powerless to interfere."

"Oh, yes! And so then I had audience of His Excellency and with permission of his mouth sent letter to you. His Excellency formed opinion right off the reel that it is not wise to send warning to mission compound, and that if I ever send word to you my head would not longer be of much use to me in T'ainan."

"Need they know of it at Kang's yamen?"

"There can not be secrets 'n yamen of great mandarin from observation eyes of other mandarin. Nothing doing!"

"Oh, I see. Spying goes on all the time, of course."

"Oh, yes! So I say farewell with tears to His Excellency, and in these old clothes of great disrepute, I"—he chuckled—"I make my skiddoo." From within the rags about his body he drew a soiled roll of paper "It has occurred to me that at Ping Yang time might roll around heavily on your hands and then, if you don't care what fool thing you do, you might bring me great honor by reading this silly little thing. It is lecture of which I spoke lightly once too often."

Absently Brachey took it. "But why can't old Kang see," he asked—"and Prince Tuan, for that matter—that if they are to start in again slaughtering white people, they will simply be piling up fresh trouble for China? Pao, I gather, does see it."

"Oh. yes, His Excellency sees very far, but now he must sit on fence and wait a bit. Kang, like Prince Tuan, is of the old."

"Didn't the outcome of the Boxer trouble teach these men anything?"

"Not these men. Old China mind is not same as Western progress mind—"

"I quite understand that, but..."

Mr. Po was slowly shaking his head. "No, old China minds dwell in different proposition. It is hard to say."

3

Toward morning, before his lamp burned out, Brachey read the lecture to which Mr. Po was pinning such great hopes. It seemed rather hopeless. There was humor, of course, in the curious arrangement of English words; but this soon wore off.

Later, sitting in the dark, waiting for the first faint glow of dawn, and partly as an exercise of will, he pondered the problems clustering about the little, hopeful, always aggressive settlements of white in Chinese Asia. Mr. Po's phrases came repeatedly to mind. That one—"Old China mind dwell in different proposition." Mr. Po was touching there, consciously or not, on the heart of the many-tinted race problems which this bafflingly complex old world must one day either settle or give up. The inertia of a numerous, really civilized and ancient race like the Chinese was in itself a mighty force, one of the mightiest in the world.... Men like Prince Tuan and this Kang despised the West, of course. And with some reason, when you came down to it. For along Legation Street the whites dwelt in a confusion of motives. They had exhibited a firm purpose only when Legation Street itself was attacked. By no means all the stray casualties among the whites in China were avenged by their governments. In the present little crisis out here in Hansi, it might be a long time—a very long time indeed—before the lumbering machinery of government could be stirred to act in an unaccustomed direction. At the present time there were not enough American troops in China to make possible a military expedition to Ping Yang; merely a company of marines at the legation. To penetrate so far inland and maintain communication an army corps would be needed; troops might even have to be assembled and trained in America. It might take a year. And first the diplomats would have to investigate; then the State Department would have to be brought by heavy and complicated public pressures to the point of actually functioning; a sentimental element back home might question the facts... Meantime, he hadn't yet so much as got Betty safely to Ping Yang.

It was "hard to say." But he found objective thought helpful. Emotion seemed, this night, not unlike a consuming fire. Emotion was, in its nature, desire. It led toward destruction.

He even made himself sleep a little, in a chair; until John knocked, at seven. Then he changed from evening dress to knickerbockers. His spirit had now sunk so low that he had John serve them separately with breakfast.

When the caravan was ready he went out to the courtyard and busied himself preparing the litter for her. She came out with John, very white, glancing at him with a timid question in her eyes. In his stiffest manner he handed her into the litter.

Then, accompanied by three soldiers, they swung out on the highway. The fourth soldier joined them outside the wall; him Brachey had sent to the telegraph station with a message to his Shanghai bankers advising them that his address would be in care of M. Pourmont, the Ho Shan Company, Ping Yang, Hansi, and further that cablegrams from America were to be forwarded immediately by wire.

Only at intervals during the forenoon did Betty and Brachey speak; for the most part he rode ahead of the litter. The luncheon hour was awkward; the dinner hour, when they had settled at their second inn, was even more difficult. They sat over their tin plates and cups in gloomy silence.

Finally Betty pushed her plate away, and rose; went over to the papered window and stared out.

Brachey got slowly to his feet; stood by the table. He couldn't raise his eyes; he could only study the outline of his plate and move it a little, this way and that, and pick up crumbs from the table-cloth. His mind was leaden; the sense of unreality that had come to him on the preceding day was now at a grotesque climax. He literally could not think. This, he felt, was the final severe test of his character, and it exhibited him as a failure. He was then, after all, a lone wolf; his instinct had been sound at the start, his nature lacked the quality, the warmth and richness of feeling, that the man who would claim a woman's love must offer her. He could suffer—the pain that even now, as he stood listless there, downcast, heavily fingering a tin plate, was torturing him to the limits of his capacity to endure, told him that— out suffering seemed a poor gift to bring the woman he loved. ... And here they were, unable to turn back. It was unthinkable; yet it was true. His reason kept thundering at his ear the perhaps tragic fact that his spirit was unable to grasp.... Braehey, during this hour—with a bitterness so deep as to border on despair—told himself that his lack amounted to abnormality. His case seemed quite hopeless. Yet here he was; and here, irrevocably, was she. The harm, whatever it might prove to be, and in spite of his sensitive, fire conquest of them emotional problem (at such a price, this!) was done. And there were no compensations. Here they were, lost, groping helplessly toward each other through a dark labyrinth.

Even when she turned (he heard her, and felt her eyes) he could not look up.

Then he heard her voice; an unsteady voice, very low; and he felt again the simple honesty, the naively child-like quality, that had seemed her finest gift. It was the artist strain in her, of course. She was not ashamed of her feeling, of her tears; there had never been pretense or self-consciousness in her. And while she now, at first, uttered merely his name—'"John!"—his inner ear heard her saying again, as she had said during their first talk in the tennis court—"I wonder if it is like a net."... Yes, she seemed to be saying that again.

But he was speaking; out of a thick throat:

"Yes?"

"What are we to do?"

He met this with a sort of mental dishonesty that he found himself unable to avoid. "Well—if all goes well, we shall be safe at Ping Yang within forty-eight hours."

"I don't mean that."

"Well..."

"I shouldn't have come."

"I couldn't leave you there, dear. Not there at T'ainan."

"It wasn't you who made the decision."

"Oh, yes—"

"No, I did it. It seemed the thing to do."

He managed to look up now, but could not knowhow coolly impenetrable he appeared to be. "It *was* the thing."

She slowly shook her head. "No... no, I shouldn't have come."

"I can't let you say that."

"It's true. Can't we be honest?"

The question stung him. He dropped again into his chair and sat for a brief time, thinking, thinking, in that, to her, terribly deliberate way of his.

"You're right," he finally came out. "We've got to be honest. It's the only thing left to us, apparently... The mistake lay back there in T'ainan. Our first talk in the tennis court. I knew then that the thing for me to do was to go."

"I didn't let you."

"But I should have. That situation was the same as this, only then we hadn't crossed our Rubicon. Now w e have. Don't you see? This situation has followed that, inevitably. And now we no longer have the power to choose. We've got to go on, at least as far as Ping Yang. But we mustn't be together..."

She glanced at him, then away.

"—no, not even like this. We have no right to indulge our moods. I'm going to be really honest now. We're in danger from these natives, yes. But that's a small thing."

She moved a hand. "Of course..." she murmured.

"The real danger is to you. And from me. Oh, my God, child, you're in danger from me!" He covered his face with his hands; then, after a moment, steadied himself, and rose. "I can't stay here and talk with you like this. I can't even help you. Already I've injured your name beyond repair."

She broke in here with a low-voiced remark the mature character of which he did not, in his self-absorption, catch. "I don't believe you know modern girls very well."

He went on: "So you see, I've hurt you, and now, when you need me most—oh, I know that!—I'm fading you. It's been a terrible mistake. But it's my job to get you to Ping Yang. That's all. No good talking. I'll go now'."

"I wish you wouldn't."

"I must. I—there we are! I'm failing you, that's all."

"I wonder if we're talking—or thinking—about the same things."

"Child, you're young! You don't understand! You don't seem to see how I've hurt you!"

"I think I see what you mean. But that—it might be difficult, of course, for a while, but it isn't what I've been thinking of. No, please let me say this! It wouldn't be fair not to give me my chance to be honest too. As for that— hurting me—I came with my eyes open."

"Oh, Betty—"

"Please! I did. I deliberately decided to come with you. I knew they'd talk, but I didn't care—much. You see I had already made up my mind that we were to be married. We'd have to be, once you were free. The way we've felt. You came way out here, and then you didn't go."

"That was weakness."

"You can call it weakness, or something else. But I'm in the same boat. And if we couldn't let each other go then, it was bound to grow harder every day. I had to recognize that. That was where I crossed my Rubicon. Nothing else mattered very much after that. I came with you because I was all alone, and miserable, and—oh, I may as well say it..."

"Oh, yes, honesty's the only thing now."

"Well, I simply had to. I couldn't face life any other way. I've been thinking it over and over and over. I see it now. I was just selfish. Love is selfishness, apparently. I fastened myself on you. I knew you had to have solitude, but I didn't seem to care. Perhaps you've hurt me. I don't know. But I am beginning to see that I've wrecked your life. I'm your job, now, just as you said. All those things you said on the ship have been coming up in my mind yesterday and to-day. Don't you suppose I can see it? My whole life right now is a demand on you." Her tone was not bitter, but sad, unutterably sad. "You said, 'Strength is better.' I'm running up with you now a 'spiritual' debt greater than I can ever pay. You said, 'If any friend of mine—man or woman—-can't win his own battles, he or she had better go. To hell, if it comes to that.'"

She was looking full at him now, wide-eyed, standing rigid, her hands extended a little way.

There was a long silence; then, abruptly, without a word, without even a change of expression on his gloomy face, he left the room.

5

That night was Betty's Gethsemane. Again and again she lived through their strange quarrel over the half-eaten dinner here in her room. Her mind phrased and rephrased the wild strong things she had said to him. And these phrases now stung her, hurt her, as had none of his.

But once again, after hours of tossing on the narrow folding cot— *his* cot—sleep of a sort came to her. She did not wake until half a hundred beams of sunshine were streaming in through the dilapidated paper squares.

She rose and peeped out into the courtyard. They were packing one of the saddles; John, and cook, and a soldier. Brachey was not in sight. He would be in his room then, across the corridor. She wondered if he had slept at all, then glanced guiltily at the cot. He would hardly lie on the unclean *kang*; very likely he had been forced to doze in a chair these two nights, while she found some real rest. There, again, she was using him, taking from him; and all he had asked of life was solitude, peace. For that he had foregone friends, a home, his country.

Then her eyes rested on a bit of white paper under the door. She quickly drew it in, and read as follows:

"My Dear, Dear Little Girl—

"As you of course saw this evening, it is simply impossible for me to speak rationally in matters of the affections. It is equally clear that by indulging my feelings toward you I have brought you nothing but unhappiness. This was inevitable. As I wrote you before I am not a social being. This fact was never so clear as now. I must be alone.

"As regards the statements you have just made, indicating that you attach the blame for the present predicament to yourself, these are, of course, absurd. I'm sure you will come in time to see that. It will be a question then whether you will be able to bring yourself to forgive me for permitting matters to go so far as they have. That has been my weakness. I allowed my admiration for you and my desire for you to overcome my reason.

"As for the course you must pursue, it will be, of course, to go on as far as Ping Yang. There I will leave you. It may even prove possible, despite the malignant enmity of Mrs. Boatwright, to convince M. Pourmont and the others that we are guilty of nothing more than an error of judgment in an extremely difficult situation. Certainly I shall demand the utmost respect for you.

"I shall make it a point to avoid you in the morning; and it will undoubtedly be best that we refrain so far as possible from speech during the remainder of our journey. I shall go on alone, as soon as you are safe at Ping Yang. I can not forgive myself for thus disturbing your life.

"I can not trust myself to write further. It is my experience that words are dangerous things and not to be trifled with. I will merely add, in conclusion, and in wishing that you may at some later time find a mate who can bring into your life the qualities which you must have in order to attain happiness, and which I unquestionably lack, that I shall hope, in time, for your forgiveness.. Without that I should hardly care to live on.

"Jonathan Brachey."

Soberly Betty read and reread this curious letter. Then for a moment her eyes rested on the cool signature, without so much as a "sincerely yours," and then she looked at that first phrase, "My Dear, Dear Little Girl"; and then her eyes grew misty and she smiled, faintly, tenderly. Suddenly, this morning, life had changed color; the black mood was gone, like an illness that had passed its climax. The curious antagonism in their talk the evening before had, it seemed, cleared the air—at least for her. And now, all at once—she was beginning to feel quietly but glowingly exultant about it—nothing mattered.

She ate all the breakfast that John brought; then hurried out. It gave her pleasure to stand aside and watch the packing, and particularly to watch Brachey as he moved sternly about. He was a strong man, as her father had been strong. He hadn't a glimmer of humor, but she loved him for that. He had all at once become so transparent. In his lonely way he had expended so much energy fighting the illusions of happiness, that now when real happiness was offered him he fought harder than ever. Her thoughtful eyes followed his every motion; he was tall, strong, clean.

His heart and mind, in their very austerity, were like a child's.

So deep ran this sober new happiness, as she stood by the litter waiting until he came—austerely—and helped her in (she was waiting for the touch of his hand, averting her face to hide the smile that she couldn't altogether control) that only a warmly up-rushing little thought of her father that came just then could restore her poise. She cared now about nothing else, about only this man whom she now knew she loved with her whole being and the father she had so suddenly, shockingly lost. If only, in the different ways, she might have brought happiness to each of these strong men. If only she could have brought them together, her father and her lover; for each, she felt, had fine deep qualities that the other would be quick to perceive.

All during the morning, feeling through every sensitive nerve-tip the nearness of this man who loved her and whom she loved, she rode through a land of rosy dreams. She felt again the power over life that she had felt during their first talk at T'ainan. Love had come; it absorbed her thoughts; it was right.... She exulted in the misty red hills with their deep purple shadows. She smiled at the absurd camels with the rings in their noses and the ragged, shaggy coats.

After a time, as the morning wore along, she became aware that he, too, was changing. Once, when he rode for a moment beside her Inter, he caught sight of her quietly radiant face and flushed and turned away. At lunch, by a roadside temple, under a tree, they talked about nothing with surprising ease. He was eager that she should draw and paint these beautiful hills of Hansi.

Late in the afternoon—they were riding down an open valley—he appeared again beside the litter. Impulsively she reached out her hand. He guided his pony close; leaned over and gripped it warmly. For a little while they rode thus; then, happening out of a confusion of impulses that, with whichever it began, was instantly communicated to the other, he bent down and she leaned out the little side door and their lips met.

The cook, from his insecure seat on the pack-saddle, carolled his endless musical narrative. John rode in stolid silence; the merely human emotions were ages old and quite commonplace. Mr. Po merely glanced up as he trudged along in the dust, taking the little incident calmly for granted.

So it was that, unaccountably to themselves, the spin of these two lovers rebounded from acute depression to an exaltation that, however sobered by circumstance, touched the skirts of ecstasy. They rode on silently as on the other days> but now their hearts beat in happy unison. No longer was the situation of their relationship unreal to them; the unreality lay with the white world from which they had come and to which they must shortly return. The mission compound was but an immaterial memory, like an unpleasant moment in a long, beautiful journey.

In the evening after dinner, they sat for a long time with her head on his shoulder dreamily talking of the mystery, their mystery, of love.

"It had to be," she said.

He could only incline his head and compress his lips as he gazed out over her head down a long vista of years, during which he would, for better or worse, for richer or poorer, protect and cherish her. The old phrases from the marriage service rang in his thoughts like cathedral bells.

"1 don't believe we'll ever have those dreadful moods again," she murmured, later. "At least, we won't misunderstand each other again. Not like that."

"Never," he breathed.

"Only one thing is wrong, dear," she added. "I wish father could have known you. He'd have understood you. That's the only sad thing."

He was silent. At last, after midnight, in a spirit of deepest consecration, he held her gently in his arms, kissed her good night, and went to his own room.

CHAPTER XVII
APPARITION

1

MEANTIME, M. Pourmont, at Ping Yang, was calling in his white assistants and sifting out the trustworthy among his native employees in preparation for withstanding a siege. He had swiftly carried out his plan of destroying the native huts that stood within a hundred yards of his compound. Such lumber and bricks as were of any value he had brought into the compound, using them to build two small redoubts at opposite comers of the walled-in rectangle and to increase the number of firing positions along the walls. From the redoubts the faces of the four walls and all of the hillside were commanded by the two machine guns. A wall of bricks and sand-bags was built up just within the compound gate so that the gate could be opened without exposing the interior to outside eyes or weapons. On all the roofs of the low stables and storehouses that bordered the walls were parapets of sand-bags.

These elaborate preparations were meant as much to impress and intimidate the natives of the region as for actual defense. In the main, and in so far as they could be understood, the natives seemed friendly. Several thousand of the young men among them had been at various times on M. Pourmont's pay-roll. The trade in food supplies, brick and other necessary articles was locally profitable. And the shen magistrate was keenly aware of the commercial and military strength represented by the foreigners.

There were—engineers, instrument men, stake-boys, supply agents, clerks, timekeepers, foremen and others—fourteen Frenchmen, eight Australians, three Belgians, six Englishmen, two Scotch engineers, four Americans, two Russians. Three of the Chinese had served as non-commissioned officers in the British Wei Hai Wei regiment in 1900. There were a few native foremen who had been trained in the modern Chinese army of Yuan Shi K'ai. The total force, including M. Pourmont himself and his immediate office force, came to forty-six white and about eighty able-bodied Chinese. These latter were now being put through hours of military drill every day in conspicuous places about the hillside.

A number of men acted as intelligence runners, and the activity of these, supplemented by occasional word from the yamen of the shen magistrate, kept M. Pourmont informed of the march of events in the province. Thus it could not have been twelve hours after Brachey bore the news of Griggsby Doane's death to the mission at T'ainan-fu before M. Pourmont as well knew of it, the word coming hy wire to the local yamen and thence passing in whispers to the compound on the hill.

Then, late one afternoon, Doane's pretty little daughter came in, escorted by the American journalist, Jonathan Brachey, and a young secretary from the yamen of the provincial judge disguised as a muleteer. Brachey at once volunteered to help and was put in charge of preparing two small lookout posts on the upper hill. He was uncommunicative and dryly self-sufficient in manner, but proved a real addition to the establishment, contributing the great Anglo-Saxon quality of confidence and tone. Though M. Pourmont would have preferred a more sociable man. His was a lonely life. He loved talk—even in broken English—for its own sake. He had, himself, vivacity and humor. And it was a disappointment that this Brachey didn't know *Chambertin* from *vin ordinaire*, and cared little for either.

Little Miss Doane touched his heart, she was so pretty, so quick in her bright graceful way, yet so white and sad. But always brave, as if sustained by inner faith. She asked at once to be put to work, and quickly adapted herself to the atmosphere of Mme. Pourmont's workroom in the residence, where Madarhe's two daughters and the English trained nurse were busy directing the Chinese sewing women.... It transpired that the Mrs. Boatwright who was in charge at the mission had refused to save herself and those in her charge, so the Mademoiselle had come on independently. This, thought M. Pourmont, showed a courage and enterprise suggestive of her father.

2

That night M. Pourmont telegraphed Elmer Boatwright confirming the news of Doane's death, and urging an immediate attempt to get through to Ping Yang.

On the preceding day he had sent a party of twelve men, white and Chinese, in command of an Australian engineer, to Shau T'ing, on the Eastern Border, to get the supplies that had been shipped down from Peking. These men returned on the following day; and among the cases and bales of supplies borne on the long train of carts they guarded were the bodies of two dead Chinese and a Russian youth with a bullet in his throat.

News came then that a large force of Lookers had started in an easterly direction from Hung Chan. And Boatwright wired that the mission party was at last under way, seven whites and fifty natives.

M. Pourmont at once sent a party of forty mounted men westward along the highway, commanded by an Englishman named Swain. This small force fought a pitched battle with the Looker band that had been evaded by Brachey, suffering several casualties. A native was sent on ahead, riding all night, with a note to Boatwright advising great haste. But it was difficult for the mission party to travel with any speed, as it had been found impossible to secure horses or carts for many of the Chinese converts, and not one of the missionaries would consent to leave these charges behind. It became necessary therefore for Swain to move a half-day's march farther west than had been intended. He joined the missionaries shortly after the advance guard of the Western Lookers had begun an attack on the inn compound. Already six or seven of the secondary Christians had been dragged out and shot or burned to death when Swain led his white and yellow troopers in among them, shooting right and left. There must have been several hundred of the Lookers; but they amounted to little more than a disorganized mob, and as soon as they found their comrades falling around them, screaming in agony and fright, they threw away their rifles and fled.

Swain at once ordered out the entire mission company, mounted as many as possible of the frightened fugitives on the horses of his troop, and with such extra carts as he could commandeer in the village for his wounded, himself and his uninjured men on foot, he pushed rapidly hack toward Ping Yang. The few Chinese who lagged were left in native houses. The horses that fell were dragged off the road and shot.

This man Swain, though he concerns us in this narrative only incidentally, was one of a not unfamiliar type on the China coast. He was hardly thirty years of age, a blond Briton, handsome, athletic, evidently a man of some education and breeding. He had once spoken of serving as a subaltern in the Boer War. A slightly elusive reputation as a Shanghai gambler had floated after him to Ping Yang. He was at times a hard drinker, as his lined face indicated, faint, purplish markings already forming a fine network under the skin of his nose. His blue eyes were always slightly bloodshot. He never spoke of his own people. And it had been noted that after a few drinks he was fond of quoting Kipling's *The Lost Legion*. Yet on this little expedition, unknown to the archives of any war department, Swain proved himself a hero. He brought all but twelve of the fifty-seven mission folk and eight of his own wounded safely to Ping Yang, leaving three of his Chinese buried back there. And himself sustained a bullet wound through the flesh of his left forearm and a severe knife cut on the left hand.... The drift of opinion among respectable people along Bubbling Well Road in Shanghai, as here in Ping Yang, was that Swain would hardly do. Certain of these mission folk, in particular Miss Hemphill, whose philosophy of life could hardly be termed comprehensive, were later to find their mental attitude toward their rescuer somewhat perplexing.

3

Though she evidently tried to be quiet about it, Mrs. Boatwright's first act was troublesome. She had been taken in, of course, with the other white women, by the Pourmonts; in the big house. Here the principal three of them—Dr. Cassin on her one hand and Miss Hemphill on the other—were put down at the dinner table on that first evening directly opposite Betty. Miss Hemphill flushed a little, bit her lip, then inclined her head with what was clearly enough meant to be distant courtesy. Dr. Cassin, already too deeply occupied with her wounded to waste thought on merely personal matters, bowed coolly. But Mrs. Boatwright stared firmly past the girl at the screen of carved wood that stood behind her.

Betty bent her head over her plate. She had of course dreaded this first encounter; all of her courage had been called on to bring her into the dining-room; but her own sense of personal loss and injury had lately been so overshadowed by the growing tragedy in which they were dwelling that she had forgotten with what complete cruelty and consistency this woman's stern sense of character could function. She had lost, too, in the mounting sober beauty of her love for Brachey, any lingering sense of wrong-doing. Here at Ping Yang Brachey commanded, she knew triumphantly, the respect of the little community.

They were thinking, he and she, only at moments of themselves. Indeed, days passed without a stolen half-hour together. She gloried in her knowledge that he would neglect no smallest duty to indulge his emotions in companionship with her; nor would she neglect duty for him........And the people here were all so kind to her, so friendly! The presence of this grim personally was an intrusion.

After dinner Mrs. Boatwright went directly to M. Pourmont in his study and told him that it would be necessary for her to sleep and eat in another building. She would give no reasons, nor would she in any pleasant way soften her demand. Accordingly, the Pourmonts, always courteous, always cheerful, made at once a new arrangement in the crowded compound. Some of the Australian young men were turned out into a tent; and the Boatwrights, accompanied by their assistants, were settled by midnight in the smaller building immediately adjoining the residence. Mr. Boatwright protested a little to his wife, but was silenced. All he could do was to make some extreme effort to treat the Pourmonts with courtesy.

And so Betty, when in the morning she again mustered her courage to enter the dining-room, found them gone. And instantly she knew why... . She couldn't eat. All day forlorn, her mind a cavern of shadows, she put herself in the way of meeting Brachey, but did not find him until late in the afternoon. He was coming in then from the outworks up the hill. She stood waiting just within the gate.

They had been thinking constantly, since the one misunderstanding, of the cablegram that would announce his freedom. In his eagerness he had expected to find it waiting at Ping Yang. Day after day native runners got through to the telegraph station and brought messages for others... To Betty now it seemed the one thing that could arm her against the stern judgment in Mrs. Boatwright's eyes.

Brachey's knickerbockers and stockings were red with mud. He wore a canvas shooting coat of M. Pourmont. He was lean, strong, quick of tread.

They drew aside, into a corner of the wall of sandbags. She saw the momentary light in his tired eyes when they rested on her; gravely beautiful eyes she thought them. Her fingers caught his sleeve; her eyes timidly searched his face, and read an answer there to the question in her heart.

"You haven't heard?"

He slowly shook his head. "No, dear, not yet."

Her gaze wavered away from him "It's got to come," he added. "It isn't as if there weren't a positive understanding."

"I know," she murmured, but without conviction. "Of course. It's got to come."

-- They were silent a moment.

"I—I'll go back to the house," she breathed, then. "Keep strong, dear," said he very gently.

"I know. I will. It's helped, just seeing you."

Then she was gone.

As he looked after her, his heart full of a gloomy beauty, he longed to call her back and in some way restore her confidence. But the appearance of the mission folk had shaken him, as well, this day. The mere presence of Mrs. Boatwright in the compound was suddenly again a living force. Up there on the hillside, driving his native workmen through the long hot hours, he had faced unnerving thoughts. For Mrs. Boatwright had brought him out of the glamour of his love; she, that sense of her, if merely by stirring his mind to resentment and resistance, restored for the time his keen logical faculty. He saw again clearly the mission compound at T'ainan-fu. And he saw Griggsby Doane—huge, strong, the face that might so easily be tender, working with passion in the softly flickering light from a Chinese lamp.

He had given Griggsby Doane a pledge as solemn as one man can give another. He had, because Doane was so suddenly dead, broken that pledge. But now he knew, coldly, clearly, that of material proof that Doane was dead neither he nor M. Pourmont nor these difficult folk from T'ainan held a shred.

4

Early on the following morning—at about three o'clock—a small shell exploded in the compound. Within five minutes two others fell outside the walls.

At once the open spaces within the walls were filled with Chinese, none fully dressed, talking, shouting, wailing. Among them, a moment later, moved white men, cartridge pouches and revolvers hastily slung on, rifles in hand, quietly ordering them back to their quarters and themselves taking positions along the walls. The crews of the two machine guns promptly joined the sentries in the redoubts. M. Pourmont went about calmly, pleasantly, supervising the final preparations. Two small parties, one led by Swain, the other by Brachey, went up the hillside to the men in the rifle pits there. A few trusted natives slipped out on scouting expeditions.

As the first faint color appeared in the eastern sky, and the darkness slowly gave way through the morning twilight to the young day, the walls were lined with anxious faces. Strained eyes peered up and down the hillside for the first glimpse of the enemy. Surmises and conjectures flew from lip to lip—the attackers were thousands strong; American, French and English troops were already on the way down from Peking; no troops could be spared; such a relieving party had already been intercepted and driven back as McCalla had been driven back in 1900; the Shau T'ing bridge was down, the telegraph lines were broken, old Kang had beheaded Pao and seized the entire provincial government, was, indeed, in personal command here at Ping Yang. So the rumors ran.

Daylight spread slowly over the hillside. Far up among the native houses and down near the village groups of strange figures could be seen moving about. They wore a uniform much like that the Boxers had worn, except that coat and trousers were alike red and only the turban yellow. At intervals shells fell here and there about the walls.

Back in his study in the residence M. Pourmont, by breakfast time, had reports from several of his scouts and was able to sift the rumors down to a basis of fact. Several thousand Lookers were already in the neighborhood and others were on the way. The Shau T'ing bridge was gone, and it was true that the local shen magistrate had been cut off from telegraphic communication with the outside world. And Kang was at the moment establishing headquarters five *li* to the westward.

The entrenched parties up the hillside lay unseen and unheard in their trenches, awaiting the signal to fire. The compound was still now. Breakfast was carried about to the men on duty.

Toward nine o'clock considerable activity was noted up the hill, beyond the outposts. Several squads of the red and yellow figures appeared in the open apparently digging out a level emplacement on the steep hillside. Then a small field gun was dragged into view from behind a native compound wall and set in position. The distance was hardly more than two hundred yards; they meant to fire point-blank.

M. Pourmont went out to the upper redoubt and studied the scene through field-glasses. The men begged permission to fire, but the bearded French engineer ordered them to wait.

The little red and yellow men were a long time at their preparations. They moved about as if confident that no white man's eyes could discern them. Finally they gathered back of the gun. There was some further delay. Then the gun was fired, and a shell whirred over the compound and on across the valley, exploding against the opposite hillside, near a temple, in a cloud of smoke and red dust.

There was still another wait. Then a shell carried away part of a chimney of the residence. The sound of distant cheers floated down-hill on the soft breeze. The little men clustered about the gun.

M. Puurmont lowered his glasses and nodded. The machine gun opened fire, spraying its stream of bullets directly on the crowded figures.

To the men standing and kneeling in the redoubt the scene, despite the rattle of the gun and the wisps of smoke curling about them and the choking smell, was one of impersonal calm. The Australian working the gun was quietly methodical about it. The crowded figures up the hill seemed to sit or lie down deliberately enough. Others appeared to be moving away slowly toward the houses, though when M. Pourmont gave them a look through his glasses it became evident that their legs were moving rapidly. Soon all who could get away were gone, leaving several heaped-up mounds of red near the gun and smaller dots of red scattered along the path of the retreat.

With a few scattering shots the Australian sat back on his heels and glanced up at M. Pourmont. "Heats up pretty fast," he remarked casually, indicating the machine gun.

5

Ashout, sounded up the hill. All turned. Swain had mounted to the parapet of his rifle pit and was waving his rifle. His half dozen men, white and Chinese, followed, all shouting now. Over to the right, from the other pit, the lean figure of Jonathan Brachey appeared, followed by others. Then they started up the hillside. Like the retreating Lookers they seemed to move very slowly; but the glasses made it clear that they were running and scrambling feverishly up the slope, fourteen of them, pausing only at intervals to fire toward the houses, where a few puffs of white smoke appeared.

They reached the Chinese sun, turned it around and, five or six of them, began running it down-hill. The others lingered, clustering together. A shot from one of the red heaps was met by a blow of a clubbed rifle; that was seen by the Australian through the glasses. There were more shots from the compound walls beyond.

The Australian quietly returned the glasses to his chief, sighted along his machine gun, and sprayed bullets along those walls, first to the left of the raiding party, then, very carefully, to the right.

M. Pourmont descended to the compound and ordered a party of coolies out with wheelbarrows. These began mounting the slope, obediently, painfully. The raiders dropped behind the little heaps of dead and waited. To the many watching eyes along the wall it seemed as if those deliberate coolies would never end their climb; inch by inch they seemed to move. Even the more rapidly moving gun, descending the slope, seemed to crawl. When it did at length draw near, the eager observers noted that the men handling it were all Chinese; the whites had stayed up there. Swain was there, and Brachey, and the others.

Betty witnessed the scene from an upper window of the residence with Mme. Pourmont and her daughters. She heard the rat-tat-tat of the machine gun; through a pair of glasses she saw the red-clad Lookers fall, all without clearly realizing that this was battle and death. It seemed a calm enough picture. But when Brachey started up the hill her heart stopped.

More and more slowly, as the climb told on the porters, the barrows moved up the slope; but at last they reached their destination. Then all worked like ants about them. Within ten minutes all were back in the compound creaking and squealing, each on its high center wheel, under the loads of shells.

Betty watched Brachey through the glasses. Naively she assumed that he would return to her after passing through such danger. And when she saw him drop casually into the little pit on the hillside it seemed to her that she couldn't wait out the day. Now that she had watched him leading his men straight into mortal danger—had so nearly, in her own heart, lost him—she began to sense the terrible power of love. All that had gone before in this strange relationship of theirs seemed like the play of children beside her present sense of him as her other self. Indeed the danger seemed now to be—she thought of it, in lucid moments, as a danger—that she should cease to care about outside opinion. Her heart throbbed with pride in him.

At dusk the outposts were relieved. When Brachey entered the gate, Betty was there, waiting, a tremulous smile hovering about her tender little mouth and about her misty eyes.

He paused, in surprise and pleasure. She gave him a hand, hesitantly, then the other; then, impulsively, her arms went around his neck.... His men straggled wearily past, their day's work done. Not one looked back. She was almost sorry, for that and for the dusk. Arm in arm they entered the compound and walked to the steps of the residence.

That night, three shells struck within the compound. One wrecked a corner of Mme. Pourmont's kitchen. Another carried away a section of galvanized iron roof and killed a horse. The third destroyed a tent, killing a Chinese woman and wounding a man and two girls. Thus, before morning, Dr. Cassam and her helpers were at the grim business of patching and restoring the piteous debris of war.

By daylight the red and yellow' lines were closed about the compound. Shells roared by at intervals all day, and bullets rattled against the walls. The upper windows of the residence were barricaded now with sandbags. Five more were wounded during the day, two of them white. Enemy trenches appeared, above and below the compound. During the following night M. Pourmont set a considerable force of men at work running a sap out to the rifle pits, and digging in other outposts on the lower slope. His night runners moved with difficulty, but brought in reports of feasts and orgies at Kang's headquarters down the valley, where, surrounded by his full retinue, the old Manchu was preparing to revel in slaughter. As the days passed, the sense of danger grew deeper; the faces one saw about the compound wore a dogged expression. An armed guard stood over the storehouses, men were killed and wounded, and women and children. They talked, heavily where the casual was intended, of settling down to a siege.

They spoke of other, larger sieges; of Mafeking and Ladysmith of recent memory. But no one, now, mentioned the prospects of early relief. One night Mr. Po went out with a Chinese soldier on a scouting trip; and neither returned. On the following night, one of the Wei Hai Wei men was sent. At daybreak they found his head, wrapped in a cloth, just inside the gate. The enemy had crept close enough, despite the outposts, to toss it over the wall... After this, for a time, no word went out or came in.

6

Elmer Boatwright slept alone in a small room; his wife, Miss Hemphill and Dr. Cassin occupied a large room in the same building. One night, tossing on his cot, the prey of nightmares, Boatwright started up, cold with sweat, and sat shivering in the dark room. Outside sounded the pop—pop, pop—of the snipers. But there was another sound that had crashed in among the familiar noises of his dreams.

It came again—a light tapping at his door. He tried to get his breath; then tried to call out, "Who is it?" But his voice came only in a whisper.

It wasn't his wife; she wouldn't have knocked. He had not before been disturbed at night; it would mean something serious, nothing good. It could mean nothing good.

Elmer Boatwright was by no means a simple coward. He rose, shivering with this strange sense of cold; struck a light; and candle in hand advanced to the door. Here, for a moment he waited.

Again the tapping sounded.

He opened the door; and beheld, dimly outlined in the shadowy hall, clad in rags, face seamed and haggard, eyes staring out of deep hollows, the gigantic frame of Griggsby Doane, leaning on his old walking stick. He was hatless, and his hair was matted. A stubble of beard covered the lower half of his face. His left shoulder, under the torn coat, was bandaged with the caked, bloodstained remnant of his shirt.

CHAPTER XVIII
THE DARK

1

Elmer Boatwrights chin sagged a little way. For a long moment he stood motionless, making no sound; then, without change of expression on his gray thin face, he moved with a slow gliding motion backward, backward, until his knees struck the bed; and stood, bent forward, his palsied hand tipping the candle so far that the hot tallow splashed in white drops on the matting.

Slowly the giant figure stirred, straightened up, came slowly into the room; closed the door, leaned back against it.

Then Boatwright spoke, slowly, huskily:

"It—it is you?"

"Yes." It was plainly an effort for Doane to speak. "But—but I don't see how you could have got through."

"Men do get through now and then." Doane spoke with the quick irritability of the man whose powers of nervous resistance have been tried to the uttermost.

"You're wounded. You must be tired." Boatwright was quite incoherent. "You'd better lie down. Here—take my bed! How did you ever find me? How did you get in in the first place?"

"I'll sit for a moment." Duane lowered himself painfully to the bed. "Betty is here?"

"Betty? Oh, yes! We're all safe."

"Where is she?"

"I—I don't know exactly."

"You don't *know!*"

"Why, Madame Pourmont has been caring for her."

"You mean that she is ill?"

"No. Oh, no! One moment. You've been hurt. I must tell the others. You must have attention at once. Mary Cassin is right here—and my wife." The little man moved to the door. His color was returning now; he was talking rapidly, out of a confused mind. "You must have had a terrible time."

"They left me for dead at the Hung Chan Gate. I crawled to the house of a convert." Doane's great eyes, staring out of shadowy hollows, burned with tragic memories. Those eyes held Boatwright fascinated; he shivered slightly. "As soon as I felt able to travel I started toward T'ainan. Several of our native people came with me, walking at night, biding by day. On the way we learned that you had left. So I came here. I must see Betty."

"But not like this," the little man blurted out. Doane's eyes wandered down over his muddy tattered clothing.

"I'll call the others first," said Boatwright He set down his candle on the wash-stand, just inside the door, and slipped out.

Doane sat erect, without moving. His eyes stared at the candle and at the grotesque wavering shadows of the wash-howl and pitcher on the wall. At each small night sound he started nervously—the scratching of a mouse, a voice in the compound, a distant sputter of shots.

Boatwright slipped back into the room.

"They're coming," he said breathlessly. "In a minute. Mary sleeps in most of her clothes anyway, these days."

"What is it about Betty?" Doane asked sharply.

"Oh—she's quite all right. We don't see much of her, not being in the same house. We're all pretty busy here, these days. It's an ugly time. I—I was just wondering. I don't know what we can dress you in. You could hardly wear my things. One of the Australians is nearly as big as you. Perhaps in the morning..."

His voice had risen a little, nearly to the querulous, as he hurriedly drew on his outer clothing. From the way his eyes wandered about the room it appeared that his thoughts had run far afield. And he was clumsy about the buttons. Even the intensely preoccupied Doane became aware of this, and for a moment studied him with a puzzled look.

The little man's tongue ran on. "Mary'll fix you up for now. Sleep'll be the best thing. In the morning you can use my shaving things. And I'll look up that Australian.... There they are!"

He hurried to the door. Dr. Cassin came in, greeted

Griggsby Doane with a warm hand-clasp, and at once examined his shoulder. Boatwright she sent over to the dispensary for bandages.

A moment later Mrs. Boatwright appeared, her strong person wrapped in a quilted robe.

"This is a great relief," she said. "We had given you up."

Duane's eyes fastened eagerly on this woman.

"Have you sent word to Betty?" he asked quickly.

Mrs. Boatwright looked at him for a moment, without replying, then moved deliberately to the window.

"Please don't move," cautioned Dr. Cassin, who was working on his shoulder.

"Have you sent word?" Doane shot the question after Mrs. Boatwright.

There was no reply.

"What is it?" cried Doane then.

"If you please!" said Dr. Cassin.

"Something is wrong! What is it?"

Mrs. Boatwright was standing squarely before the window now, looking out into the dark courtyard.

"What is it? Tell me! Is she here?"

"Really, Mr Doane"—thus the physician—"I can not work if you move. Yes, she is here."

"But why do you act in this strange way?"

Dr. Cassin compressed her lips. All her working adult life had been spent under the direction of this man. Never before had she seen him in the slightest degree beaten down. She had never even seen him tired. In her steady, objective mind he stood for unshakable, enduring strength. But now, twitching nervously under her firm hands, staring out of feverish eyes after the uncompromising woman by the window, his huge frame emaciated, spent with loss of blood, with suffering and utter physical and nervous exhaustion, he had reached, she knew', at last, the limits of his great strength. He had, perhaps, even passed those limits; for there was a morbid condition evident in him, he seemed not wholly sane, as if the trials he had passed through had been too great for his iron will, or as if there was something else, some consuming fire in him, burning secretly but strongly, out of control. All this she saw and felt. His temperature was not dangerously high, slightly more than two degrees above normal. His pulse was rapid, but no weaker than was to be expected. Worry might explain it; worry for them all, but particularly for Betty. Though she found this diagnosis not wholly satisfactory. Of course it might be, after all, nothing more than exhaustion. Sleep was the first thing. After that it would be a simpler matter to study his case.

Then, starling up suddenly, wrenching himself free from her skilful hands, Doane stood over her, staring past her at the woman by the window'.

"Will you please go to Betty," he said, in a voice that trembled with feeling, "and tell her that I am here. Wake her. She must know at once. And try to prepare her mind—she mustn't see me first like this."

There was a breathless pause. Then Mrs. Boatwright turned and moved deliberately toward the door. Then she paused.

"You'll see her?" cried the father. "At once?"

"No," replied Mrs. Boatwright. "No. I am sorry. I would like to spare you pain at this time, Griggsby Doane. But I do not feel that I can see her. I'll tell you though, what I will do. I'll tell Monsieur Pourmont." And she went out.

2

She was closing the door when it abruptly opened. Elmer Boatwright stood there, looking after his wife as she went along the dark hallway. He came in then.

"I brought the bandages," he said.

"You must sit down again," said the physician.

Doane, evidently bewildered, obeyed. And she began bandaging his shoulder.

He even sat quietly. He seemed to be making a determined effort to control his thoughts. When he finally spoke he seemed almost his old self.

"Elmer, something is wrong with Betty. Whatever it is, I have a right to know."

Boatwright cleared his throat.

Dr. Cassin broke the silence that followed.

"Mr. Doane," she said, "sit still here and try to listen to what I am going to tell you. We have been disturbed about Betty. I won't attempt to conceal that. This Mr. Brachey—"

"Brachey? Is he—"

"Please! You must keep quiet!"

"But what is it? Tell me—now!"

"I'm trying to. Mr. Brachey came to the compound the morning after you left—"

"But he gave me his word!"

"You really must let me tell this in my own way. He brought the news of your death. He had it from Pao's yamen. He demanded that we all leave T'ainan at once, with him. If he gave you his word, it is probable that he regarded your death as a release. Well...." For a moment she bent silently over her task of bandaging.

"Yes. Tell me?" Doane's voice was quieter still. More and more, to Boatwright, who stood by the wash-stand lingering a towel, he looked, felt, like the old Griggsby Doane... except his eyes; they were fixed intently on the matting; they were wide open, staring open.

"Well... Mrs. Boatwright felt that it was not yet the time to go. She distrusted this man. So we stayed a few days longer."

"You are not telling me."

"Yes. I am coming to it. Betty... Betty felt that she couldn't let him go alone."

In a hushed, almost a reflective voice Doane asked: "So she came with him?"

Dr. Cassin bowed. Elmer Boatwright bowed. Doane glanced up briefly, and took them in; then his gaze centered again on the matting.

"And they are here now?"

"Betty is staying with Madame Pourmont. Mr. Brachey is living in a tent."

"Where? What tent?"

Elmer Boatwright did not wait to hear this question answered, or the rush of other palliative phrases that were pressing nervously on the tip of Dr Cas-sin's not unsympathetic tongue. Never had he heard the quiet menace in Griggsby Doane's voice that was in it as he almost calmly uttered those three words, "Where? What tent?" He could nut himself think clearly; his mind was a blur of fears and nervous impulses. Doane wasn't normal; that was plain. Dr. Cassin's bare announcement was a blow so severe that even as he framed that tense question he was struggling to control the blind wild forces that were ravaging that giant frame of his. Once wholly out of control, he might do anything. He might kill Brachey. Yes, easily that!

It was in his eyes.... And so, without a plan, all confused impulses, Elmer Boatwright slipped out, closing the door behind him. On the outer sill of the little building he paused, trying desperately to think; but, failing in this effort, harried through the night to Brachey's tent.

He was, of course, far from understanding himself. It was a moment in which no small dogmatic mind, once touched by the illogic of merely human sympathy, could hope to understand itself. Though he and Brachey were barely speaking, he had watched the man during the capture of the Chinese gun and ammunition. And since that incident he had observed that Brachey was steadily winning the respect of all in the compound. The confusing thought was that a sinner could do that. For he believed, with his wife, and Miss Hemphill, that Brachey and Betty had sinned. Dr. Cassin had been more guarded in her judgment but probably she believed it, too. Sin, of course, to what may without unpleasant connotation be termed the professionally religious mind, is a definite, really a technical fact. In the faith of the Boatwrights it could be atoned only by an inner conviction followed by the blessing of the Holy Spirit. No mere good conduct, no merely admirable human qualities, could save the sinner. And neither Betty nor Brachey had shown the slightest sign of the regenerative process. In Mrs. Boatwright's judgment, therefore, since she was a woman of utter humorless logic, of unconquerable faith in conscience, the two stood condemned. But her husband, in this time of tragic stress, was discovering certain merely human qualities that were bound to prove disconcerting to his professed philosophy. He wanted, now, to help Brachey; and yet, as he ran through courtyard after courtyard, he couldn't wholly subdue certain strong misgivings as to what his wife might think if she knew.

3

Before the tent he hesitated. The flap was tied; he shook it, with a trembling hand. He heard, then, the steady breathing of the man within. He tried knocking on the pole, through the canvas, but without effect on the sleeper. Then, with a curious sensation of guilt, he reached in and untied the flap, above, then below; and passed cautiously in. The night was warm. Brachey lay uncovered, dressed, as Boatwright saw when he struck a match to make certain of his man, in all but coat, collar and shoes.

Boatwright blew out the match. For another moment he stood wondering at himself; then laid a hand on the sleeper's shoulder. Brachey started up instantly; swung his feet to the floor; said in a surprisingly alert, cautious voice:

"What is it?"

"It's Elmer Boatwright."

"Oh!" was Brachey's reply to this. He quietly lighted the candle that stood on a small table by the head of his cut. Then he added the single word, "Well?"

"I have come on a peculiar errand, Mr. Brachey..." Boatwright was fumbling for words.

"Yes?"

"There is little time for talk. A queer situation... let me say this—when you came to the mission and asked us to leave T'ainan with you it was under the supposition that Griggsby Doane was dead."

"Yes.... You mean that now... that the news was inaccurate?"

Boatwright inclined his head.

"He is alive, then?"

Another bow.

"Where is he?"

"Well... it is... I must ask you to consider the situation calmly. It is difficult."

Boatwright felt the man's eyes on him, coolly surveying him. It did seem a bit absurd to be cautioning this strange being to be calm. Had he ever been otherwise? Here he was, roused abruptly from slumber, listening, and looking, like a judge. He said now with quick understanding:

"He is here?"

Boatwright's head inclined.

"How did he ever get through?"

"We haven't heard the details yet. There's so much else.... I want to make it plain to you that he isn't altogether himself. He has evidently been through a terrible experience. He was wounded. He has some fever now, I believe.... Let me put it this way. He has just now learned that you are here—-that you—"

"That I brought his daughter here?" The remark was cool, clear, decisive.

"Well—yes. Now please understand me. He isn't himself. The news shocked him. I could see that. My suggestion is—well, that you move over to the residence for the rest of the night."

"Why?"

"You see—Mr. Doane asked where you might be found, in what tent. He has had no time to reflect over the situation. His present mood is—well, as I said, not normal. I've thought that to-morrow—after he has slept—some—we can prevail on him to consider it calmly."

"You mean that he may attack me?"

"Well—yes. It's quite possible. Monsieur Pour-mont would take you in now. I'm sure. In the morning you'll be back in your trenches. That will give us time to..."

His voice died out. His gaze anxiously followed Brachey's movements. The man had buttoned on his collar, and was knotting his tie before the little square mirror that hung on the rear tent-pole. Next he brushed his hair. Then he got into his coat. And then he discovered that he was in his stocking feet. That bit of absent-mindedness was the only sign he gave of excitement.

"If I might suggest that you hurry a little," thus Boatwright... "it's possible that he's on his way here now."

"Who?" asked Brachey coolly, raising his head. "Oh—you mean Doane."

"Yes. I really think—"

Brachey waved him to be still. He moved to the tent opening, peered out into the night, then turned and looked straight at his caller, slightly pursing his lips.

"Where is Mr. Doane?" he asked.

"He was in my room. But you're not—you don't mean—"

"I'm going to see him, of course."

"But that's impossible. He may kill you."

"What has that to do with it?"

This blunt question proved difficult to meet. Boatwright found himself saying, rather weakly, "I'm sure everything can be explained later."

"The time to explain is now."

With this, and a slight added sound that might have been an indication of impatience, Brachey strode out.

4

For a moment Boatwright stood in the paralysis of fright; then, catching his breath, he ran out after this strangely resolute man; quickly caught up with him, but found himself ignored. He even talked—incoherently—as his short legs tried to keep pace with the swift long stride of the other. He didn't himself know what he was saying. Nor did he stop when Brachey's arm moved as if to brush him off; though he perhaps had been clinging to that arm.

Brachey stopped, looking about.

"This is the house, isn't it?" he remarked; then turned in toward the steps.

The door burst open then, and a huge shadowy figure plunged out. A woman's voice followed: "I must ask you to please come back, Mr. Doane. Really, if you—"

At the name—"Mr. Doane"—Brachey stopped short (one foot was already on the first of the three or four steps) and stiffened, his shoulders drawn back, his head high, Doane, too, stopped, peering down.

"Mr. Doane," said the younger man, firmly but perhaps in a slightly louder tone than was necessary, "I am Jonathan Brachey."

A hush fell on the group of them—Brachey waiting at the bottom step, Boatwright just behind him. Dr. Cassin barely visible in the shadows of the porch, silhouetted faintly against the light of a candle somewhere within, and Griggsby Doane staring down in astonishment at the man who stood looking straight up at him.

Brachey apparently was about to speak again. Perhaps he did begin. Boatwright found it impossible afterward to explain in precise detail just what took place. But the one clear fact was that Doane, with an exclamation that was not a word, seemed to leap down the steps, waving his stick about his head. There was the sound of a few heavy blows; and then Brachey lay huddled in a heap on the the walk, and Doane stood over him, breathing very hard..

Dr. Cassin hurried down the steps and knelt lie-side the silent figure there. To Elmer Boatwright she said, briskly: "My medicine case is in your room. Bring it at once, please? And bring water."

Boatwright vaguely recalled, afterward, that he muttered, "I beg your pardon," as he finished past Doane and ran up the steps. And he heard the sound of some, one running heavily toward them.

When he came out the scene was curiously changed.

Some of the natives were there, and one or two whites. An iron lantern with many perforations to let out the candle-light stood on the tiles. One of the Chinese held another. Dr. Cassin was seated on the ground examining a wound on Brachey's scalp; and the man himself was struggling back toward consciousness, moving his arms restlessly, and muttering.

But the voice that dominated the little group that stood awkwardly about was the voice of M. Pourmont.

Doane had sunk down on the steps, his head in his hands. And over him, somewhat out of breath, gesturing emphatically with raised forefinger, the engineer was speaking as follows:

"Monsieur Doane, it gives me ze great plaisir to know zat you do not die. To you here I offair ze vel-come viz all my 'eart. But zis I mus' say. It is here la guerre. It is I who am here ze commandair. An' I now' comman' you, Alonsieur Doane, zer mus' be here no more of ze mattair personel. We here fight togezzer, as one, not viz each ozzer. You have made ze attack on a gentleman zat mus' be spare' to us, a gentleman ver' strong, ver' brave, who fear nozzing at all. It is not pairmit' zat you make 'arm at Monsieur Brashayee. Zis man is one I need. It is on 'im zat I lean."

Here Boatwright found himself breaking in, all eagerness, all nerves:

"If you had only known how it was! Mr. Brachey insisted on coming straight to you."

"Monsieur Boatright, if you please! I mus' have here ze quiet! Monsieur Doane, you vill go at once to bed. It is so I order you. Go at once to bed!" Doane slowly lifted his head and looked at M. Pour-munt. "Very well," he said quietly. "You are right, of course." On these last few words his voice broke, but he at once recovered control of it. He rose, with an effort, moved a few slow steps, hesitated, then got painfully down on one knee beside the limp groaning figure on the walk. He looked directly at Dr. Cassin, as he said:

"Is he badly hurt?"

"I don't think so," replied the physician simply, wholly herself. "The skull doesn't seem to be fractured. We may find some concussion, of course." Doane's breath whistled convulsively inward. He knelt there, silent, watching the deft fingers work. Then he said—under his breath, but audibly enough: "What an awful thing to do! What a terrible thing to do!" And got up.

Boatwright hurried to help him.

"I'll go with you, Elmer," said Doane.

CHAPTER XIX
LIVING THROUGH

1

WHEN Griggsby Doane moved, pain shot through his lame muscle. A vaguely heavy anxiety clouded his brain, engaged as it still was with the specters of confusedly ugly dreams.

The speckled area overhead was gradually coming clear; it appeared to be a plastered ceiling, very small; a little cell of a place... oh, yes, Elmer Boatwright's room!

Faintly through the open window at the foot of the bed came the sound of a distant, shot; another; a rattle of them. And other, nearer shots. Then a slow whistling shriek and a crash. Then the rattle of a machine gun, quite clear. Then a lull.

He sensed a presence; felt rather than heard low breathing; with an effort that was as much of the will as of the body he turned his head.

Betty was sitting there, close by the bed, gently smiling. Almost painfully his slow eyes took her in. She bent over and kissed him, then her little hand nestled in his big one. They talked a little; he in a natural enough manner, if very grave, spoke of his joy in finding her safe. But as he spoke his mind, not yet wholly awake, took on a morbid activity. Did she know what he had done in the night? Had they told her? Anxiously, as she answered him, he searched her delicately pretty face. How young she was! Dwelling amid tragedy, in a degree sobered by it, the buoyancy of youth glowed in her brown eyes, in the texture of her skin, in the waving masses of fine hair, in the soft vividness of her voice; the touch of tragedy would, after all, rest lightly on her slim shoulders. To her the world was young; of the bitter *impasse* of middle age she knew no hint. Men loved her, of course. Men had died for less than she.... He pondered, swiftly, gloomly, the problem her very existence presented. And he looked on her and spoke with a finer tenderness than any he had before felt toward any living creature, even toward the wife who had left her soul on earth in the breast of this girl.

He decided that they hadn't told her. After all, they wouldn't. They were, when all was said, adult folk. He couldn't himself tell her. But his predicament was pitiful. He knew now, from the honest love in her eyes, that not the least black of his sins had been the doubting her. Never again could he do that. But this realization brought him to the verge of an attitude toward Jonathan Braehey that it was impossible for him to entertain; the mere thought of that man roused emotions that he could not control. But emotions, all sorts, must be controlled, of course; on no other understanding can life be lived. If direct effort of will is insufficient, then counter-activity must be set up.

Betty protested when he told her he meant to get up at once. But it was afternoon. He assured her that his wound was not serious; Dr. Cassin had admitted that, and he had slept deeply. H is muscles were lame; but that was an added reason for exercise.

They had brought in some of the clothing of the large Australian. As he pieced out a costume, he shaped a policy He couldn't, at once, fit into the life of the compound. He couldn't face Brachey. Not yet. The only hope of getting through these days of his passion lay in keeping himself desperately active. He weighed a number of plans, finally discarding all but one. Then he rang for a servant; and sent, while he ate a solitary breakfast, a chit to M. Pourmont.

2

The engineer received him at three. Neither spoke of the incident that had brought them together in the night. To Doane, indeed, it was now, in broad daylight and during most of the time, but a nightmare, unreal and impossible. During the moments when it did come real, he could only set his strong face and wait out the turbulence and bewilderment it stirred in him.

M. Pourmont found him very nearly himself; which was good. He seemed, despite the bandaged shoulder and the thinner face, the Griggsby Doane of old. But his proposal—-he was grimly bent on it—was nothing less than to make the effort, that night, to get through to the telegraph station at Shau T'ing.

M. Fourmunt took the position that the thing couldn't be done. After losing two natives in the attempt, he had decided to conserve his meager manpower and fall back on the certain fact that the legations knew of the siege and were doubtless moving toward action of some sort. Besides, he added, Duane with his courage and his extensive knowledge of the local situation was the man above all others he could least well spare.

Doane, however, pressed his point. "Getting through the lines will be difficult, but not impossible," he said. "Remember I did get through last night. I believe I can do it again to-night. Even if I should be captured they may hesitate to kill me. I would ask nothing better than to be taken before Kang. He would have to listen to me, I think. And if I do succeed in establishing communication with Peking I may be able to stir them to action. The Imperial Government can hardly admit that they are backing Kang. It may even be possible to force them, through diplomatic pressure alone, to repudiate him and use their own troops to overthrow him. But first Peking must have the facts."

M. Pourmont smiled.

"If you vill step wiz me," he said, and led the way down a corridor to his spacious dining-room. There on the table, stood a large basket heaped with apples and pears. "Vat you t'ink, Monsieur Doane! But yesterday comes *un drapeau bianc* to ze gate viz a let-tair from zis ol' Kang. He regret vair' much zat ve suffair *ici ze derangement*, an' he hope zat vair' soon ve are again *confortable*. In Heaven, perhaps he mean! *Chose donnante!* An' he sen' *des fruits* viz ze *compliments of Son Excellence* Kang Hsu to Monsieur Pourmont. *Et je vous demande, qu'est-ce que cela fait?*"

Doane considered this puzzle; finally shook his head over it. It was very Chinese. Kang doubtless believed that through it he was deluding the stupid foreigners and escaping responsibility for his savage course.

Finally Doane won M. Pourmont's approval for his forlorn sally. He was, in a wild way, glad.

During the few hours left to him he must work rapidly, think hard. That, too, was good. He decided to write a will. If he had little money to leave Betty, at least there were things of his and her mother's. Elmer Boatwright would help him. And he must tell Betty he was going. It was curiously hard to face her, hard to meet the eye of his own daughter. He winced at the thought.

She had returned to the residence before him. He asked for her now.

M. Pourmont, giving a moment more to considering this man, whom he had long regarded with a respect he did not feel toward all the missionaries, wondered, as he sent word to the young lady, what might underlie that strange quarrel of the early morning. The only explanation that occurred to him he promptly dismissed, for it involved the little Mademoiselle's name in a manner which he could not permit to be considered. M. Pourmont was a shrewd man; and he knew that the Mademoiselle was ashamed of nothing. Nothing was wrong there. Like his wife he had already learned to love the busy earnest girl. And then, leaving M. Doane in the reception-room waiting for her, he returned to his study and dismissed the whole matter from his mind. For the siege was cruel business. One by one, some one every day, men and women and children, were dying. The living had to subsist on diminishing rations, for he had never foreseen housing and feeding so large a number. There were problems—of discipline and morale, of tactics, of sanitation, of burying the dead—that must be met and solved from hour to hour.

On the whole, as he settled again into his endless, urgent task, M. Pourmont was not sorry that M. Doane had won his consent to this last desperate effort to reach those inhumanly deliberate white folk up at Peking; men whose minds dwelt with precedents and policies while their fellows, down here at Ping Yang, on a hillside, held off with diminishing strength the destruction that seemed, at moments, certain to fall.

3

Doane, watching Betty as she entered the room attired in a long white apron over her simple dress, knew that he must again beg the question that lay between them. He could no more listen to the burden of her heart than to the agony of his own. Sooner or later, if he lived, he would have to work it out, decide about his life. If he lived....

"My dear," he said, quickly for him, holding her hand more tightly than he knew, "I have some news which I know you will take bravely."

He could feel her steady eyes on him. He hurried on. "I am going out again to-night. There seems a good chance that I may get through to Shau T'ing, with messages. I'm going to try."

His desire was to speak rapidly on, and then go. But he had to pause at this. He heard her exclaim softly—"Oh, Dad!" And then after a silence—"I'm not going to make it hard for you. Of course I understand. Any of us may come to the end, of course, any moment. We've just got to take it as it comes. But—I—it does seem as if—after all you've been through, Dad—as if—"

He felt himself shaking his head.

"No," he said. "No. It's my job, dear."

"Very well, Dad. Then you must do it. I know. But I do wish you could have a day or two more to rest. If you could"—this wistfully—"perhaps they'd let me off part of the time to take care of you. You know, I'm nursing. I'd be stern. You'd have to sleep a lot, and eat just what I gave you." She patted his arm as she spoke; then added this: "Of course it's not the time to think of personal things. But there's one thing I've got to tell you pretty soon, Dad. A strange experience has come to me. It's puzzling. I can't see the way very clearly. But it's very wonderful. I believe it's right—really right. It's a man."

She rushed on with it. "I wanted you to meet him to-night. He's—out in the trenches, all day, up the hill. We're expecting word—a cablegram—when they get through to us. And when that comes, I'd have to tell you all about it. He'll come to you then. But I—well, I had to tell you this much. It's been a pretty big experience, and I don't like to think of going through it like this without your even knowing about it from me, and knowing, too, no matter what they may say"—her voice wavered—"that it's—it's—all right." Her hands reached suddenly up toward his shoulders; she clung to him, like the child she still, in his heart, seemed.

He could trust himself only to speak the little words of comfort he would have used with a child. He felt that he was not helping her; merely standing there, helpless in the grip of a fate that seemed bent on racking his soul to the final Emit of his spiritual endurance.

"This won't do," she said. "I have no right to give way. They need me in the hospital. I shall think of you every minute, Dad. I'm very proud of you."

She kissed him and rushed away. He walked back to Elmer Boatwright's room fighting off a sense of unreality that had grown so strong as to be alarming. It was all a nightmare now—the manly dogged faces in the compound, the wailing sounds from the native quarter, the intermittent shots, the smells, the very sun that blazed down on the tiling. Nothing seemed really to matter. He knew well enough, in a corner of his mind, that this mood was the most dangerous of all. It lay but a step from apathy; and apathy, to such a nature as his, would mean the end.

So he busied himself desperately. The simple will he left for Boatwright with instructions that it was to be given to Betty in the event of his death. It seemed that the little man was one of a machine-gun crew and could not be reached until well on in the evening; he had turned fighter, like the others.

He sewed up his tattered knapsack and filled it with a sort of iron ration. He wrote letters, including a long one to Henry Withery, addressed in care of Dr. Hidderleigh's office at Shanghai. He framed with care the messages that were to go over the wires to Peking. He ate alone, and sparingly. And early, as soon as darkness settled over the scene of petty but bitter warfare, he clipped out of the compound and disappeared, carrying no weapon but his walking stick.

CHAPTER XX
LIGHT

1

DOANE walked, carelessly erect, to a knoll something less than a hundred yards northeast of the compound and off to the left of the ride pits. Here he stood for a brief time, listening. He purposed going out through the lines as he had come in through them, by crawling, hiding, feeling his way foot by foot. The line was thinnest in front of the rifle pits, and just to the left where the upper machine gun commanded a defile.

He had allowed two hours for the journey through the lines, but it consumed nearly four. At one point he lay for an hour behind a stone trough while a squad of Lookers built a fire and brewed tea. A recurring impulse was to walk calmly in among those yellow men and go down fighting. It seemed as good a way as any to go. He found it necessary to hold with a strong effort of will to the thought of his fellow's in the compound; that to save them, and to save Betty, he must carry through.

Toward one o'clock in the morning, now well to the eastward of the besieging force, he swung into his stride. It seemed, in the retrospect, absurdly like the play of children to be hiding and crawling about the hillsides. But he was glad now that he had somehow, painfully, kept his head. Barring the unforeseen, the diplomatic gentlemen up at Peking would find the news awaiting them when they came to their desks in the morning. After that noting that he might do would greatly matter. He could follow these powerfully recurring impulses if he chose; let the end come. That was now his greatest desire. Life had become quite meaningless. Except for Betty....

2

Shau T'ing was but another of the innumerable rural villages that dot northern China. Though there were a railway station, and sidings, and a quaintly American water tank set high on posts. The inns were but the familiar Oriental caravansaries; no modern hotel, no "Astor House," had sprung up as yet to care for newly created travel.

As he approached the stream that ran through a loess canyon a mile or more west of the village he glimpsed, ahead, a group of soldiers seated about a fire. Just behind them were stacks of rifles; this much he saw and surmised with the help of the firelight. And the first glow of dawn was breaking in the east. He left the highway and swung around through the fields, passing between scattered grave mounds from whose tops the white joss papers fluttered in the gray twilight like timid little ghosts.

He crossed the gorge by the old suspension footbridge, with the crumbling memorial arches at either end bearing, each characteristic inscriptions suggestive of happiness and peace. Looking down-stream he could dimly see that the railway bridge lay, a tangle of twisted steel, in the stream, leaving the abutments of white stone rearing high in the air with wisps of steel swinging aimlessly from the tops.

He half circled the village, and waited outside the eastern gate until the massive doors swung open at sunrise.

He went to the leading inn, and gave up an hour to eating the food in his knapsack and cleaning his mud-dyed clothing. The innkeeper informed him, when he brought the boiled water, that another white man had been there for three days. After this Doane went down to the station. A solitary engine was puffing and clanking among the sidings, apparently making up a train.

A number of the blue-turbaned military police stood sentry-go here and there about the yard, each with fixed bayonet. Within the room that was at once ticket office and telegraph station sat the Chinese agent cheerfully contemplating a slack day.

Doane wrote out his messages, and stood over the man until they were sent; then walked slowly back toward the inn. His task, really, was done. He would wait until night, of course; there might be replies. But at most his only further service would be in carrying hopeful messages to the beleaguered folk at Ting Yang. Beyond that he would be but one more human unit to fight and to be fed. Debit and credit, they seemed just about to balance, those two items. Fastening his door he stretched out on the *kang*.

He was awakened at the close of day by the innkeeper bringing food. The man set out two plates on the dusty old table. Doane sat on the edge of the *kang* and drowsily wondered why. He had slept heavily. He stood up; moved about the room; he was only a little stiff. Indeed his strength was surely returning. He felt almost his old self, physically.

There was a knock at the door. In Chinese he called, "Enter!"

The door slowly opened, and a drab little man came in, walking with a slight limp, and stood looking at him out of dusty blue eyes. He carried a packet of papers.

"Grigg!" he exclaimed softly.

"Henry Withery!" cried Doane, "What on earth are you doing here?"

Withery smiled, and laid hat and packet on the table.

"I've arranged to dine with you," he explained. "You won't mind?"

"Of course not, Henry. But why are you here?"

"My plans were changed."

"Evidently. Do sit down."

"I came back to find you. I've been waiting here for a chance to get through. We've worried greatly, of course. A rumor came from the Chinese that you were killed."

"I nearly was," said Doane quietly. A cloud had crossed his face as he listened. At every point, apparently, at each fresh contact with life, he was to be brought face to face with his predicament. It would be pitiless business, of course, all the way through, for the severest judge of all he had yet to face dwelt within his own breast; long after the world had forgotten, that judge would be pronouncing sentence upon him.

"You got through to Shanghai?" he asked abruptly.

Withery, touched by his appearance, a little disturbed by his nervously abrupt manner, inclined his head.

"Well, it's out, I suppose. What are they saying about me, Henry? Really, you'd better tell me. I've got to live through this thing, you know. I may as well have the truth at once."

Withery lowered his eyes; fingered the chopsticks that lay by his plate.

"No," he said slowly. "No, Grigg, it's not out."

"But you know of it. Surely others do, then. And they'll talk. It's the worst way. It'll run wild. I'd rather face a church trial than that." He was himself unaware that he had been constantly brooding upon this aspect of his trouble, yet the words came snapping out as if he had thought of nothing else.

"Now, Grigg," said Withery, in the same deliberately thoughtful way, "I want you to let me talk. I've come way back here just to do that. Hidderleigh showed me your letter. Then in my presence, he destroyed it. I have promised him I would speak of it to no one but you. ... Neither you nor I could have foreseen just how Hidderleigh would take this. He is, of course, as he has always been, a dogmatic thinker. But like others of us, he has grown some with the years. He's less narrow, Grigg. He knows you pretty well—your ability, your influence. He respects you."

"Respects me?" Doane nearly laughed.

"Yes. He sees as clearly as you or I could that any human creature may slip. And he knows that no single slip is fatal. Grigg, he wants you to go back and take up your work."

Doane could not at once comprehend this astonishing statement. He was deeply moved. Withery by his simple friendliness had already done much to restore in his mind, for the moment, a normal feeling for life.

"But he feels, Grigg, that you ought to marry again."

Doane shook his head abruptly.

"No," he cried, "I can't consider that. Not now."

"As he said to me, Grigg, 'It is not good for man to be alone!'"

Withery let the subject rest here, and asked about the fighting. The whole outside world was watching these Hansi hills, it appeared. The Imperial Government was already disclaiming responsibility. Troops were on their way, from Hong Kong, from the Philippines, from Indo-China.

"It will be a month or so before they can get out here," mused Doane.

"Oh, yes! At best."

"Meantime, the compound will fall at the first really determined attack. They've been afraid of Pour-mont's machine guns—I heard some of their talk last night, and the night before—but let Kang come to a decision to drive them in and they'll go. That will settle it in a day."

"Will they have the courage?"

"I think so. You and I know these people, Henry. They're brave enough. All they lack is leadership, and organization. And this crowd have a strong fanaticism to hold them up. Once let Kang appeal to their spirit and they'll have to go in to save face. For if they can't be seen the only danger is of an accident here and there. And, for that matter, Kang may simply be waiting for Pourmont to use up his ammunition. It can't last a great while, not in a real siege, which this is."

"By the way," said Withery a little later, "here is a lot of mail for Pourmont's people. It's been accumulating. There was no way to get it to them."

"I'll take it in," said Doane.

"You? You don't mean that you're going to ran that gauntlet again, Grigg?"

"Yes." He untied the packet, and looked through the little heap of envelopes. One was a cablegram addressed to Jonathan Brachey. He held it in tense fingers; gazed at it long while the pulse mounted in his temples. "Oh, yes," he said, almost casually then, "I'm going hack in. They'll be looking for me." But his thoughts were running wild again.

Withery said, before he left, "I'm going to ask you not to answer Hidderleigh's request until you've thought it over carefully. My own feeling is that he is right."

"Suppose," said Doane, "my final decision should be—as I think it will—that I can't go back. What will they do?"

"Then I've promised him, I'll go in and take up your work. As soon as this trouble is over."

"That knocks out your year at home, Henry."

"Yes, but what matters it? Very likely I shall find more happiness in working, after all. That isn't what disturbs me.... Grigg, if you leave the church it will be, I think, the severest blow of my life. I—I'm going to tell you this—for years I've leaned on you. You didn't know, but I've made a better job of my life for knowing that you too were hard at it, just beyond the mountains. We haven't seen much of each other, of late years, but I've felt you there."

Doane's stern face softened as he looked at his old friend.

"And I've felt you, Henry," he replied gently.

"Your blunders are those of strength, not of weakness, Grigg. Perhaps your greatest mistake has been in leaning a little too strongly on yourself. What I want you to consider now is giving self up, in every way."

But Duane shook his great head.

"No, Henry—no! I've given to the uttermost for years. And it has wrecked my life—"

"No, Grigg! Don't say that!"

"Well—put it as you will. The trouble has been that I was doing wrong all the time—for years—as I told you back in Tiaman, I was doing the wrong thing. It led, all of it, to sin. For that sin, of course, I've suffered, and must suffer more. The best reason I could think of for going back would be to keep this added burden off your shoulders. But that would be wrong too.

It's getting a little clearer to me. I know now that I've got to face my doubts and my sins, take them honestly for whatever they may be. Each life must function in its own way. In the eagerness of youth I chose wrong. I must now take the consequences. Good-by, now! There's barely time to slip through the lines before dawn."

Withery rose. "I'll go with you," he said.

"No. I won't allow that. You haven't the strength. You're not an outdoor man We should have to separate anyway; together we should almost certainly be caught. No. You stay here and get word through to them from day to day if you can find any one to undertake it. It will mean everything to them to hear from the outside world. Good luck!"

He took the packet and went out.

3

Again it was dawn Griggsby Doane stood on the crest of a terraced hi'! looking off into the purple west. But a few miles farther on lay Ping Yang.

Beneath him, near the foot of the slope, four coolies were already at the radiating windlasses of a well, and tiny streams of yellow water were trickling along troughs in the loess toward this and that field, where bent silent farmers waited clod in hand to guide the precious fluid from furrow to furrow. Still farther down, along the sunken highway, a few venturesome muleteers led their trains. No outposts in the Looker uniform were to be seen. And he heard no shots. It would be a lull, then, in the fighting.

He descended the hill, dropped into the road, and walked, head high, toward Ping Yang. As he swung along he heard, far off, the shots his ears had strained for on the hill; one, another, then a spattering volley; but he walked straight on. The Mongols and Chihleans on the road gave him no more than the usual glance of curiosity. He passed through a village; Ping Yang would be the next. The railway grade—here an earthen rampart, there a cutting, yonder a temporary wooden trestle—paralleled the highway, cutting into the heart of old China like a surgeon's knife, letting out superstition and festering poverty, letting n the strong fluids of commerce and education. He felt the health of it profoundly, striding on alone through the cool, dear morning air. It was imperfect, of course, this Western civilization that he had so nearly come to doubt; yet, materialistic in its nature or not, it was the best that the world had to offer at the moment. It was what the amazing instinct in man to push on, to better his body and his brain, had brought the world to. It seemed, now, a larger expression of the vitality he felt within himself, the force that he had so lavishly expended in a direction that was wrong for him.

He felt this, which could not have been less than the beginning of a new focus of his misdirected, scattered powers, and yet he walked straight on toward the red army that was sworn to kill all the whites. And though his brain still told him, coolly, without the slightest sense of personal concern, that he would probably be slain within the hour, his heart, or his rising spirit, as calmly dismissed the report.

It might come, of course. He literally didn't care. Death might come at any moment to any man. The present moment was his; and the next, and the next, until the last whenever it should come. He walked with a thrilling sense of power, above the world. For the world, life itself, was suddenly coming back to him. He had been ill—for years, he knew now—of a sick faith. Now he was well. If the old dogmatic religion was gone, he was sensing a new personal religion of work, of healthy functioning, of unquestioning service in the busy instinctive life of the world. He would turn, not away from life to a mystical Heaven, but straight into life at its busiest, head up, as now on the old highway of Hansi, trusting his instinct as a human creature. No matter how difficult the start he would plunge in and live his life out honestly. Betty remained the problem; he knit his brows at the thought; but the new flame in his heart blazed steadily higher. Whatever the problems, he couldn't he headed now.

"What a morbid, sick fool I've been!" It was the cry of a heart new born to health. It occurred to him, then, as he heard his own voice, that this new sense of light had come to him as suddenly as that other light that smote Paul on the Damascus road. It had the force, as he considered it now, of a miracle....

4

The road was blocked ahead. Drawing near, he saw beyond the mules and horses and men of the highway and the curious, pressing country folk a considerable number of yellow turbans crowding the road canyon. There must have been a hundred or more, with many rifle muzzles slanting crazily above them. After a moment the rabble broke toward him.

Doane did not wait for them to discover him, but raising his stick and calling for room to pass he walked in among them. He stood head and shoulders above them, a suddenly appearing white giant whom a few resisted at first, but more gave way to as he pushed firmly through. Emerging on the farther side he walked on his way without so much as looking back. And not a shot had been fired.

The road wound its way between steep walls of loess, so that ii was impossible at any point to see far ahead. He came upon other, smaller groups of the Lookers. Only one man, the largest of them, threatened him, but as the man raised the butt of his rifle Doane snatched the weapon from him and knocked him down with it; then tossed it aside and strode on as before.

He came at length to a scenic arch in a notch. Through the arch Ping Yang could be seen in its valley.

He stopped and looked. Near at hand were the tents of some of the Looker soldiery; beyond lay the village; and beyond that on the hillside, the compound of the company, lying as still as if it were deserted. There were no puffs of smoke, no sounds along the village street; between the outlying houses small figures appeared to Le bustling about, but they made no noise that could be heard up here. The scene was uncanny.

Doane, however, went on down the hill. None of the Lookers were in evidence now on the winding street, but only the silent, curious villagers; this until two soldiers in blue came abruptly out of a house; and then two others firmly holding by the arms a man in red and yellow with an embroidered square on the breast of his tunic that marked him as an officer of rank. Other soldiers followed, one bearing a large curved sword.

Doane stopped to watch.

Without ceremony the officer's wrists were tied behind his back. He was kicked to his knees. A blue soldier seized his queue and with it jerked his head forward. The swordsman, promptly, with one clean blow', severed the neck; then wiped his sword on the dead man's clothing and marched away with the others, carrying the head.

Duane shivered slightly, compressed his lips, and, paler, walked on. He passed other blue soldiers in the heart of the village, and a row of Lookers standing without arms. Emerging from the straggling groups of houses beyond the village wall he took the road up the hill. Away up the slope he could see the men of the outposts standing and sitting on the parapets of the rifle pits. At the gate of the compound he called out.

The gate opened, and closed behind him. Within stood men of the garrison, and women, and behind them the Chinese. All looked puzzled. Many tongues greeted him at once, eagerly questioning.

He looked about from one to another of the thin weary faces with burning eyes that hung on his slightest gesture, and slowly shook his head. He could answer none of their questions. He was searching for one face that meant more to him than all the others. It was not there. He walked on toward the house occupied by the Boatwrights. Just as he was turning in there he saw Betty. She was tunning across from the residence.

"On, Dad!" she cried. "You're back!" Her arms were around his neck. "How wonderful! And you're well—like your old self."

"Better than my old self, dear"

"Better than my old self, dear," he said, with a tender smile, and kissed her forehead.

"I can't stay, Dad. I just ran out. Wasn't it strange—I saw you from the window! But what's happened? What is it? Everybody's so puzzled. Have the troops come?".

He shook his head.

"But it's something. Everybody's terribly excited."

"I don't understand it myself, dear. Though I walked through it, apparently."

"Oh, look! They're opening the gate! What is it?" She hopped with impatience, like a child, and clapped her hands. "Oh, I mustn't stay! But tell m, do you think this dreadful business is over?"

"I believe it is, Betty."

She ran back to her post. And he returned to the gate.

An odd little cavalcade was moving deliberately up the hill. In front marched a soldier in blue bearing a large white flag (an obviously Western touch, this). Behind him came a squad in column of fours, on foot and unarmed; then a green sedan chair with four pole-men; behind this three pavilions with carved wooden tops, of the sort carried in wedding processions, each with four bearers; and last another squad of foot soldiers.

Just outside the gate they came to a halt. The soldiers formed in line on either side of the road. An officer advanced and asked permission to enter. This was granted. At once the chairmen set down their burden. The carved door opened, and a young Chinese gentleman stepped out. He was tall, slim, with large spectacles; and moved with a quiet dignity that amounted to a distinction of bearing. His long robe was of shimmering blue silk embroidered in rose and gold; and the embroidered emblem on his breast exhibited the silver pheasant of a mandarin of the fifth class. On his head, the official, bowl-shaped straw hat with red tassel was surmounted with a ball or button of crystal an inch in diameter set in a mount of exquisitely worked gold. His girdle clasp also was of worked gold with a plain silver button. The shoes that appeared beneath the hem of his robe were richly embroidered and had thick white soles.

Calmly, deliberately, he entered the compound. One of the engineers, an American, addressed him in the Mandarin tongue. He replied, in a deep musical voice, with a pronounced intonation that gave this mellow language, to a casual ear, something the sound of French.

The engineer bowed, and together they moved toward the residence, where a somewhat mystified M. Pourmont awaited them. But first the mandarin turned and signaled to the pavilion bearers, who still waited outside the gate. These came in now, and it became evident that the ornate structures were laden with gifts. There were platters of fruits and of sweetmeats, bottles of wine, cooked dishes, and small caskets, some carved, others lacquered, that might have contained jewels.

Doane, quietly observing the scene, found something familiar in the appearance of the envoy. Something vaguely associated with the judge's yamen at T'ainan-fu. Certainly, on some occasion, he had seen the man. He stood for a brief time watching the two figures, a white man in stained brown clothing, unkempt of appearance but vigorous in person, walking beside the elegant young mandarin, appearing oddly crude beside him, curiously lacking in the grace that marked every slightest movement of the silk-clad

Oriental; and the picture dwelt for a time among his thoughts—the oldest civilization in the world, and the youngest. Crude vigor, honest health, contrasted with a decadence that clung meticulously to every slightest subtlety of etiquette. And behind the two, towering above the heads of the ragged bearers, the curving pointed roofs of the three pavilions, still gaily bizarre in form and color despite the weatherbeaten condition of the paint; a childish touch, suggestive of circus day in an American village. Suggestive, too, whimsically, of the second childhood of the oldest race.

Doane, reflecting thus, slowly followed them to the residence.

5

Jonathan Brachey sat moodily on the parapet. Down below, the compound (a crowded mass of roofs within a rectangle of red-gray wail) and below that the straggling village, stood out as blocked-in masses of light and shadow under the slanting rays of the morning sun.

A French youth, beside him, polishing his rifle with a greasy rag, looked up with a question.

Brachey shook his head; he had no information. He looked over toward the other pit. The Australian in command there (three nights earlier they had buried Swain) waved a carelessly jocular hand and went on nibbling a biscuit.

The thing might be over; it might not. Brachey found himself almost perversely disturbed, however, at the prospect of peace. He had supposed that he hated this dirty, bloody business. He saw no glory in fighting, merely primitive blood-lust; an outcropping of the beast in man; evidence that in his age-long struggle upward from the animal stage of existence man had yet a long, long way to climb. But from the thought of losing this intense preoccupation, of living quietly with the emphasis again placed on personal problems, he found himself shrinking. What a riddle it was!

He spoke shortly to the French youth, took up his own rifle, and led the way up the hill to the bullet-spattered farm compounds. They were quite deserted. Only the huddled, noxious dead remained. He went on up the hillside, searching all the hiding-places of those red and yellow vandals who had filled his thoughts by day and haunted his sleep at, night; but all were empty of human life. A great amount of rubbish was left—cooking utensils, knives, old Chinese-made rifles and swords, bits of uniforms. He found even a jade ring and a few strings of brass cash.

Weary of spirit he returned to the rifle pits only to find these, too, deserted. From the upper redoubt a man was waving, beckoning. Apparently the compound gate was open, and a group of soldiers standing in line outside; but these soldiers wore blue. Through his glasses he surveyed the moving dots near the village; none wore red and yellow.

The man was still waving from the redoubt. The French youth, he found now, was looking up at him, that eager question still in his eyes. He nodded. With a sudden wild shout the boy ran down the hill, waving bis rifle over his head.

So it was peace—sudden, enigmatic. Brachey sat again on the parapet. Griggsby Doane was doubtless there (Brachey knew nothing of his journey; he had not seen Betty. What could he say to him, to the father whom Betty loved?

This wouldn't do, of course. He rose, a set dogged expression on his long, always serious face, and went slowly down the hill; and with only a nod to this person and that got to his tent. Once within, he closed the flaps and sat on the cot. He discovered then that he had brought with him one of the strings of cash, and jingled it absently against his knee.

Voices sounded outside. Men were standing before the tent.

Then the flaps parted, and he beheld the spectacled, pleasantly smiling face of Mr. Po.

"Oh," he said, more shortly than he knew. "Come in!"

Mr. Po stepped inside, letting the flaps fall together behind him. He made a splendid figure in blue and gold, as he removed the round hat with its red plume and crystal ball and laid it on the rude table.

"I'm glad to see you're still sound of life and limb and fresh as a daisy," he remarked cheerfully. "With permission I will sit here a bit for informal how-do chin-chin, and forget from minute to minute all ceremonial dam-foolishness."

CHAPTER XXI
THE SOULS OF MEN

1

WELL," continued Mr. Po expansively, "I've certainly had a pretty kettle of fish about my ears."

Brachey filled and lighted his pipe, and yielded his senses for a moment to the soothing effect of the fragrant smoke.

"Is the fighting really over?" he asked.

"Oh, yes!"

"But why? What's happened?"

Mr. Po indulged in his easy, quiet laugh.

"To begin at first blush," he said, settling comfortably back as If launched on a long narrative, "while out on scouting leap in dark I stumbled plump on Lookers, and by thunder, it was necessary to trust broken reed of lying on stomach hi open ground!"

"They caught you?"

"Oh, yes! For hell of a while I held breath, but with dust in nose it became unavoidable to sneeze. I would then have lost head promptly but officer of yamen entourage of Kang spotted me and said, 'What the devil you doing_ here!' With which I explain of course that I escape by hook or crook from white devils. Then I appear before general and demand audience discussion with old Kang. Old reprobate received me and made long speech. Perfectly absurd! He said I must go to T'ainan-fu as his particular guest and speak to His Excellency Pao Ting Chuan his message, like this:

"'For many years I have known and respected your abilities as scholar and statesman of huge understanding ability. We have both seen, you and I, continuing unprincipled encroachment of foreign devil on preserves of our ancient and fruitful land, while the sorrow of our own Hansi Province under heel of foreign mining syndicate despot is matter of common ill repute to us both. Now as loyal friend and unswervingly determined on destroying all evil influence of foreign devils, I invite you as guest to share with me pleasure of witnessing capture and utter destruction of foreign compound at Ping Yang. Omens agree on midnight of to-day week, following banquet of state and theatrical performance at my headquarters, at which favorite amateur actor Wang Lo Hsu will recite historical masterpiece, "The Song of Wun Hsing." And as my cooks are all wretched creatures, unworthy of catering to poorest classes, I beg of you bring delicately expert cook of Canton that I may again rejoice in delightful memory of sweet lotus soup.'"

Mr. Po paused to light a cigarette.

"So you went back to Tiainan?" asked Brachey.

"Oh, no, I was taken back against grain as prisoner of large armed guard."

"And you delivered the message?"

"Oh, yes!"

"Pao didn't accept, of course. Though I don't see how he could get out of it. He had no soldiers to speak of, did he?"

"Oh, yes, some. These he sent by northern road to region of Shan Tang, only thirty *li* away from Ping Yang. And then he accept, for His Excellency is great statesman. Nobody yet ever put it over on His Excellency, not so you could notice it. Without frown or smile he assemble secretaries, runners and lictors of yamen. banner-men, some concubines and eunuchs and come post-haste."

"So he's here now?"

"Oh, yes. We have large establishment at temple over on neighboring hill. And everything's all right. O. K."

"You'll forgive me if I don't at all understand why."

"Naturally. I am going to make clear as cotton print. For a day or so everything was as disorderly as the dickens, of course. You couldn't hear yourself think. And sleep? My God, there wasn't *any*. And of course after death of old reprobate Lookers went to pieces and raised Ned. It became necessary to punish leaders and all that sort of thing. You see, Dame Rumor gets move on in China, runs around like scared chicken, faster than telegraph, I sometimes think. And when Lookers heard stories, that Imperial Government up at Peking wasn't so crazy about giving them support, and might even hand them double-cross lemon, they began to think about patching holes in fences. They just blew up. And His Excellency"—he chuckled—"he grasped situation like chain lightning. Oh, but he's whale of a fellow, His Excellency!" Brachey smoked reflectively as he studied this curiously bloodless enthusiast. Evidently behind the humorously inadequate English speech of Mr. Po there was, if it could be got at, a stirring drama of intrigue. A typical Oriental drama, bearing a smooth surface of silken etiquette but essentially cruel and bloody. The difficulty would be, of course, in getting at it, drawing it out piecemeal and putting it together.

"His Excellency will now clean up whole shooting match," Mr. Po went on. "No more Ho Shan Company!" And he waved his cigarette about to indicate the compound.

"Oh, that goes, too?"

"Oh, yes! His Excellency has at once telegraphed agent-general at Tientsin for final show-down price on surrender of all leases, agreements, expenses, bribes and absolute good riddance. They say three million taels cash. To-morrow we shall throw it at their heads. And so much for that!"

"H'm!" mused Brachey. "Pretty quick work. Rather takes one's breath away."

"Oh, yes! But His Excellency's son of a gun."

"Evidently. But I'm still in the dark as to how this rather extraordinary change came about. Did I understand you to say that Kang is dead?"

"Oh, yes! Night before last."

"How did that happen?"

"Oh, well—it's just as well not to give this away—on arrival at Ping Yang His Excellency made at once prepare bowl of sweet lotus soup and send it with many compliments and hopes of good omens to old devil."

"You mean—there was poison in it?"

"Oh, yes! Pretty darned hard to put it over His Excellency. After that it was no trouble at all to behead commanders of Looker troops."

"Naturally," was Brachey's only comment. He proceeded to draw out, bit by bit, other details of the story.

Some one stepped before the tent, and a strong voice called:

"Mr. Brachey."

With a nervously abrupt movement Brachey sprang up and threw back the flaps; and beheld, standing there, stooping in order that he might see within, the giant person of Griggsby Doane.

2

Brachey bowed coldly. Doane's strong gaunt face worked perceptibly.

Brachey said:

"Won't you come in, sir? The tent is"—there was a pause—"the tent is small, but... You are perhaps acquainted with Mr. Po Sui-an of the yamen of His Excellency Pao Ting Chuan."

Mr. Doane bowed toward the Chinese gentleman.

"I think I have seen Mr. Po at the yamen," he said, speaking now in the slow grave way of the old Griggsby Doane. "You bring good news?"

"Oh, yes!" Mr. Po lighted a cigarette. "We shall doubtless in jiffy see you again at T'ainan-fu."

Doane looked thoughtfully, intently at him, then replied in the simple phrase, "It may be." To Brachey he said now, producing a white envelope, "I found this, cablegram held for you at Shau T'ing, sir."

Brachey took the envelope; stood stiffly holding it unopened before him. For a moment the eyes of these two men met. Then Doane broke the tension by simply raising his head, an action which removed it from the view of the men within the tent.

"Good morning," he said rather gruffly. And "Good morning, Mr. Po."

He was well out of ear-shot when Brachey's gray lips mechanically uttered the two words, "Thank you." From a distant corner of the compound came the fresh voices of young men—Americans and Australian and English—raised in crudely pleasant harmony They were singing *My Bonnie Lies Over the Ocean*. As they swung into the rolling, rollicking refrain, women's voices joined in faintly from here and there about the compound.... Brachey seemed to be listening. Then, again, abruptly starting into action, he stepped outside the tent and stared across the courtyard after Griggby Doane.... Then, as abruptly, he remembered his guest and returned within the tent, with an almost muttered "I beg your pardon."

"Oh, go on—read your cablegram!" said Mr. Po good-humoredly.

Bradley looked at him; then at the envelope—turning it slowly over. His hands trembled. This fact appeared to disturb him. He held one hand out before his face and watched it intently, finally lowering it with a quick nervous shake of the head. He seated himself again on the cot; tore off an end of the envelope; caught his breath; then sat motionless with the bit of paper that meant to him everything in life, or nothing, hanging between limp fingers. A puzzling reminder of the strange man, Griggsby Doane, was the painful throbbing in his head.... They were singing again, about the compound—it was the college song of his youth, *Solomon Levi*.

He thought, with another of those odd little mental and physical jerks, again of his guest; and heard himself saying—weakly it seemed, like a man talking in dreams—"You will think me..." But found himself addressing an empty enclosure of canvas. Mr. Po had slipped out and dropped the flaps. That he could have done this unobserved frightened Brachey a little. He looked again at his trembling hand.

Again he raised the envelope. Until this moment he had assumed that it could be but one message to himself and Betty; but now he knew vividly better.

Anything might have happened. It was unthinkable that he should want the courage to read it. He had foreseen no such difficulty. Perhaps if it had come by any other hand than that of Griggsby Doane....

His thoughts wandered helplessly back over the solitary life he had led... wandering in Siam and Borneo and Celebes, dwelling here and there in untraveled corners of India, picking up the quaint folklore of the Malay Peninsula, studying the American sort of social organization in the Philippines... eight years of it! He had begun as a disheartened young man, running bitterly away from the human scheme in which he found no fitting niche. Yes, that was it, after all; he had run away! He had begun with a defeat, based his working life on just that. The five substantial books that now stood to his name in every well-stocked library in America, as in many in England and on the Continent, were, after all, but stop-gaps in an empty life. They were a subterfuge, those books.........All the hard work, the eager close thinking, was now, suddenly, meaningless. That he had chosen work instead of drink, that he had been, after all, a decent fellow, pursuing neither chance nor women, seemed immaterial.

The curse of an active imagination was on him now, and was riding him as wildly as ever witch rode a broomstick.

The very bit of paper in his hand was nothing if not the symbol of his terrible failure in the business called living. As he had built his work on failure, was he, inevitably, to build the happiness of himself and Betty on the same painful foundation. Even if the paper should announce his freedom? Bitterly he repeated aloud the word, "Freedom!" Then "Happiness?"... What were these elusive things? Were they in any sense realities?

He nerved himself and read the message:

"Absolute decree granted you are free."

He tossed it, with its unpunctuated jumble of words, on the table.

A little later, though he still indulged in this scathing self-analysis, the habit of meeting responsibilities that was more strongly a part of his nature than in this hour of utter emotion he knew, began to assert itself. The strong character that had led him, after all, out to fight and to build his mental house, was largely the man.

He slowly got up and stood before the square bit of mirrror that hung on the rear tent-pole; then looked down at his mud-stained clothes. Deliberately, almost painfully, he shaved and dressed. It was characteristic that he put on a stiff linen collar.

There was, to a man of his stripe, just one thing to do: and that thing he was going at directly, firmly. Until it was done he could not so much as speak to Betty. Of the outcome of this effort he had no notion; he was going at it doggedly, with his character rather than with his mind. Indeed the mind quibbled, manufactured little delays, hinted at evasions. He even listened to these whisperings, entertained them; but meanwhile went straight on with his dressing.

3

As he emerged from the tent sudden noises assailed his ears. A line of young men danced in lock step, doing a serpentine from one areaway to another, and waving and shouting merrily as they passed. There was still the singing, somewhere; one of the songs of Albert Chevalier, who had not then been forgotten. He heard vaguely, with half an ear, the enthusiastic outburst of sound on the final line:

"Missie 'Enry 'Awkins is a first-class nyme!"

So it was a day of celebration! He had forgotten that it would be. But of course! Even the Chinese were at it; he could hear one of their flageolets wailing, and, more faintly, stringed instruments.

He walked directly to the building occupied by the Boatwrights; sent in his card to Mr. Doane.

He was shown into a little cubicle of a room. Here was the huge man, rising from an absurdly small work table that had been crowded in by the window, between the wall and the foot of the bed. He was writing, apparently, a long letter.

Brachey, an odd figure to Doane's eyes, in his well-made suit and stiff white collar, stood on the sill, as rigid as a soldier at attent ion.

"I am interrupting you," he said, almost curtly,

For the first time Griggsby Doane caught a glimpse of the man Brachey behind that all but forbidding front; and he hesitated, turning for a moment, stacking his papers together, and with a glance at the open window laying a book across them.

He had said, kindly enough, "Oh, no, indeed! Come right in." But his thoughts were afield, or else he was busily, quickly, rearranging them.

Brachey stepped within, and closed the door. Here they were, these two, at last, shut together in a room. It was a moment of high tension.

"Sit down," said Doane, still busying himself at the table, but waving an immense hand toward the other small chair.

But Brachey stood... waiting... in his hand a folded paper.

Finally Doane lifted his head, with a brusk but not unpleasant, "Yes, sir?"

Brachey, for a moment, pressed his lips tightly together.

"Mr. Doane," he said then, clipping his words off short, "may I first ask you to read this cablegram?"

Doane took the paper, started to unfold it, but then dropped it on the table and stepped forward.

And now for the first time Brachey sensed, behind this great frame and the weary, haggard face, the real Griggsby Doane; and stood very still, fighting for control over the confusion in his aching head. This was, he saw now, a strong man; a great deal more of a personality than he had supposed he would find. Even before the next words, he felt something of what was coming, something of the vigorous honesty of the man. Doane had been through recent suffering, that was clear Something—-and even then, in one of his keen mental dashes, Brachey suspected that it was a much more personal experience than the Looker attack—something had upset him. This wasn't a man to turn baby over a wound, or to lose his head in a little fighting. No, it was an illness of the soul that had hollowed the eyes and deepened the grooves between them. But it didn't matter. What did matter was that he was now, in this gentle mood, surprisingly like Betty. For she had a curious vein of honesty; and she said, at times, just such unexpectedly frank, wholly open things as he felt (with an opening heart) that the father was about to say now.

"Mr. Brachey"—this was what he said, with extraordinary simplicity of manner—"can you take my hand?"

If Brachey had spoken his reply his voice would have broken. Instead he gripped the proffered hand. And during a brief moment they stood there.

"Now," said Doane quietly, "sit down." And he read the cablegram. After some quiet thought he said, "Have you come to ask for Betty?"

The directness of this question made speech, to Brachey, even more nearly impossible than before. He bowed his head.

Doane had dropped into the little chair by the little table. He sat, now, thinking and absently weighing the cablegram in one hand. Finally, reaching a conclusion, he rose again.

"The best way, I think, will be to settle this thing now." He appeared to be speaking as much to himself as to his caller. "I'll get Betty. You won't mind waiting? They don't have call bells in this house." And he returned the cablegram and went out of the room, leaving the door ajar behind him.

Brachey stepped over to the window, thinking he might see Betty when she came, but it gave on an inner court. He stared out at the gray tiling. The moment was, to him, terrible. He stood on the threshold of that strange region of the spirit that is called happiness. The door, always before closed to him (except the one previous experience when it proved but an entry into bitterness and desolation) had opened, here at the last, amazingly, at his touch. And he was afraid to look.

It seemed an hour later when footsteps sounded outside, and the outer door opened. Then they came in, father and daughter.

Betty, rather white, stood hesitant, looking from one to the other. Doane placed a gently protecting arm about her slim shoulders.

"I haven't told her," he said. "That is for you to do. I want you both to wait while I look for the others."

He was gone. Betty came slowly forward. Brachey handed her the cablegram.

"I—I can't read it," she said, with a tremulous little laugh. "John—I'm crying!"

4

The door squeaked. Miss Hemphill looked in; stopped short; then in a sudden confusion of mind in which indignation struggled with bewilderment for the upper hand, stepped back into the hall. Before she could come down on the decision to flee, Dr. Cassin joined her; curiously, carrying her medicine case.

To the physician's brisk, "Mr. Doane sent word to come here at once. Do you know what is the matter?" Miss Hemphill could only reply, rather acidly, "I can't imagine!"

Mrs. Boatwright came into the corridor then, followed by Doane. She walked with firm dignity, her enigmatic face squarely set. And when he ushered them into the room, she entered without a word, but remained near the door.

For a long moment the room was still; a hush settling over them that intensified the difficulty in the situation. Miss Hemphill stared down at the matting. Mrs. Boatwright's eyes were fixed firmly on the wall over the bed. The one audible sound was the heavy breathing of Griggsby Doane, who stood with his back to the door, brows knit, one hand reaching a little way before him. He appeared, to the shrewd eyes of Dr. Cassin, like a man in deep suffering. But when he spoke it was with the poise, the sense of dominating personality, that she had felt and admired during all the earlier years of their long association. Of late he had been ill of a subtle morbid disease of which she had within the week witnessed the nearly tragic climax; but now he was well again.... Mary Cassin was a woman of considerable practical gifts. Her medical experience, illuminated as it had been by wide scientific reading, gave her a first-hand knowledge of the human creature and a tolerant elasticity of judgment that contrasted oddly with the professed tenets of her church, with their iron classification as sin of much that is merely honest human impulse, that might even, properly, be set down as human need. She saw clearly enough that the quality in the human creature that is called, usually, force, is essentially emotional in its content—and that the person gifted with force therefore must be plagued with emotional problems that increase in direct ratio with the gift. Unlike Mrs. Boatwright, who was, of course, primarily a moralist, Mary Cassin possessed the other great gift of dispassionate, objective thought. I think she had long known the nature of Doane's problem. Certainly she knew that no medical skill could help him; her advice, always practical, would have taken the same direction as Dr. Hidderleigh's. It brought her a glow of something not unlike happiness to see that now he was well. The cure, whatever it might prove to have been, was probably mental. Knowing Griggsby Doane as she did, that was the only logical conclusion. For she knew how strong he was.

"There has existed among us a grave misapprehension"—thus Doane—"one in which, unfortunately, I have myself been more grievously at fault than any of you. I wish, now, before you all, to acknowledge my own confusion in this matter, and, further, to clear away any still existing misunderstanding in your minds.... Mr. Brachey has established the fact that he is eligible to become Betty's husband. That being the case, I can only add that I shall accept him as my only son-in-law with pride and satisfaction. He has proved himself worthy in every way of our respect and confidence."

Mary Cassin broke the hush that followed by stepping quickly forward and kissing Betty; after which she gave her hand warmly to Brachey. Then with a word about her work at the hospital she went briskly out.

Miss Hemphill started forward, only to hesitate and glance in a spirit of timid inquiry at the implacable Mrs. Boatwright. To her simple, unquestioning faith, Mr. Doane and Mary Cassin could not together be wrong; yet her closest daily problem was that of living from hour to hour under the businesslike direction of Mrs. Boatwright. However, having started, and lacking the harsh strength of character to be cruel, she went on, took the hands of Betty and Brachey in turn, and wished them happiness. Then she, too, hurried away.

Elmer Boatwright was studying his wife. His color was high, his eyes nervously bright. He was studying, too, Griggsby Doane, who had for more than a decade been to him almost an object of worship. Moved by an impulse, perhaps the boldest of his life—and just as his wife said, coldly, "I'm sure I wish you happiness," and moved toward the door—he went over and caught Betty and Brachey each by a hand.

"I haven't understood this," he said—and tears stood in his eyes as he smiled on them—"but now I'm glad. Betty, we are all going to be proud of the man you have chosen. I'm proud of him now."

CHAPTER XXII
BEGINNINGS

1

THE day of sudden and dramatic peace was drawing near its close. Seated on the parapet of a rifle pit Betty and Brachey looked out over the red-brown valley. Long, faintly purple shadows lay along the hillside and in the deeper hollows. From the compound, half-way down the slope, a confusion of pleasant sounds came to their ears—youthful voices, snatches of song, an energetically whistled Sousa march, the quaintly plaintive whine of Chinese woodwinds—while above the roofs of tile and iron within the rectangle of wall (that was still topped with brown sand-bags) wisps of smoke drifted lazily upward.

"It seems queer," mused he, aloud, "sitting here like this, with everything so peaceful. During the fighting I didn't feel nervous, but now I start at every new sound. I loathed it, too; but now, this evening, I miss it, in a way." He gazed moodily down into the short trench. "Right there," he said, "young Bartlett was hit."

"And you brought him in under fire."

"A Chinaman helped me."

"Oh, it was you," she said. "He wouldn't have done it. I watched from the window." Her chin was propped on two small lists; her eyes, reflective, were looking out over the compound and the valley toward the walled temple on the opposite slope with its ornate, curving roofs and its little group of trees that were misty with young foliage. "I've been thinking a good deal about that, and some other things. All you said, back there on the ship, about independence and responsibility."

"I don't believe I care to remember that," said he quietly.

"But, John, if you will say startling, strong things to an impressionable girl—and I suppose that's all I was then—you can't expect her to forget them right away."

His face relaxed into a faint, fleeting smile. But she went earnestly on.

"Of course I know it wasn't really long ago. Not if you measure it by weeks. But if you measure it by human experience it was—well, years."

He was sober again; cheek on hand, gazing out into those lengthening, deepening shadows.

"That was what we quarreled about, John. I felt terribly upset. I was blue—I can't tell you! Just the thought of all your life meant to you, and how I seemed to be spoiling it."

A strong hand drew one of hers down and closed about it. "I'm going to try to tell you something, dear," he said. "You thought that what I said to you, on the ship, was an expression of a real philosophy of life."

"But what else could it have been, John?"

"It was just a chip—right here." He raised her hand and with it patted his shoulder. "It was what I'd tried for years to believe. I was bent on believing it. You know, Betty, the thing we assert most positively isn't our real faith. We don't have to assert that. It's likely to be what we're trying to convince ourselves of.... I'm just beginning to understand that, just lately, since you came into my life—and during the fighting. I had to bolster myself up in the faith that a man can run away, live alone, because it seemed to be the only basis on which I, as I was, could deal with life. The only way I could get on at all. But you see what happened to me. Life followed me and finally caught me, away out here in China. No, you can't get away from it. You can't live selfishly. It won't work. We're all in together. We've got to think of the others..... I'm like a beginner now—going to school to life. I don't even know what I believe. Not any more. I—I'm eager to learn, from day to day. The only thing I'm sure of"... he turned, spoke with breathless awe in his voice... "is that I love you, dear That's the foundation on which my life has got to be built. It's my religion, I'm afraid."

Betty's eyes filled; her little fingers twisted in among his; but she didn't speak then.

The shadows stretched farther and farther along the hillside. The sun, a huge orange disc descending amid coppery strips of shining cloud, touched the rim of the western hills; slid smoothly, slowly down behind it, leaving a glowing vault of gold and rose and copper overhead and a luminous haze in the valley. Off to the eastward, toward Shau T'ing and the crumbling ruins of the Southern Wall (which still winds sinuously for hundreds of miles in and out of the valleys, and over and around the hills) the tumbling masses of upheaved rock and loess were deeply purple against a luminous eastern sky.

"Will you let me travel with you, John? I've thought that I could draw while you write. Maybe I could even help you with your books. It would be wonderful—exploring strange places. I'd like to go down through Yunnan, and over the border into Siam and Assam and the Burmah country. I've been reading about it, sitting in the hospital at night."

"There would be privation—and dangers."

"I don't care."

"You wouldn't be afraid?"

"Not with you. And if—if anything happened to you, I'd want to go, too.... Of course, there'd be other problems coming up. Don't think I'm altogether impractical, dear."

"What are you thinking of?"

She hesitated. "Children, John. I know we shan't either of us be satisfied to live just for our happiness in each other. I couldn't help thinking about that, watching you here, during the siege."

"No, we shan't."

"And with your work what it is—what it's got to be there's our first problem."

"We'll have to take life as it comes."

"Yes, I know." They were silent again. Gradually the brilliant color was fading from the sky and the distant hills softening into mystery.... "Father says that we'll find marriage a job—"

"Oh, it's that!"

"Full of surprises and compromises and giving up. He says it's very difficult, but very wonderful."

"I should think," said Brachey, his voice somewhat unsteady, "that it would be the most wonderful job in the world. Its very complexities, the nature of the demands it must make."

"I know!"

After a long silence he asked, so abruptly that she looked swiftly up:

"Do you ever pray, dear?"

"Why—yes, I do."

"Will you teach me? I've tried—up here in the trenches. I've thought that maybe I'd pick up a copy of the English prayer-book. They'd have it at Shanghai or Tientsin...."

Dusk was mounting the hill-slopes.

"It was a strange talk father and I had. Nearly all the afternoon—while you were checking up ammunition and things. It's the first time he's really sat down with me like that like a friend, I mean—and talked out, just as he felt. Oh, he's been kind. But it's queer about father and me. You see, when they sent me over to the States, I was really only a child. Mother was dead then, you know. Father was always hoping to get over to see me, but there was all the strain of building up the missions after the Boxer trouble, and then he'd had his vacation. And he couldn't afford to bring me out here just for the journey."

Brachey broke in here. "Did you ask him if he would marry us?"

She nodded. "Yes. And he won't. That's partly what I'm going to tell you. He's resigned."

"From the church?"

"Yes. He thought of having Mr. Boatwright do it. But it seems that his position is rather difficult. On account of his wife. She'll never be friendly to us."

"Oh, no!"

"I could see, though, that Dad was glad about our plan for an early wedding. Of course, he's had me to think of, every minute. He did say that the certain knowledge that I'm cared for will make it easier for him to carry out his plans. But he wouldn't tell me what the plans are. It's odd. He doesn't like to think of me as a responsibility. I could see that. I mean, that he might have to do something he didn't believe in in order to earn money for me. He said that he's been for years in a false position. I never saw him so happy. He acts as if he'd been set free."

"Perhaps he has," Brachey reflected aloud. "It is strange—almost as if we represented opposite swings of the pendulum, he and I. Perhaps we do. I've not had enough responsibility, he's had too much. Probably one extreme's as unhealthy as the other."

"I've worried some about him, John. But he begs me not to. He's planning now to sell all his things."

"All?"

"Everything. Books, even. And his desk, that he's had since the first years out here. Mr. Withery is going to be in charge at T'ainan, and Dad's leaving the final arrangements to him."

"You speak as if your father were going away, far off. And in a hurry."

"He is. That's the strange thing. Just to tell about it, like this, makes it seem'—well, almost wild. But when you talk with him you feel all right about it. He's so steady and sure. Just as if at last he's hit on the truth."

The night drew its cloak swiftly over the valley. For a long time after this conversation they sat there in silent communion with the dim hills; she nestling in his arms; he dreaming of the years to come in which his life—such was his hope—might through love find balance and warmth.

3

Doane was at the residence when Brachey left Betty there—at the door, chatting with M. Pourmont. He walked away with Brachey. And the tired but still genial Frenchman looked after them with a puzzled frown.

"Stroll a bit with me, will you?" said Doane. "I've got a few things to say to you." And outside the gate, he added soberly: "About the beastly thing I did."

"I've forgotten that," said Brachey; stiffly, in spite of himself.

"No, you haven't. You never will. Neither shall I. What I have to say is just this—it was an overwrought, half-mad man who attacked you."

"Of course, I've come to see that. All you'd been through."

"What I'd been through, Brachey, wasn't merely hardship, fighting, wounds. It was something else, the wreck of my life. I'd had to stand by, in a way, and look at the wreckage. I was doing the wrong thing, living wrong, living a lie. For years I fought it, without being able to see that I was fighting life itself. You see, Brachey, the power of dogmatic thinking is great. It circumscribed my sense of truth for years."

He fell silent for a moment, looking up at the stars. Then, simply, he added this:

"I want you to know the whole truth. I feel that it is due you. My struggle ended in sin. The plainest kind—with a woman—and without a shred of even human justification. Just degradation.... I can see now that it was a terrific shock. It nearly pulled me under, very nearly. They want me to stay in the church, but I can't, of course."

"No," said Brachey, "you wouldn't want to do that."

"I couldn't. I went through the more or less natural morbid phases, of course. That attack on you—"

"That was partly exhaustion," said Brachey. "You weren't in condition to analyze a situation that would have been difficult for anybody. And of course I was in the position of breaking my pledge to you."

"It was more than that, Brachey. The primitive resurgence in me simply reached its climax then. No—let me have this out! I suspected you because I had learned to suspect myself. That blow was a direct result of my own sin. And I want you to know that I've come to see it for what it was."

"H'm!" mused Brachey. They were standing by a pile of weathering timbers, beside the old Chinese highway. "Shall we sit a while?" Then—"I'd have to think about that." Finally—"I don't know but what your analysis is sound. But"—he mused longer, then, his voice clouded with emotion, broke out with—"God, man, what you must have suffered! And after our row…. I can't bear to think of it." And then, quite forgetting himself, he rested a hand on Doane's arm. It was perhaps the first time in his adult life that he had done so demonstrative a thing.

Doane compressed his lips, in the darkness, and stared away.

"Oh, yes," he replied, after a moment, "I've suffered, of course. I even made a rather cowardly try at suicide."

"No—not—"

"On my return from Shau T'ing I walked into the Looker lines in broad daylight. I rather hoped to go out that way. But the fighting was over. I couldn't even get killed."

He seemed as confiding as a child, this grave powerful man. And he was Betty's father! Brachey was sensitively eager to help him.

"Betty said you had new plans. I wonder if you would feel like telling me of them."

"Yes. I've meant to."

"Are you going back to the States?"

"No. Not now. Not with things like this. My worldly possessions, when everything is sold, will probably come down to a thousand or fifteen hundred dollars. My library is worth a good deal more than that, but won't bring it. I have a little in cash; not much. I've estimated that two hundred dollars—gold, not Mex.—will get me down to Shanghai and tide me over the first few delays. I'm giving Betty the rest, and arranging for Withery to turn over to her the proceeds of any sale."

"But what are you going to do down there?"

"Work. Preferably, for a while, with my hands."

"You don't mean at common labor?"

"Yes. Why not? I have a real gift for it. And I'm very strong."

"That would mean putting yourself with yellow coolies. The whites wouldn't like it; probably they wouldn't let you. And you have a brain. You're a trained executive."

"I won't take a small mental job. A large one—-that would really keep me busy—yes. But there'll be no chance of that at first. And I must be fully occupied. I want to be outdoors. I may take up some branch of engineering, by way of private study. But at the moment I really don't care...." He smiled, in the dark. Brachey felt the smile in his voice when he spoke again. "I was forty-five years old this spring, Brachey. That's young, really. I have this great physical strength. And I'm free. If I have sinned, I have really no bad habits. I probably shan't be happy long without slipping my shoulders under some new burden—a good heavy one. But don't you see how interesting it will be to start new, at nothing, with nothing? What an adventure?"

"It won't be with nothing, quite. There's your experience, your mental equipment. With that, and health, and a little luck you can do anything."

"Yes," said Doane, "it is, after all, a clean start. I've been terribly shaken."

"So have I," said Brachey gently. "And I'm starting new, too." He rose; stood for a moment quietly thinking; then turned and extended his hand. "Mr. Doane, here we are, meeting at life's crossroads. You're starting out on something pretty like my old road, and I'm starting on a road not altogether unlike yours. The next few years are going to mean everything to each of us. And what we both do with our lives is going to mean everything to Betty. Let's, between us, make Betty happy." His voice was a little out of control, but he went resolutely on. "Let's, between us, help her to grow—enrich her life all we can—give her every chance to develop into the woman your daughter has a right to become!"

Doane sprang up; stood over him; enveloped his hand in a huge fist and nearly crushed it.

4

The Reverend Henry Withery came in that night, on a shaggy Manchu pony, with his luggage behind on a cart. And late the following afternoon a wedding took place at the residence. A great event was made of it by the young people of the compound. The hills were searched for flowers. A surprising array of presents appeared. Mrs. Boatwright was prevented from attending by a severe headache, but her husband, at the last moment, came. The other T'ainan folk were there. His Excellency, Pao Ting Chuan, with fifteen attendant mandarins, in full official costume, among whom was Mr. Po Sui-an, lent the color of Oriental splendor to the occasion. His Excellency's gift was a necklace of jade with a pendant of ancient worked gold. Withery performed the ceremony; and Griggsby Doane gave the bride.

The young couple were leaving in the morning for Peking, at which city the groom purposed continuing for the present his study of the elements of unrest in China.

Directly after the wedding and reception a remarkably elaborate dinner was served in the large diningroom, at winch Griggsby Doane appeared for a brief time to join in the merrymaking with an appearance of *savoir faire* that M. Pourmont, shrewdly taking in, found reassuring; but he early took a quiet leave.

At dusk, after the talking machine had been turned on and the many young men were dancing enthusiastically with the few young women, the newly wedded couple slipped out and walked down to the gate. Here, outside in the purple shadows, they waited until a huge man appeared, dressed in knickerbockers, a knapsack on his back and a weatherbeaten old walking stick in his hand.

The bride clung to him for a long moment. The groom wrung his hand. Then the two stood, arm in arm, looking after him as he descended to the highroad and strode firmly, rapidly eastward, disappearing in the village and reappearing on the slope beyond, waving a final farewell with stick and cap—very dimly they could see him—just before he stepped through the old scenic arch at the top of the hill.